CHRYSALIS

· A THRILLER ·

LINCOLN CHILD

corsair

To Veronica

CORSAIR

First published in the United States in 2022 by Doubleday,
A division of Penguin Random House LLC
First published in the United Kingdom in 2022 by Corsair
This paperback edition published in 2023

1 3 5 7 9 10 8 6 4 2

Front-of-jacket images: pattern © zf L / Moment / Getty Images;
texture © oxygen / Moment / Getty Images
Jacket design by Michael J. Windsor

A CIP catalogue record for this book is available from the British Library.

ISBN: 978-1-4721-5778-2

Printed and bound in Great Britain by Clays Ltd, Elcograf S.p.A.

Papers used by Corsair are from well-managed forests
and other responsible sources.

Corsair
An imprint of
Little, Brown Book Group
Carmelite House
50 Victoria Embankment
London EC4Y 0DZ

An Hachette UK Company
www.hachette.co.uk

www.littlebrown.co.uk

Technology is a useful servant but a dangerous master.

—CHRISTIAN LOUS LANGE

1

Randall Pike crouched in his tent, disassembling his surveying gear—transit theodolite and retroreflector—and thrusting the delicate equipment into foam-fitted cases. He'd spent almost every waking minute of the last two weeks with them, knew every plummet and reticle as well as if it was family: but here he was, manhandling everything.

"Randy!" the feminine voice floated in from outside. "The chopper will be here in five minutes."

"I know!" he called back, louder than necessary. Then, modulating his voice: "I'll be ready."

He should have expected this: he was annoyed. As always on the last day of each annual pilgrimage to the Kalimatsu Glacier.

He rolled up his North Face bag with practiced twists, then stuffed it into its sack and pulled the lanyard tight. He glanced around. Backpack, scientific gear, laptop, notebook, toilet kit—everything was ready. The ice core equipment was lashed together. All that remained was to break down the tent, and he could do that in sixty seconds. He pushed all the gear out ahead of him, then ducked through into the open air.

Even though he'd been inside the tent only a quarter of an hour, the dazzling glare of the glacier temporarily blinded him. As the glare faded he could make out his lone companion, Wing Kaupei, standing outside her own setup thirty yards away. Her gear, of course, was already stowed in a neat pile, with just a few items sitting off to one side.

Five minutes. He took a deep breath of the frigid air and slowly turned, boots crunching in the hard-packed snow, to take one final look around before they departed. As always, the rugged beauty of the place, so majestic in its solitude, was overwhelming. His annoyance drained away, replaced by awe. To the north, the peaks of the Alaska Range glittered like diamonds in the arctic sun, Denali rising like a king among princes. The white blanket of glacier ran away from it, the smooth surface becoming rougher as it approached the accumulation zone. There was no sound save for a faint whisper of wind. The closest human habitation was forty miles away, the closest city an hour by chopper. Anchorage. In an hour, he'd be there. And then, twenty-four hours later, back in New England.

"Want me to take a picture?" Wing asked as she checked her gear. "You know how lousy you are with selfies."

"No. Thanks, though." It was a thoughtful gesture, but a photo was the last thing he wanted. He had little interest in remembering how this place looked today. Because he knew when he returned next year, the view would have changed—and not for the better.

In the decade he'd been coming to this spot, the Kalimatsu had shrunk in dramatic fashion, the ablation zone around his drill site contracting fourteen inches in the last twelve months alone. Over ten years, its surface had fallen a total of six linear feet. The glacier was aging prematurely, advancing with the speed of some frantic silent comedy. Every day, icebergs the size of skyscrapers were calving into the ocean as their terminus grew increasingly unstable. As the snowpack receded, curiosities now and then had begun appearing out of the ice: ancient seeds, nuts, buried for countless millennia, seeing sun again well before their intended time.

This—ironically—was a benefit of the receding glacier: the natural, ancient treasures buried within it. Two years back, a woolly mammoth had emerged from the Siberian melt—that, along with the more recent find that accounted for Wing's presence this year. The ground he stood on had once been jungle. Eventually that jungle, too, would once again emerge into the sun. Pike smiled mirthlessly. By then, of course, global warming would have raised the sea level sixty feet—and mankind would have other things on its mind besides geologic research.

This was the first year he'd actually felt the glacier moving. As he lay in bed at night, tapping readings and measurements into his tablet, he could feel the Kalimatsu groaning beneath him like a living thing. Since they'd arrived, a large crevasse—fifty feet long, its knife-edged depths unguessable—had opened with a shattering crack, just yards from Wing's tent. Pike had quickly offered to help move her to a safer location, but she'd refused with the same quiet, philosophical manner in which she seemed to approach everything. She hadn't explained, but he thought he understood anyway: Wing believed one's fate had long ago been determined, and there was nothing we could do to change it.

He glanced again at Wing. He really hadn't gotten to know her well over the last two weeks—she'd been busy cataloging and running tests on the ice cores he'd brought up—but she had proved a decent companion. She seemed to share his grief at how the Kalimatsu Glacier was dying around them, although it was clear she was more interested in his discovery the previous year . . . and in his theories about it. He'd probably talked more about those than he should: after all, she was practically management. But it was lonely up here, and Wing was a good listener. Besides, at the end of the day they were both on the same team.

He walked toward her, heaving a sigh as he navigated around the crevasse. This annoyance bubbled up every time he left the glacier. Within a week or two, he'd forget all about it as he busied himself with sample data. If he was honest, it had become a kind of hypocritical gesture, easing his guilt about not feeling enough guilt. Because the discoveries made possible by this retreating glacier were now a primary focus: measuring melt and shrinkage was almost passé.

And those discoveries had proved more promising than he'd ever hoped.

There it was: something that would make him feel better. He pulled his tablet out of a pocket of his parka, connected it to the sat phone, and sent a brief message. It was Carewell protocol to maintain radio silence during an expedition—one never knew what academic competitor might find a way to listen in—but the expedition was done now, and he could at least send a thumbs-up to the Complex without going into detail.

Wing was stuffing the last few of her items into a canvas carryall. "Listen," he began as he walked toward her, "I just wanted to thank you—" Then he frowned. "Are those core samples?"

She turned suddenly, fingers rising to stroke a small mole, situated in the perfect center of her throat. It was an unconscious gesture he'd seen before: clearly, she hadn't heard him approach over the soft snow.

"Yup," she said after a brief pause. She put the last of half a dozen frosted tubes into the carryall, then zipped it up briskly and stowed it with the rest of her gear. Odd that he hadn't seen her with them before.

"I didn't realize your work involved taking full cores, too," he said. "I assumed it was minimally invasive."

"That just shows how unobservant you are," Wing said with a giggle. "You're always so busy fussing over your equipment, it's like you've been wrapped in your own private world the last two weeks."

Pike shook his head ruefully. "You're right. I suppose I've been a terrible companion."

Wing waved this away, leaning on an ice ax for support. Then she cocked her head, listening. Pike could hear it, too: the drone of a chopper, distant but growing closer.

"Look at you," she said with mock reproach. "Our ticket out of here is arriving, and you're on your tablet instead of packing away your tent. Come on, I'll give you a hand." And she began making her way over to Pike's tent.

Pike, embarrassed, hurried to get ahead of her.

"Did you send back a report?" she asked. "Prematurely?"

"Just to pass on the good news." The helicopter was still a few minutes away; that would give them time to—

"Naughty boy," Wing said from behind him.

Suddenly, he heard a grunt of effort, followed by a sharp, deep pain between his shoulder blades. He looked around in shock and saw Wing standing a foot away, ice ax raised, its sharp edge glistening crimson.

She brought the ax down again, this time splitting his breastbone, and Pike cried out as the pain exploded. He fell backward, feet and hands windmilling. Wing, a strange, determined look on her face, was prodding him farther backward with the ax. As she did so, she glanced around at her feet. Despite his agony and vast surprise, Pike realized she was checking for bloodstains.

And then suddenly he was falling: limbs flailing helplessly as he hurtled into the fresh crevasse that had opened near Wing's tent. Above he could see a crack of receding blue sky, and—briefly—Wing's booted foot, kicking the phone and tablet into the fissure after him.

It seemed that he fell forever, crying out as he went. And then he caromed off an ice wall with such force it crushed his ribs and took his breath and voice away forever. But as he fell farther still, the white of the ice turning to blue and then to black, he could still hear the faint sounds of the chopper and what sounded like Wing's voice, calling out desperately for help.

2

As Susan Chambers walked into the executive conference room, she felt a familiar sense of dread. The crisp, postmodern space was immaculate: the three Rothko paintings were perfectly arrayed along the inside wall; the long glass conference table polished almost to invisibility; the floor-to-ceiling windows opposite freshly cleaned, ensuring the jaw-dropping view of Manhattan's Central Park remained unobscured by even the smallest splat of pigeon shit. But none of these accounted for her apprehension: it was the chilled bottles of Tasmanian Rain—their seals already cracked, weeping frosted beads of moisture, set atop coasters and placed, with an empty crystal glass, before every chair—that made her mouth go dry. Tasmanian Rain was one of the purest, healthiest, most expensive bottled waters in the world, captured as raindrops and never allowed to touch the ground. It was also the only brand J. Russell Spearman would drink.

So he *was* coming to the meeting. *Shit.*

Her boss, Art Wegler, was already at the table, and he gave her a wan smile as she took a seat next to him. As much as she might covet his stature in the entertainment industry, she was glad she wasn't in his shoes right now. It would be funny if it wasn't so unsettling. Art Wegler—one of the most promising film directors in decades, a man who'd already won an Oscar and been nominated for another—looking like a schoolboy about to receive a caning. That, in microcosm, was the effect of the shadow cast by Mr. Spearman.

Chrysalis Studios had been fashioned from a series of smaller movie companies and cable television networks into a twenty-first-century media giant. But like every other media giant, it had an Achilles heel. Its cachet, and stock valuation, was only as good as last year's gross receipts. One or—God forbid—two more flops at the box office, and the new studio's reputation—an asset beyond price—would come into question.

The studio already had its dog for the year. *Stone Cold in Love,* a rom-com with top stars and A-list talent behind the camera, the film that couldn't possibly tank, had done just that. And that meant the lineup for the rest of the year—especially the holiday season—had to perform.

The Christmas before last, *Crystal Champions* had been a massive hit, one of the few superhero films to gross $2 billion worldwide. A captive comic-book audience had helped launch it into the stratosphere. But that was twenty months ago—a lifetime in the entertainment industry. *Crystal Champions II: The Dark Matrix* was being fast-tracked for release in December, with Art as director. But problems had slowed development. Integrating digital cameras with the new, cloak-and-dagger Omega virtual technology—supplied by the Chrysalis parent company—was proving harder than expected. Just as troubling were the disagreements over the screenplay. Principal photography was already far along, even though a finished script had yet to be green-lighted. Hence, this meeting.

And the presence of Russell Spearman.

Chambers glanced around the conference table. Everybody had now seated themselves: everybody save one. The meeting had been scheduled for five minutes ago, but the chair at the head of the table remained empty. That, too, was par for the course.

The balance of power had shifted significantly since Chaplin, Mary Pickford, and the rest formed United Artists to ensure creative talent got a say in making films. These days, it was directors who were influential—not the old moguls like Sam Goldwyn or Louis B. Mayer. The exception was Chrysalis Studios and Russell Spearman. He was a producer still capable of striking fear into the heart of the bravest directorial enfant terrible—a man who, through his influence and breadth of industry connections, could make or break a film even before it got off the ground. Like many powerful people, he had his eccentricities—once he'd approved a project, he never revisited his decision. But it was the initial approval process that had strewn the corpses of cinematographers, executive directors, and other auteurs before him, like so many gnawed bones lying outside an ogre's den.

Suddenly, there was a commotion at the entrance. Chambers looked up to see a young woman move quickly around the table, slipping black folders in front of everyone: the most recent screenplay revision. Half a dozen yellow notes protruded from each. These were the sticking points keeping production from going forward—and Russell Spearman would deal with them all, one way or another.

A brief, collective shudder, rippling through the room, announced the producer's arrival. He was in his mid-seventies but looked a decade younger, with a tan dark as Cary Grant's and a thick shock of platinum-white hair. He was thin and fit for his age, and he wore a beautifully tailored suit that gleamed faintly in the artificial light.

For a minute, it felt to Chambers as if the air had been sucked out of the room. Then Spearman cleared his throat and opened his folder, and she found she could breathe again.

Without opening pleasantries, he flipped to the first yellow note. Everyone in the room followed along with a subdued rustle of paper.

"Scene twenty-two," Spearman said, looking at the screenplay. He read quickly through some scribbled notes in the margin. "What exactly is the problem here?"

Colin Wriston, head of Creative, spoke up. "It's Melissa, sir. The actress portraying Galaxielle."

"I know damn well who she is. What's the *problem*?"

Wriston was a little pale. "It's the way she—well, it's her death scene. She thinks it's too early. She's holding out for the act two climax."

"Holding out?" Spearman glared at Wriston as if it was his fault.

"She says she'll refuse the part if we don't rewrite her role."

Spearman glanced back at the page for a minute. Then he abruptly exploded. "But she's *vital* to the film! She had the final line in *Crystal Champions*!"

"I know that, sir. The problem is, she knows it, too. She doesn't like the direction we're taking with the character, and wants her role to be expanded to—"

"Ungrateful bitch!" Spearman growled in a low voice. "*Crystal Champions* fucking *made* her." He tore the page out of his binder and shook it at the room. "The answer is simple. The way she dies here—crushed when two battle drones collide—it's shit. She needs a bigger death: that's all."

Susan Chambers knew all the work that had gone into that scene already: the countless hours of choreographing a space battle, the CG prep they'd been working on since the beginning of the month.

"Mr. Spearman," Wriston said, "excuse me, but I don't think it's quite that simple. Melissa's really put her foot down, and—"

"*And* I don't want to hear any more whining! It *is* that simple. No actress can resist a death scene—if it's good enough. Have your people write her one: the kind audiences will talk about afterward. Not this drek!" He threw the page at the head of Creative. "Keep it to a page and a half. And up her paycheck by half a million."

What Spearman just proposed would mean unraveling half a dozen scenes, teams of writers working twenty-four-hour days. But Wriston merely nodded, scribbling notes on his own copy of the screenplay.

Now Spearman unscrewed his bottle of Tasmanian Rain and filled his glass partway. A fizz of carbonation filled the room as half the others did likewise. Spearman took a deep sip and banged the glass down, shivering the tabletop. Chambers noted the producer was even more irritable than usual. He plucked at his collar, adjusted his perfect necktie as if it was askew. He cleared his throat again, louder, almost a bark. Then he flipped the pages of his binder to the next note. There was a tense silence as he read a page, then another. And then he shouted, *"Jenkins!"*

The head of the digital effects department abruptly jumped to his feet. "Mr. Spearman."

Spearman looked him up and down with ill-disguised contempt. Then he glanced back at the script. "It says here the kamikaze ship can't explode."

Jenkins swallowed painfully. "Well, it's a little more complicated than that."

"Complicated? Filmmakers have been blowing up models for a hundred years. Slip a fucking M-80 inside it, light the fuse, and run away. Any chimp can do that."

"The issue isn't so much with the explosion, sir, as what triggers it. As written, the ship misses its target, loses control, and plows into a dwarf star. We're having real problems integrating that particular effect with the Omega tech. In six months, maybe, the platform will be sufficiently robust. But that visual just can't be done with the tools currently at our disposal, and we were thinking that if instead of a dwarf star, the kamikaze ship was to—"

"Six months," Spearman said.

Susan had already heard this unwelcome piece of news. Since Omega was a new VR imaging technology, the darling of the conglomerate parent of Chrysalis Studios—and since that conglomerate was the only earthly power Spearman answered to—this wasn't what he wanted to hear.

Jenkins swallowed again. "That's what our tech team says. So—"

"So the dwarf star is integral to *the whole damned story*!" Spearman had jumped to his feet as well, brandishing his rolled-up screenplay like a cudgel. "The birth sequence. The transformation sequence. We can't wait six months—we're releasing at Christmas. Are you suggesting we take those sequences out of the film?"

"No, Mr. Spearman, of course not." Jenkins reached into his case, pulled out a sheet of paper. "My team has a couple of ideas, strong ideas, that would work just as well and not push the existing technology past the—"

"*Get out!*" Spearman said in a voice that was almost a scream. His face had gone beet red. "Get the hell out! You know what you can do with your 'strong ideas'! I don't want to see or hear of them again. *Or* you—until you've figured out how to solve this."

Spearman walked over to the floor-to-ceiling windows and stared out, hands clasped behind him. Susan Chambers could see the tailored cloth covering his shoulders moving up and down as he breathed, trying to control an anger that could never, it seemed, be fully tamed. Jenkins wouldn't be back. And at the next meeting, there would be somebody else sitting in the digital effects chair.

Now Spearman swiveled away from the window. His face had returned to its normal color, and he walked back to the table and sat down, smoothing the screenplay in front of him. He turned to the next flag, tore it away, read for a moment. Then he said quietly, without looking up: "Art."

Susan could sense her boss freeze in his chair.

She knew that Spearman—as much as he liked anybody—liked Art Wegler. Spearman admired the director's wits and guts. He was one of the few people Spearman called by their first name. But none of that mattered right now. The sequel was everything, and anyone was expendable.

Spearman took a gulp of his Tasmanian Rain. "It says here you want to do the martial arts sequence outside the capital ship in seventy millimeter."

"That's right."

"In fact, you've started filming in seventy."

"Yes, sir."

"But those green-screen effects won't work with this Omega shit—and Chrysalis can't very well be the conglomerate that takes virtual reality mainstream if its own movies don't leverage the technology." Spearman plucked at his collar again.

"But this approach might help Jenkins with his visual issues. It could really stand out. Like the way we undercranked the dream montage in *Crystal I.*"

Spearman took another gulp, put down his glass. "I admire your vision. To be honest, I agree with it. But we just don't have the time. We're already going to get killed in postproduction; we'll barely make deadline."

"Sir, I've calculated that if we—"

"Art!" Spearman rose once more, his gaze locking with that of his director. The mogul cleared his throat yet again, smoothed his tie. Then he turned and walked back to the wall of windows.

Susan snuck a glance at her boss. He looked committed. Stricken, but committed—like a finalist in a game of Russian roulette.

"Sir," he said in a steady voice, "without this approach, we won't *make* the deadline."

But Spearman didn't seem to notice.

Susan heard Wegler take in a breath. "The fact is, we haven't just started filming. Yesterday we wrapped photography on the sequence."

For a moment, the entire table sat in shock. There was a strangled silence. In Spearman's productions, this was heretical, unheard of: a director, taking such a decision on himself.

Spearman continued to look out the window. At last, he spoke. "You finished the sequence."

"Yes."

"In seventy mil."

"Yes, sir."

"Knowing full well it was a red-flag item for today's meeting."

"Yes," Susan's boss whispered.

Abruptly, Spearman whirled around. Once again, his gaze was locked on Wegler. But the producer's expression was different now. Instead of fury, it was more like panic—pleading, beseeching. One hand reached toward Wegler. His mouth opened, but no sound came. Murmurs began to circle the table. As Susan watched, the whites of Spearman's eyes suddenly blossomed crimson, like blotting paper dipped in ink.

And then, with an inarticulate cry, Spearman fell heavily across the table, shattering it into a thousand shards.

In an instant, pandemonium. People screaming, running to get away, grabbing their phones to dial 911. Susan stared, frozen in horror, as J. Russell Spearman lay impaled, jerking like a marionette gone mad. Daggers of glass blossomed in the air, followed by expensive arcs of Tasmanian Rain, and then—inevitably—blood that rose in gouts of awful regularity, staining everything in sight and clashing with the Rothkos that hung, oblivious, on the inner wall of the room.

3

Jeremy Logan nudged the accelerator of his Lotus Elan and felt it leap ahead on the highway with a low growl. He was all too familiar with the route up 91 from the Connecticut coast to Hartford—he'd attended, spoken at, and been bored by enough conferences in the state capital to last a lifetime. But the area beyond—leading to Springfield and Holyoke, Massachusetts—was relatively unknown to him. He'd veered west onto 44, then north on 202, surprised at how quickly the densely populated southern area of his home state gave way to tiny hamlets dozing in the afternoon sunshine, occasional boutique inns or wineries, and picturesque farms. As he continued north, and the land began to rise and pastures gave way to forest, even those vestiges of civilization began to fall away, until at last—after seeing no sign of human activity for five miles—he came across a gas station, where he pulled the vintage coupe in. The facility was so old that an attendant in bib overalls insisted not only on filling the tank, but cleaning the front and rear windshields as well.

Logan glanced at the battered map of Connecticut he always carried in his duffel—it was more a nostalgic relic now than useful tool—and then the screen of his phone. It showed empty green terrain, crazed with tiny crooked side roads that didn't seem to lead anywhere . . . and, of course, the usual message: PLEASE ACTIVATE OMEGA INTERFACE.

He paid the attendant and then, with a sigh, reached into his jacket pocket and pulled out the device that had rarely left his side the past six months. He'd originally purchased an older model, but new ones arrived now and then in the mail: each better looking, less intrusive, and quicker to integrate with his other devices and daily chores.

Starting the motor, he turned the device over in his hands. This latest model he'd synchronized—the Omega Venture 7a— was slender and stylish: a blend, he'd read somewhere, of plastic, silicone, and trade secret polymers. It looked something like an oversize hearing aid, as imagined by a high-end Italian designer: beautifully proportioned, with a pair of thin rimless glasses attached by one of the temple bars. A tiny QR code etched into the device identified it as his and his alone.

Logan fitted the device behind his ear and let the glasses rest lightly on the bridge of his nose, automatically activating it. Looking in the rearview mirror, he could barely see it: the Omega designers were obsessed not only with making you forget you were wearing it, but with making it barely detectable to others as well.

He pulled back onto the road. "Syncing," came the silky feminine voice. And then, almost immediately: "Sync complete." That meant, Logan knew, that the Venture had updated itself with his mobile phone.

Logan glanced toward the passenger seat. "Kit," he said to his wife, "it seems Arthur C. Clarke was right: any sufficiently advanced technology is indistinguishable from magic. Do you think that's going to put me out of a job one of these days?"

Kit did not answer, of course. She had died of cancer six years before. But Logan still enjoyed speaking to her from time to time when he was alone. It was mostly a one-way conversation; only rarely did she answer back.

The view remained as before, but now other things changed significantly. The Venture was in communication with all the orbiting satellites and server farms that held the petabytes of data making up his digital life. The glasses now displayed a semitransparent map, altitude, heartbeat, and half a dozen other things marginally useful: all he'd had to do was snug his Omega into place.

When the Venture first came out some eighteen months before, he'd dismissed it as another expensive byproduct of the Internet of Things that would prove a passing fad. But instead, it seemed to be filling a niche nobody had even known existed. When the conglomerate behind the device finally took it public, Logan's curiosity got the best of him and he joined twenty million other Americans, perhaps against his better instincts, and purchased a unit. At some point along the way, he must have drunk the Kool-Aid.

It tasted good.

"Pythia," he said, "find the best route to One Thousand Mobius Strip."

What have I gotten myself into? he wondered at the same time.

"Thank you, Jeremy," said the voice from somewhere in the vicinity of his right ear. "Route calculated. Certain details of this route are secure and should not be divulged. Destination fifteen point three miles ahead. Estimated arrival, twenty-one minutes."

A new image came up on the eyeglasses: a route through the maze of back-hamlet roads, like a trail of breadcrumbs through a shadowy forest.

"Audio directions, Pythia," he said.

"Thank you, Jeremy. Turn left in two miles onto Unnamed Road."

The trees thickened around him and he realized he was entering the foothills of the Berkshires. This corner of New England, once given over to hardscrabble farms, had more or less surrendered again to the woods and low mountains, along with a few towns full of summer homes. And then of course there was his destination, which was no longer on any normal map.

After a reminder from Pythia, Logan turned onto Unnamed Road. Here the elevation began increasing in earnest. There were no road signs. The forest closed in on both sides, beautiful and remarkably virgin. The sun was low, its descent accelerated by the heavy tree cover. He turned onto another nameless road, still climbing through the woods. No vehicles passed the other way. It seemed undisturbed since the days of Lewis and Clark, and he half expected Sacagawea to step out of the forest and offer directions.

But something odd was happening. At first he couldn't tell what it was. Then he realized: the car wasn't bumping over cracked, ancient highway anymore. The road was new and smooth. And as he watched, it widened ahead of him, from two lanes to four. The wild forest remained, but it too had changed subtly: it looked more cultivated somehow, the understory less dense and unkempt.

"Estimated arrival time six minutes, Jeremy," said Pythia. "Be prepared to stop."

The early evening sky was beginning to make it difficult to see the trees around him. He turned a sharp corner, then slowed in surprise. Ahead, set into the woods as carefully as a dovetail joint, a building stretched across the road, metal lift gates in each direction. A sign on the shoulder said STOP AHEAD.

There was nobody in line, and Logan drove up to the nearest entry window. A man in an unmarked uniform looked down at him with a smile. "Can I help you?"

"The name's Jeremy Logan." Grabbing a thin envelope from the passenger seat, Logan handed it to the guard.

The man opened the envelope, looked at the letter inside.

Logan expected he'd be asked for his driver's license. But instead, the guard simply reached out of the window and aimed a small wand at Logan's Venture. There was a chirrup. The guard smiled again, then put the paper back in the envelope and handed it to Logan.

"Go straight on, Dr. Logan," he said. "Where the road divides, make a right toward the processing station."

"Thanks," Logan said. What looked like an industrial laser ran a beam quickly over his car. Then the lift gate rose. At the same time, Logan noticed that a spike strip, camouflaged the color of asphalt, was retracting beneath the surface of the road. Apparently, security here was not quite as laid-back as it seemed.

Maybe I should have asked for more money.

He drove on. The grade grew abruptly steeper, switchbacking around a large outcrop of granite that protruded through the deciduous forest. And then suddenly, the Lotus crested the mountain.

"Holy shit," Logan breathed. He pulled the car over for a better look.

Ahead in the dusk lay a bowl-shaped valley, almost perfectly symmetrical, as if the hand of God had carved it out with an ice cream scoop. The upper edge of the valley was of almost uniform height, like the crater surrounding the throat of a volcano, its circular crest softened by the autumn covering of red, yellow, and green. At the four ordinal points, airplane beacons blinked intermittently. But their lights were almost drowned by the glow radiating up from the valley itself.

Looking down, Logan saw a hulking, torus-shaped structure, seemingly carved right out of the flanks of the hills, circling the entire valley. Countless lights winked up from countless windows, arranged in serried rows like the portholes of an ocean liner. The bowl of the valley was aglow with them.

From its interior side, four bridge-like structures—each of gleaming steel—ran along the same ordinal points as the beacons. They joined in the center of the valley, where a tower rose at least fifty stories—more than half the distance to the mountaintop. Logan stared at it in wonder. It, too, was dotted with the lights of countless windows. Here and there were large balconies, arching around the sides of the tower. Some were occupied by people, no larger than ants from this distance. On one particularly large balcony, they were chatting and mingling at what appeared to be a cocktail party. Logan thought he could even make out the faintest susurrus of conversation, the strains of a jazz band, floating toward him on the evening breeze. At its base were small dots of activity. The sun was sinking now, throwing the eastern edge of the valley into dark relief and making the lights of the vast and humming city—for there was really no other word to describe it—seem to shine all the brighter.

Naturally, he'd heard of the Complex. He'd seen grainy renderings of it in online magazines and Wikipedia. But those images didn't do it justice. Much like the product perched lightly on the bridge of his nose, the Chrysalis Torus looked like something slightly out of time: something from a future world.

The email that brought him here had arrived just five hours earlier, as he was returning from an early lunch with a Yale colleague. Logan was used to receiving urgent and sometimes odd requests, many of which were jokes. But this email contained a notarized link to a secure server, and the text got right to the point:

Dr. Logan, as head legal counsel to the Chrysalis Corporation, I wish to retain your services immediately regarding an urgent and highly confidential matter. . . .

"Jeremy," Pythia prompted.

"Yes?" Logan replied, staring.

"There are no delays to your destination, One Thousand Mobius Strip. Estimated arrival time remains at six minutes."

"Okay. Don't get your virtual knickers in a bunch." And tearing himself away from the view, he pulled back onto the road and began descending the inside curve of what, when it was allowed a name, had been known as Hurricane Valley.

4

Over the next hour, things happened at dizzying speed. There were two more outer checkpoints, after which Logan found himself easing the car down into an underground structure that looked as if it were made of seamless titanium. An armed valet opened his door, took his keys with a dazzling smile, and handed him off to a bellhop. This man in turn led the way into the towering lobby of what Logan assumed must be guest accommodations for visitors to the Chrysalis Advanced Research Center. With a marble front desk, several fountains, and a string quartet playing earnestly on an orchid-framed stand, it looked and sounded like a four-star hotel.

The bellhop led him to the front desk, where he was escorted discreetly across the ornate lobby, through an unmarked door, and into a small room with two chairs and a table, on which sat some kind of screening device. A young woman in a dark suit entered from a back door and, smiling and offering endless apologies, ran a wand over Logan himself, then his bags. Then she asked him to sign a series of nondisclosure and noncompete agreements, along with others Logan didn't bother to ask about. Ordeal complete, she escorted him out of the room and down a corridor. Reaching a bank of elevators, she entered one, spoke into her Omega module—rather different than his—then pressed the top button. They were whisked twenty floors to a sky lobby, dimly lit and comparatively elegant, obviously within the central spire of the complex. A final elevator ride brought them to what appeared to be a sprawling executive suite. The woman led Logan into a conference room, asked him to make himself comfortable, and then left, closing the door behind her.

Logan put his duffel on the long table, which he now noticed bore the distinctive yellow and red striped hues of canary wood. He took a minute to catch his breath. The first thing he felt was relief—he'd been afraid a body cavity search was next on the menu. This was quickly followed by curiosity. He walked over to the windows that spanned one wall of the huge, elegant room. They curved slightly, following the skin of the tower, and were covered with some semi-translucent material. They distorted the view below, but he was able to make out the faint twinkle of countless lights that could only represent one flank of the Torus, running along the bowl-shaped valley over which night had now fallen.

The door opened again and Logan turned to see another woman—older and taller than his guide—enter the room. She looked to be in her mid-forties, about Logan's own age, and was dressed conservatively and rather expensively, and she was the first person Logan had seen who wasn't wearing a badge.

"Dr. Logan," she said, extending her hand. "Welcome to the Complex. I'm Claire Asperton, general counsel to the Chrysalis Management Group. We spoke earlier." She had dark blond hair with just a few strands of gray, cut in an elegant, shoulder-length blowout.

"Pleasure to meet you," Logan said, shaking the proffered hand. "It's only been six hours, but I feel like we're practically old friends."

"Thank you for coming so quickly," she said with a tight smile.

Logan was used to assignments with heavy veils of secrecy and confidentiality. What he wasn't used to was such urgency: he'd been asked, in the politest of terms, to drop everything, make whatever excuses were necessary, and rush to this remote complex—that very day. His generous consultancy fee would take into account this inconvenience and haste.

"Please take a seat," Asperton said. "I apologize for the urgency of our call, and the vetting process you were just subjected to."

"The trials of the Redcrosse Knight?"

The lawyer chuckled. "And to think you still have Archimago to look forward to."

Logan laughed despite himself. It was nice to know, somehow, that this person had read something other than law books. "Actually, I'm used to it. I find it comes with the territory."

"Well, it's a territory that's new to me. You call yourself an—enigmalogist, is that correct?"

Logan nodded. "It started as a kind of hobby, really. It's not something one studies for. But when it became a vocation, I decided I'd better give the job a name."

"I've seen your face on the cover of several magazines, though usually with a more sensational job title. Like 'ghost-breaker' or 'supernatural detective.'"

"Sensational, yes. Accurate, perhaps not so much."

"But from what I understand, you've participated in some fairly high-profile investigations. Is it true you dispelled the curse of some Egyptian king's tomb?"

"I did the best I could."

"And you solved the mystery of the Taos Hum?"

"Most of the work I do is more . . . terrestrial. I prefer to stay under the radar when I can. It helps weed out the cranks."

"But still, the cases you specialize in are always, for lack of a better term, out of the ordinary."

"Yes. I'm not a detective—I investigate circumstances, or phenomena, the authorities either won't or can't deal with. Sometimes it's because they refuse to spend time with something ridiculous. Other times, they haven't any idea what to do."

"But you do."

"I've had an excellent success rate so far."

Asperton nodded. "And you're extremely discreet. That's important: along with the fact you do most of your work on a corporate scale, rather than taking on private individuals. And you have a willingness to travel."

"Even to places that don't exist," Logan said. "Like Hurricane Valley." The way Chrysalis had removed the names of the surrounding roads, and supposedly paid mapping apps to pixelate their images of the valley, reminded him of something that—like the Roman emperor Maxentius—was in the process of being erased from history, both victims of *damnatio memoriae*.

Asperton nodded. "As a conglomerate, Chrysalis is unique in having so many high-tech lines of business: defense work, robotics, medicine, personal tech. Why scatter your technological resources all around the world, when you could build a single entity to house them all?"

"And in a beautiful, unspoiled location, free from distracting urban surroundings." *With security easier to enforce,* Logan thought to himself.

"A remote location wasn't only agreeable—believe it or not, it was central to the conception. We're a hundred miles from two of the planet's cultural hubs—New York and Boston—and yet our own campus is so self-contained that few feel the need to leave. In fact, it makes poaching high-level talent almost easy. With so many lines of business in one place, we've been able to provide a facility with a dozen fine restaurants, four gyms, two live theaters, a hospital, a tech university for cross-discipline study, a sixty-acre wooded park, spacious living quarters with first-class furnishings—all provided without cost. Not to mention the most important thing: the psychological and professional benefits of working with so many others, in so many fascinating lines of research, pushing so many envelopes."

The lawyer paused. Her contralto voice with its faint finishing-school accent was still light, but now her smile vanished. "In any case, I wanted to speak with you as soon as you arrived, if only to explain the urgency. We're still waiting on your final security clearance, but we hope to have it completed late tonight. In the meantime, there's a good deal of background I'd like to give you."

She shifted in her chair. "Chrysalis has come a long way from John Christie's original automobile and farm-implement manufacturer. As with other large international entities, we've diversified into areas such as medical devices, a motion picture studio, nanotechnology. But we've also learned you can't be Sony and IBM and Exxon all at the same time. So rather than duking it out with the established competition, we've been focusing our major attention, and research, into technological backwaters not yet fully exploited. And the most promising avenue—and where we've funneled tremendous resources—is developing software codecs from our entertainment division that, combined with neural engineering, will create a fully immersive, existential telepresence. The result is *that*." The lawyer pointed at the device currently protruding from Logan's pocket.

"Omega," Logan said.

"Virtual reality is going to revolutionize the world—it's not a question of if, but when. And since our technology has been under development for some time, it's now almost fully mature—while our competition is just beginning to realize what they're missing out on. They've continued to think of VR as primarily a game technology. But it's got the potential to be much, much more. Which is why we bought Infinium—and the brain behind it."

Logan nodded. He had, of course, read about this. Infinium had originally been the brainchild of Matthew Wrigley, an MIT postdoc who'd developed a passion for 3D and augmented reality literally in his dorm room. The press had been full of stories about how, by buying Infinium for a staggering sum—and bringing the famously difficult Wrigley along to supervise its growth—

Chrysalis had spent far too much on a passing fad. But the union of Wrigley's vision and Chrysalis's funding had formed Omega: a technology now seeping slowly into daily life.

"The device you have there in your pocket," Asperton went on, "and the others snugged behind people's ears everywhere—they're marvelous, but they're only the first phase of our business plan. The second is far more ambitious . . . and, best of all, it's being quietly rolled out as we speak. All the infrastructure is in place for announcing Omega's new incarnation, the Voyager—and taking it live next week. We've poured hundreds of millions into this, Jeremy. That's how much we believe in Omega."

Abruptly, she sat forward and her expression changed.

"But we've run into an issue. That's why you, you specifically, were brought here on such short notice—to make sure it's only an *issue*, not a *problem*. As the top lawyer for Chrysalis, it's my job to be paranoid. I'm bringing you in for a six-figure fee as a precaution. Too much is riding on the phase two rollout, which is why your presence here at this critical juncture is an occupational necessity. And this decision comes from the highest perch in the company."

"The highest perch," Logan repeated in a low voice.

Asperton nodded slowly. Then she pressed a button on a console built into the table, spoke quietly into it. A minute passed. And then a door on the far side of the conference room opened and a form slowly emerged.

Logan, who had seen a great many strange things, thought he was inured to surprise. But as he looked at the person who'd just stepped into the room, he stood up automatically, astonished. Asperton did the same.

Standing at the far end of the conference table was a phantom. Yet Logan had no doubt this phantom was real: the heavy brow, the hooked nose, and the unmistakable scar across the left jawline—testament to an accident on the factory line fifty years ago—identified him beyond question. John Christie IV, descendant of the Christie who had founded the auto empire now known as Chrysalis. Nobody outside the company had glimpsed him for almost twenty years. It was rumored he was long dead from his factory's carcinogens. But here he was, beyond question, in the flesh. He was thin, almost gaunt, and his bespoke suit hung on his skeletal limbs. After a brief silence, he came forward, along the edge of the table, to where Logan was standing.

The two looked at each other for a moment. And then the aged man took Logan's hand in both of his.

"It's a pleasure to meet you, Jeremy," he said in a whispery voice. "The work being done here is precious. It's the future of technology—the future of man. We have our own people looking into this tragedy, but the time element is critical. Even if it turns out to be a police matter, the authorities would only impede our progress unnecessarily. Besides, we have police of our own. That's why *you* are here. I know what you did for Lux: please do the same for us now. You're the only person in the world I felt comfortable contacting. You're our Hail Mary, Jeremy. You're our *just in case*."

As Christie spoke, the pressure of his hands on Logan's increased. For such an old man, he had a remarkable grip. At last, Christie relaxed his hands. He patted Logan's shoulder. Then he turned and walked slowly away. The door closed with a soft click and it was as if he had never been there.

But he *had*. And Logan understood why. This was the conglomerate's way of telling him how seriously they took this problem.

Asperton broke the gathering silence. "It's quite late. You'll find a corporate prospectus, org charts, and a stack of other reading matter waiting in your suite. We'll send dinner as well. Get acclimated; get some rest. Because at some point tonight, your clearance will come through—and then the real work begins."

And with that, she smiled slightly, then led the way out of the conference room.

5

Logan stepped into the suite he'd been assigned in the hotel embedded within the tower. His luggage was there waiting for him, looking pristine and inviolate despite having been pawed through by security just a few hours earlier.

The room had the feel of a typical upscale hotel suite, with a separate bedroom and a wall of windows, currently hidden by neutral curtains. Logan walked over, lifted a curtain aside with the back of his hand. Beyond, in the dark, he could make out—several floors below—the nearest skyway leading from the central spire out to the gently curving flank of the Advanced Research Torus, lights gleaming from windows on various levels. It was as if a vast, ring-shaped spacecraft had settled into this bowl of a mountain valley and taken up residence.

He reflected on the odd conversation he'd just had in the executive suite. Asperton had said a major development strategy of long gestation was under way, and phase two was on the brink of being rolled out. The company was clearly at a crossroads. Christie had used the word "tragedy"—which Logan presumed involved this second phase in some way. Christie had also told Logan he was their "Hail Mary"—but in the same breath, the man had also called him their "just in case." It was odd, almost a paradox.

One thing was clear: somehow, probably an old-boy network of billionaires, Christie had heard of Logan's mission at Lux, the reclusive think tank. That helped explain why he, of all people, had been summoned. Something strange had happened here—precisely what, he'd learn tomorrow.

With a sigh, he pulled the Venture module out of the front pocket of his jacket and attached the device. For a few seconds nothing happened, but this was normal: one of Omega's many stylish features was that it did not interrupt your life with updates and reboots—it came to life only when fully linked.

There it was: through the lens, he could see characteristic blue-green glows emanating from various objects in his suite. He glanced at the faint flicker around the refrigerator. Instantly, the glow sharpened into a distinct outline. A nod of his head brought up an interior view, showing its contents. Along one side of his vision was a menu for increasing or decreasing temperature, setting a timer, ordering online food delivery, and several other options, all of which would be triggered by blinks or certain movements of his head.

He looked away, and his virtual interface with the refrigerator decoupled. At the lower edge of the lens, another menu was available. He hadn't seen this before; it was probably some enhancement available only to Complex visitors. There were two items in the menu: the first was apparently an email from Asperton, and the second was something called "Flight."

Focusing his gaze on the email brought up directions to tomorrow morning's meeting, other attendees unnamed.

Next he turned to "Flight." It was some kind of interactive demonstration of the Omega technology—more eye candy for impressing important visitors.

In his job as an enigmalogist, Logan had dealt with things explainable by science, as well as things that most emphatically were not. As a result, his tool set was exotic and necessarily broad: deep reading in ancient and medieval history; studies of chemistry, astronomy, astrology, and biology—as well as everything from EMF meters to gris-gris. But one of his most useful tools was his innate intuition. He was a "sensitive"—instinctually empathetic to his surroundings. It was a gift to be used sparingly, but with it he could sense not only people's hidden emotions, but also—rarely—the proximity of evil, either present or past.

He felt fatigued, but not sleepy. Too much had happened today for sleep to come just yet. Venture still in place, he removed his jacket, lay down on the bed, focused again on the "Flight" menu item, and blinked carefully to activate it.

There was a slow fade to black. Then, astoundingly, he felt himself rise off the bed and float, suspended and motionless, in his hotel suite. Distantly, he could still feel the reassuring presence of the bed beneath him, but the sense of realism projected was extraordinary, unlike anything he'd ever felt. After several moments, as if allowing him time to adjust to this novel sensation, he saw . . . no, he *felt* . . . himself begin to rise again, through the ceiling and up through various levels of the tower, past dormitories and machine rooms and swimming pools and offices, until he was outside, above the structure, the Torus glimmering far below and the forested mountain flanks swaying in the faint breeze.

Still he kept rising, above the tops of the mountains, until the remote landscape was spread out below him like a carpet of dark green in the night. The wonder of it, the sensation of floating above the earth with little artificiality at all, was intoxicating. He began to rise again. . . .

And then, suddenly, the spell was broken and he was tumbling headlong toward the earth. Distantly, he was aware that the breeze had grown chill and angry. The lights of the Torus, the menacing point of the spire, drew closer and closer, as he prepared for the excruciating pain of impact—

Suddenly, the imagery vanished and he was back in his suite, sitting up, breathing hard. His Venture device was in a corner of the room, near the door, where he must have thrown it. He had no recollection of tearing it from his head, yet he must have taken it off and, in so doing, stopped the nightmare.

The nightmare. Surely this was not the innocent demo that guests were supposed to experience? Logan wondered if his abilities as a sensitive had somehow interacted, or interfered . . . with unpleasant results.

He rose from the bed, retrieved his Venture, and slipped it back into the pocket of his jacket. And as he did so, he became aware of a presence, rising as if to envelop the entire valley in its grasp: something dark and full of pitiless greed, like a rotten core at the heart of this technological marvel.

6

At 7 a.m., Logan was awakened by a chirp from his bedside. A message from Claire Asperton told him that his clearance had come through, and she'd like to meet at 7:45, if possible.

Logan showered and dressed, and in short order he was making his tentative way through the Tower, Chrysalis employees moving purposefully around him, until Pythia told him he'd reached his destination: an unmarked door on one of the low floors. He frowned. After a moment, he knocked. The door opened and Logan found himself face-to-face with the trim figure of Claire Asperton.

"Ms. Asperton," he said.

The lawyer smiled as she gestured Logan inside. "Call me Claire, please. This isn't my regular office. It's a refuge I use from time to time."

The office was not nearly as large as last evening's conference room, but it was pleasantly, if severely, appointed. There were no bookcases or paintings to soften the monochromatic walls: just a few leather chairs, a desk, a table, some screens that were currently dark, and a wall of glass looking out over the Advanced Research campus. A bowl of macadamia nuts sat on the table, along with a tray of breakfast pastries and two tall mugs that smelled richly of coffee. Asperton ushered him to one chair and took a seat in another.

"Last night, I explained our goal for Omega: to create a product nobody knows they need, but in a couple years won't be able to live without—with our competition receding in our rearview mirror. But the only thing more difficult than deceiving the competition has been developing the technology itself. And that's why the next few days are so critical—not just for the success of Omega, but for Chrysalis as a conglomerate."

Logan sat back. "I'm all ears."

"Good, because with your clearance out of the way, I can get you up to speed. In a nutshell, we—I guess I should say Matthew Wrigley—has devised a comprehensive three-stage rollout, as I touched on last night. The Venture we introduced last year, your device, was phase one: technology that lets people accomplish many things in a more intuitive way. Here and there, we've allowed this technology to bring two different mediums together—such as in movies like the upcoming *Crystal Champions II*—but we don't make a big deal about it. The primary effort has been to broaden the tech beyond games, let people grow comfortable with the devices and a degree of virtual immersion. And we've succeeded: someone using a Venture isn't seen as a bleeding-edge geek, or a person with a severe hearing problem, anymore. Meanwhile, behind the scenes, we've been frantically preparing for phase two."

She sipped her coffee, grabbed a few macadamias. "Care for some?"

"No, thanks."

"Phase two, the Omega Voyager, is where the real magic starts to happen. We're leveraging our virtual reality into a persistent, viable commercial environment."

Logan's blank look must have registered, because Asperton smiled. "I'll give you an example. Imagine being an avid golfer living in Tulsa—and being able to pick out a new set of golf clubs . . . while standing in the Pro Shop at Pebble Beach. Or St. Andrews. The smells, the sights—even the feel of the wind—all utterly realistic. And, of course, since this virtual world will be interacting seamlessly with the Voyager interface, those clubs you buy will be perfectly sized and you'll be able to pick out the grips that feel best in your hand. In later iterations, you'll be able to have a virtual drink at the nineteenth hole afterward."

Logan listened intently. It sounded like a far cry from the little Venture unit of his.

Asperton scooped up a few more nuts. "It will be a perfect purchasing experience—because 'purchasing' becomes fun, an outing or adventure of sorts. And with our licensing fees and the per-usage charges, we'll recoup our investment quickly. There isn't a major retailer who won't want to build out a store on our proprietary platform."

She let that sink in. Logan realized the financial ramification would be staggering.

"We've finished beta-testing phase two, and the first one hundred thousand Voyager units are arriving on the doorsteps of early adopters as we speak. Another two hundred thousand will be synced and shipped to additional customers in coming weeks, but the first Voyagers will go live on Monday."

Monday. That was five days away.

"And phase three?" he asked.

"Still in preproduction—probably sometime later next year." Asperton paused and refocused. "Now, for the reason you're here. Bad news can be told more quickly than good, I'm afraid: the day before yesterday, a member of the Chrysalis board died."

"I'm sorry to hear that. Which member was it?" Logan asked, slipping a tablet out of his duffel and thinking of the organizational chart he'd studied the previous evening.

"Russell Spearman, producer at Chrysalis Film Studios. Something happened at a staff meeting—he had some kind of seizure. Or fit. One eyewitness said it was almost like he went insane. Then he plunged through a plate-glass conference table. Whether he died of blood loss, shock, or a combination is still an open question."

Logan nodded, making notes on the tablet.

"On its own, his death would be a tragic circumstance for our studio and would present a vacancy on our board. But that's not the crux of the problem. Fifteen minutes after I heard about Spearman's death, I received a strange message on my own Omega device. At first, I thought it was gibberish. But then, on a hunch, I tried unscrambling it with my private key—all executives within the company have one. Unfortunately, that worked—and the message speaks for itself."

She tapped a tablet of her own, then turned its display toward Logan. The text it displayed was brief.

Spearman Was the First. No Accident.
The Second Will Drop the Day After Tomorrow.

Logan read, then reread, the message in silence. As Asperton withdrew the tablet, he made a quick mental calculation. "You said his death was the day before yesterday."

"Yes," she said, gaze leveled on Logan.

"Which means today is the 'day after tomorrow.'" Logan thought a moment. "I assume you've forensically analyzed that message?"

"Very quietly, using only our top-level assets in security and logistics. We know nothing more than what you can read from it yourself."

"You don't know what the 'second' is, or what 'drop' signifies."

"No. But I can't see any happy ending."

Nor could John Christie, I expect, Logan thought. It was becoming clearer why Christie, knowing personally of Logan's expertise, would have thought of bringing him in: so much at stake, so little to go on.

"You said unscrambling the message with a private key was unfortunate. Why?"

"It means whoever sent the message has the ability to infiltrate our systems using asymmetric cryptography."

Logan took a few more notes. "This message contains no specific threat. No blackmail. The red flags are simply that Spearman wasn't an accident, and that a second drop would take place today."

Asperton nodded. "Our concern—our *primary* concern, beyond grief at Spearman's death—is the timing."

"The rollout of phase two."

The lawyer nodded.

"Any autopsy or police reports yet?"

"Preliminary. Inconclusive."

"Chances of suicide? Murder?"

Asperton sighed. "Hard to know. So far, no evidence of either."

"Conglomerates like Chrysalis have fingers in many pies. Is there some other important spin-off, or anything, that will happen in the near future?"

After a brief hesitation, Asperton shook her head. "There's the *Crystal Champions* sequel Spearman was producing, but that's months away and they're already scrambling to replace him. Voyager is the big event. And I mean *big*—if we have to hold off the rollout, we'd lose tens of millions of dollars a day. But more importantly, we'd lose the initiative and untold credibility with both the public and our corporate partners. It would be a crippling blow, not only to the subdivision but Chrysalis as a whole."

"I'm going to ask a stupid question, and it's stupid because, if it was relevant, you would probably have mentioned it already. Can you think of any person, company, or entity of any sort who'd like to see Chrysalis or this product compromised? Or, for that matter, who'd be powerful enough to make such a thing happen?"

"Well, there's the magic question. Corporate espionage is always a possibility. But as I've told you, we've done a superb job of misdirection with Omega. And the retailers partnering with us in this next phase have almost as much to lose as we do. You could posit a whole raft of things—a disaffected stockholder, a jilted business rival, a psycho—but within minutes you'd be drowning in hypotheticals."

"Fair enough. Yet you called me, in particular, because—as soon as you got this message—you assumed it had to do with the impending launch. Right?"

"I hoped—and still hope—it doesn't. But it's too serious and unsettling to ignore. We need you to investigate this in any way you see fit."

Logan nodded, then put his tablet aside. "I assume that's all you can tell me."

"As of this moment, that's all I've got. But we can now give you unrestricted access to the Chrysalis databases." She stood up, smoothed her skirt, walked over to the desk, and pressed a button. "We've set up a space for you to operate; I'll have you taken there now. Maybe you can learn something about Spearman, or the message, that will shed light on this and help you anticipate what's next. While you're here, I can grant you access to anyone and anything within the company. Where necessary, we'll tell people you're working on a high-level data analysis for my office."

There was a knock on the door. Logan, assuming it was his escort, stood up. But Asperton stopped him. "Just a moment, Dr. Logan."

He paused.

"There's one thing I want to make clear. It may be helpful; it may not. Last night, I told you I was aware of your work as a paranormal sleuth. I know you've solved several nonsupernatural cases as well, but those don't make headlines. When an emergency meeting was called Monday afternoon, I was the person—once

Mr. Christie mentioned your name—who insisted you be called in. Obviously, not because of your affinity for ghosts, but because of what you call yourself: an *enigmalogist*. You confront—and solve—problems nobody has encountered before, that stymie normal methods of investigation, rules of engagement. Is that an accurate appraisal?"

"I may well add it to my CV."

She gave a wintry smile. "Then you understand what's at stake and why I hired you. This is a problem we've never encountered, and frankly aren't sure how to define, let alone handle. And we'd like to keep it quiet. I wanted you here on-site, fully briefed, as quickly as possible. Let's hope I acted from an overabundance of caution." She gestured toward the door. "Good luck, Jeremy."

7

Piers Bridger sat, pleasantly alone, in the left-hand seat of his twin-engine Beechcraft King Air. At 15,000 feet, the atmosphere was quiet and the ride smooth: puffy cumulus clouds floated lazily beneath his wings. Now and then, he'd fly through the upper wisps of a particularly tall formation, and the windshield would be briefly obscured, like a car in a fogbank. Then he'd be out in the late-afternoon sun again; the wipers would clear the droplets away; and he'd continue flying northeast in his pressurized cocoon.

He gazed around the cockpit, then back into the cabin. The plane was much more enjoyable to fly than his single Pilatus had been. Naturally, he'd had it heavily customized from the usual six-by-six configuration into a small two-room suite where his family could be comfortable. But his kids were off leading their own lives now, and his wife was down at their winter home in Jupiter. Actually, in the past couple of years, what had once been a "winter home" was now, in truth, her permanent residence: they saw each other only half a dozen times a year. But they had come to a quiet understanding: Candice was content spending time with her nouveaux-riche friends, and he had his company to keep him busy.

Funny, how he didn't miss spending time with her or the kids. After reaching sixty, he seemed to have become a different person, finding more comfort in solitude than among other people. Take this flight, for instance: although he could have used one of the AmTex corporate jets and the pilot who came with it, he'd decided to make the flight himself. The hours he logged would help his license stay current, of course, but the truth was that up here—three miles above the earth, without another living soul capable of disturbing him—was the only place he ever felt truly, comfortably alone.

As he cleared the upper edge of another cloud, he felt a moment of turbulence. It was so brief it didn't even register on the instruments, but he'd been flying so long that he'd felt it nevertheless, like a sixth sense. It wasn't uncommon to get a little turbulence with these kinds of clouds, and so far everything had been clear sailing. Nevertheless, it gave him an excuse to check the instrumentation. The plane was trimmed out; he'd leaned the engines and was cruising at 250 knots, with a twenty-five-knot tailwind. Naturally, the GPS was synced and the Garmin autopilot locked on—though pilots didn't like to admit it, a monkey could fly a plane once cruising altitude had been reached. He'd heard stories about pilots falling asleep, or even dying of heart attacks, and their autopilots would just keep happily flying along to the preloaded destination . . . where the plane would circle and circle until it ran out of gas.

He glanced out the windshield: no more clouds ahead, just dark blue sky. At this rate, he would arrive in half an hour.

On cue, his radio came alive. "King Air Kilo Romeo 753," came the metallic voice. "Leaving New York airspace. Contact Boston Approach on 124.1. Good day."

"Seven five three, good day," Bridger said into his headset. He decided he might as well complete the handoff. He cleared his throat, then spoke again: "Good afternoon, Boston Approach. King Air Kilo Romeo 753, with you on 124.1. Squawk one five zero seven and ident."

"Good day, 753," came the response—a woman speaking this time. There was a pause as the altitude calibration information was gathered. Then: "King Air 753, at flight level 150, altimeter 29.13."

"Seven five three," Bridger replied, signing off. Now he was in Boston's airspace, and he wouldn't have to talk to ATC again until he was on the glideslope to Hartford.

He shifted in his seat, grunting slightly at the old, familiar pain in his knee—now much reduced, thank God—and lapsed back into thought while the autopilot did the flying. One always heard that a preference for being alone was somehow wrong: you had a social phobia, or perhaps were somewhere on the spectrum. He knew himself well enough to realize that wasn't the case. He'd raised two children, run AmTex as chairman and CEO for ten years, dealt with clients both military and civilian, hired and fired and presided over innumerable meetings. If he and Candice weren't seeing eye to eye anymore, well . . . it was too bad, but such things weren't exactly rare.

Suddenly, he felt turbulence again—only this time much stronger, enough to jolt his entire body. His first reaction was alarm, but this was quickly replaced by an instinct for problem-solving. Almost subconsciously, he checked all the important instrumentation, saw nothing unusual. The sky ahead looked clear, the altimeter had been set, and he'd received no weather warnings. He tuned the radio to the ATIS frequency to listen in on the conditions at Hartford. Again, nothing out of the ordinary. But he'd logged enough hours for his instincts to tell him that—

And then, just as suddenly, there it was again: turbulence that was almost like a physical blow, causing him to reflexively, protectively, duck his head, spasming in his seat. Heart beating fast now, he glanced more carefully at the instrumentation, glanced out the window for any signs of smoke or damage, then examined the autopilot settings.

Nothing. *Jesus.*

A thought came into his mind. It wasn't something he cared to dwell on, but now and then he was forced to consider it, if only for self-preservation. Some of AmTex's military contracts were highly classified. The people he employed were meticulously vetted. But there were entities out there who'd pay a great deal of money for his corporation's crown jewels . . . and, no doubt, several unfriendly nation-states that would be just as happy if Pierson Bridger was no longer around. That was, in fact, one reason he preferred to fly himself . . . just as he let his bodyguard double as his chauffeur. Still, it wouldn't require a rogue suicide pilot to do the job: somebody with the right skills could hack the complex elements of a modern autopilot system, and achieve results just as effective.

Thinking along these lines, he grew increasingly unnerved by the autopilot's lack of response. After a jolt like that, it should at least have slowed the engine, corrected for any variation in altitude—after all, you couldn't just force your way through rough turbulence at full speed: not if you wanted to keep the wings on the fuselage.

As a precaution, he disengaged the autopilot and put the controls on manual, throttling back and reducing speed. He'd take it himself for ten minutes or so, make sure everything was copacetic. A little extra seat-of-the-pants flying was probably a good—

Another jolt out of nowhere, even worse than before, like a baseball bat slamming against his headrest; he tried to compensate, but the violence of it sent a galvanic shock through his limbs, jerking the yoke closer to his chest. He tried to push it away, but it was as if his fingers were paralyzed. Then came a noise he'd only heard in a simulator: the stall horn, warning of interrupted airflow over the wings and consequent loss of lift. A split second later, the wing broke hard left and the plane began to corkscrew downward. Bridger stayed calm even in this crisis, remembering the steps required to break out of a spin. PARE: power pulled out, ailerons neutral, rudder kicked out opposite the spin while pushing the elevator forward. But even as he tried to follow through, he felt his hands growing cold, while perversely a terrible warmth spread through his head—could G forces be acting on him already? How had the plane gone out of control, so fast? And then for the briefest moment he recalled a nightmare he'd had during flight school, of looking over and finding his instructor pilot had vanished. The warmth increased, along with a noise that had nothing to do with the screaming of the engines . . . and then, just before he exploded in blinding pain, he realized it was the voice of the plane's ground warning system, calmly giving him audible confirmation that his altitude had fallen below the recommended minimum.

8

At a few minutes before ten the next morning, Logan sat in his office—suite, actually—not far from Claire Asperton's own private hidey-hole. The sun had not yet risen above the eastern ridgeline, and the landscape beyond the window was veiled in mysterious shadow. Directly below him was one of the four massive skyways, running from the central spire out to the Torus. As he watched, a helicopter came in for a landing on a helipad atop the massive western spoke.

His gaze drifted up the flank of the Torus itself, toward where the works of man ended and nature reasserted itself in dense forest. It amazed him: this vast, ring-shaped technological hive, running completely around the perimeter of the valley. Leaving the Complex unnecessarily was frowned upon, but—from what he'd seen already, walking the concourses and parapets—employees were delighted to be here. Not only was the cuisine varied and excellent, but every form of entertainment one could wish for—from symphonies to rock concerts, vast digital libraries to celebrity lectures, squash courts to climbing walls to bowling alleys—were easily accessible day and night.

He turned back to his desk, where he'd spent the previous day and much of the night familiarizing himself with Chrysalis and Russell Spearman. He'd learned a great deal about both—but nothing that shed light on either Spearman's death or the mysterious note.

But now, all that had changed. Yesterday, there had been a single folder on his computer desktop; this morning there were two.

Logan had gone to bed feeling relieved there had been no second catastrophe. But he'd been awakened at 4 a.m. by Claire Asperton. Her tight voice still rang in his ears: *Jeremy, a rural police department just reported the crash of a private jet. The pilot and sole occupant on the manifest was Pierson Bridger, CEO of AmTex—and a board member of Chrysalis.*

He'd been flying from Philly to Hartford when his flight path became erratic. He'd transmitted a final, garbled message, then gone silent. His plane had crashed in a remote section of the Pootatuck State Forest: rescue teams had not found the site until after midnight, and another hour had passed before the body was identified.

An autopsy had been fast-tracked, Asperton told Logan, but was still ongoing. Meanwhile, she'd routed all data she had on Bridger to Logan's temporary office. There had been no further communication from the mysterious messenger, but it seemed all too likely Bridger was this second "drop"—especially when Asperton informed Logan that Bridger, like Spearman, was a member of the Chrysalis board.

He turned from the folders to the computer screen. *Spearman. Bridger.* His investigation could begin in earnest now, starting with a search for any commonality between the two men.

The computer came awake immediately, the display showing a menu busy with options. Speaking the name of an option allowed his Venture unit to control the menu system. More than that, his Venture seemed to have grown more perceptive, guessing his commands and affording him access to a remarkably comprehensive data library, covering not only Chrysalis and its history but just about any other fact or document imaginable.

In retrospect, he was secretly relieved he'd had the previous afternoon and evening to familiarize himself with the place and its operations, uninterrupted. Because boot camp was clearly over . . . and he was on the front lines.

"Pythia, please display personnel folders for J. Russell Spearman and Pierson Bridger." Almost instantaneously, the two encrypted folder icons opened. *My fourth-grade librarian, old Miss Pew, would have traded her maidenhood for magic like this,* he thought. One of the folders—Spearman's—he'd already examined. But now, with the death of Bridger, it had taken on a new meaning entirely.

Two deaths, unrelated save for their connection to Chrysalis. Was the threat in that cryptic note credible? What could be the motivation? With so little to go on, it posed a riddle as difficult to solve as the Riemann hypothesis; the "lonely runner" conjecture; Linear A.

Logan lined the folders up on the desktop and, for the next hour, buried himself in them.

It was an arduous slog. Pathology and toxicology tests weren't in yet on Bridger, although they were due soon. Spearman had certain well-known psychological issues—a narcissistic mood disorder, obsession that manifested in constant insistence on perfection—but if anything, these had been integral to his success, and would not account for falling through a glass table. Logan had already requested Asperton to—beyond the standard metabolic and toxicological panels—run as many special assays as the condition of the bodies allowed: "full-30" heavy metal tests, volatile scan panels. Asperton objected this would take at least ten days, well past the scheduled Voyager rollout; Logan had been polite, but persistent.

Bridger, aged fifty-four, had IBD, but kept it under control with diet and exercise. The condition itself was mild and posed little danger of developing into something like Crohn's disease.

No history of serious injuries except a torn knee a decade before. His psych evals were clean—unusually so for a high-performing executive.

Logan pushed the files to one side of his screen. Both men had apparently been in good overall health, given their ages and genetics.

Time for somebody—or something—else to do the work. "Pythia," he said to his Venture device, "please reconfigure all personal biographical records on Russell Spearman and Pierson Bridger so I can review them side by side for similarities."

He sat back in his chair while a great deal of data—some on the screen, some already converted to Omega-ready 3D—streamed past his gaze. Other than the fact that Spearman seemed a thoroughly unpleasant person, with more than his share of divorces and wrecked competitors, there was nothing that stood out. Nor with Bridger.

He forced himself to sit up. "Pythia," he said, "please run a query to determine when both subjects were together—same times, same locations."

Another set of data ballooned on the screen. A gala at the Waldorf, seven years ago, to welcome Spearman to the board. A ribbon-cutting ceremony for the Torus, four years ago. A symposium on the role of private industry in government defense . . .

"Scroll forward," Logan said. "Display last calendar year only."

He rubbed his eyes, then watched as another list scrolled past. Harvard reunion for alumni of extraordinary achievement; award recipients at the Institute for . . .

"Pythia," Logan said suddenly. "Freeze."

But this command was superfluous. Pythia had reached the end of the list. The final entry was a board meeting—and a tour of the advanced products division—within the very Complex he now sat in.

Two weeks ago.

He stared at the screen a moment. Then he told his Venture unit to ring Asperton's private line.

"Jeremy," came the lawyer's voice a moment later.

"Did you know that both Spearman and Bridger—not to mention the other members of the board—were here recently?"

"Of course. There's a meeting every six months—"

"Hold on. Spearman and Bridger were together just two weeks ago."

"So were the other ten members of the board."

"I know. That's what I'm worried about."

Asperton gave a brief exhalation. "Jeremy, we brought you in because you could bring a unique perspective to this situation—"

"And that's exactly what I'm doing."

"Fair enough. But I've just come from a briefing with the heads of security and infrastructure, and it's their opinion that we're being played. There was nothing in that note to imply Spearman's death was in any way related to Chrysalis."

"The note was sent to you . . . wasn't it?"

"Yes. It mentioned a death and made a vague reference to some second calamity. But it's so vague that we can't jump to conclusions."

Logan could imagine just what the overly defensive security wonks had told Claire Asperton: what would most fully absolve Chrysalis.

"You know," Asperton went on, "it's possible somebody read about Spearman, then went down to the hangar and sabotaged Bridger's plane. Or maybe the two deaths weren't even related: Bridger wasn't especially liked, I understand. Or maybe it was a simple case of engine failure. Why assume it's murder?"

"I wasn't the one to bring up murder," Logan said. "But what makes you sure it wasn't?"

"While Bridger was in the middle of flying back here? It doesn't make sense."

"Wait a minute. Bridger was on his way to the Torus when his plane went down?"

"He was coming back for some special service."

"Special service? You sound like a garage mechanic."

A laugh. "He's got a bad knee. Our medical department gave him a prototype implant that helps with the side effects. Call it a perk of being on the board."

Logan thought quickly. "So Bridger had an implant—a prototype implant—designed by Chrysalis?"

"Yes: designed by BioCertain, to be precise—one of our subsidiaries."

"And he was coming back here for what, exactly? A replacement?"

"God, no. We don't do procedures on-site. You'd have to ask Frank Purchase."

"Who?"

"Frank Purchase. He heads the implants research division." Finally, her voice was beginning to show concern. "What are you driving at?"

"I'm looking for any connections whatsoever. If Bridger was coming back because of some implant he had, I'm assuming he talked to this Frank Purchase about it, two weeks ago, to make the necessary arrangements."

"I suppose so." A brief silence. "Yes, that's correct: Bridger did spend fifteen minutes in BioCertain."

Logan felt a sudden chill. "Did any other board members go off on their own that day? Special consultations or appointments?"

Another brief silence. "No."

"Not even Spearman?"

"I'm looking at their schedules now, including inbound and outbound flights. Nobody."

"In that case, I think you need to take me over to BioCertain. And right away, please."

9

"The entire morning was taken up with group business," Claire Asperton told Logan as they descended the elevator. "Nothing out of the ordinary—balance sheets, growth predictions, and so forth. Then they had lunch before heading out for an update on Omega Two."

The doors opened onto a large, high-ceilinged sky lobby—what seemed a common architectural feature—and Asperton led the way along what Logan soon realized was one of the massive spokes that led out, in ordinal directions, from the central spire to the Torus itself. They were on the highest level of the skyway, judging by the semicircle of glass overhead, affording spectacular views. As usual, they were surrounded by workers walking alone or in small groups, badges of various colors displayed on their casual attire or lab coats. Several seemed surprised to see Asperton among the hoi polloi, and a few others evidently recognized Logan, and they were given a deferentially wide berth.

"I'm no industrial designer," Logan said, "but I'm guessing the Tower is where all the corporate and administrative offices are housed—along with residential and leisure facilities—and the Torus is where the actual work takes place."

"That's basically accurate. The Torus is divided into eight discrete sections—arcs—each devoted to the R&D division of a Chrysalis subsidiary. They're labeled A through G."

"A through G. Seems pretty banal."

"Nobody could think of anything better. Can you?"

Logan thought a moment. "The eight flavors of schizophrenia. The eight different cancers currently detectable by a DNA test."

"I'm not sure that would go down well." She paused, apparently listening to the small device cradled over her ear. "The prelims on Bridger's autopsy are in."

"And?"

"Nothing unusual. No traces of suspicious drugs in his system, and nothing to indicate a stroke, SDS, or any other cardiac death." She paused to listen again. "The body was in poor condition, and we fast-tracked that autopsy just to learn the cause of death was nonspecific."

Other than crashing into the ground at three hundred miles an hour. "How about mechanical failure?"

"It's possible. They're looking into it. But the plane was state-of-the-art and scrupulously maintained, and just passed an annual inspection last week. The preflight check was exhaustive, I understand—it seems Bridger was a stickler about that."

Logan knew the answer to his next question, but asked it anyway. "Any psychiatric issues?"

"You've seen the files. Nothing relevant. Neither of them presented with any depression or suicidal ideation—especially not Spearman, with that ego of his."

They had now reached the point where the northern skyway intersected the curve of the Torus. Asperton led them down an escalator, threaded her way briefly through a crowded sky lobby, larger than the ones Logan had seen in the spire, then guided them onto a people mover that protruded slightly from the inner flank of the Torus—probably to improve its views, Logan realized. It was surrounded by a cradle of tinted glass, and now he recalled seeing it from his suite: running laterally along the Torus like the mud vein of an endless, circular shrimp.

"We're headed for B," Asperton said. "That's where the labs, think tanks, and segmented area of BioCertain is located."

"The pharmacological division?"

Asperton shook her head. "You're thinking of Carewell Pharmaceuticals. BioCertain develops medical hardware: everything from surgical lasers to lithium CFx pacemakers to small-footprint hyperbaric chambers."

She guided Logan off the people mover and onto the main concourse, which curved on gently ahead of them. To the left were windows facing the spire; to the right was the bulk of the Torus, where the labs and offices were housed and all the proprietary work performed. Its walls were punctuated here and there by windows—some clear, some smoked—and doors equipped with security scanners. There was a plaza nearby, with couches and tables and a bustling food court. Logan guessed this was a natural division between Arc B—their destination—and whatever mysteries were contained in A, which they'd just hurried past.

"The rest of the board went somewhere else before visiting the Omega division?" he asked.

Asperton nodded. "Agrinox. Some very interesting things are happening there, like an organic manure hybrid that repels pests. We're taking it to market in just over a month, by the way."

"Hell, I'd knock people over in my hurry to see that, too."

Asperton shot him a disapproving look. "Several of our board members represent companies with interests in crop production, livestock, or similar agribusiness."

She stopped at a large door, pressed her hand against a palm analyzer, and it opened onto a wide, sterile-looking hallway, with a female receptionist-cum–security guard seated to one side. Ahead, Logan could hear the chatter of conversation and the hum of light machinery.

The receptionist stood when she saw Asperton enter; they

exchanged a few words, and then the woman spoke into her Omega device—which, like all the rest here, looked different from Logan's. Within sixty seconds, a tall, thin man of about forty emerged from a door near the end of the hallway and strode purposefully toward them. He had reddish hair and, as he drew nearer, Logan saw that his eyes were of a piercing blue shade.

"Ms. Asperton," he said, shaking the lawyer's hand. "I've been expecting you."

"Dr. Purchase—Frank—thanks for taking the time on such short notice." She turned to Logan. "Frank, this is Jeremy Logan. He's doing some data analysis for us on the corporate level—streamlining resources . . . you know the kind of thing."

Dr. Purchase did, apparently, know the kind of thing: Logan was a moneyman, out to cut jobs and expenses. Purchase's attitude, already friendly, now became faintly deferential. Luckily, it seemed he hadn't heard of Logan; in retrospect, Logan realized, it might have been better if they'd given him a new name to go along with this phony position at Chrysalis.

Purchase opened a nearby door that gave onto a small conference room, and they all took seats around the lone table. "We won't take up much of your time," Asperton said. "We understand Piers Bridger is on his way back—to see you, I believe."

"Yes, that's correct. We've blocked out an hour in one of the labs for four p.m. this afternoon."

Logan had to admit this was masterful: it put Purchase, a big deal in BioCertain, in the spotlight. He'd be too concerned wondering if he'd made some faux pas to ask questions of his own. Asperton spent a moment fussing with her tablet and smoothing down her skirt. Logan realized that, if Purchase knew Bridger was already dead, he'd obviously be talking about it right now . . . instead of the visit scheduled for late afternoon. Apparently, it was too early for the news to have spread—or perhaps, Chrysalis had controlled access to it in here, within the Complex. Either way, the head of Implants Research was in for a nasty surprise.

"And this was the outgrowth of a conversation you had with him after the recent board meeting?"

Purchase nodded. "He and the rest of the board were on a tight schedule. I showed him mock-ups of our latest devices."

Logan nodded. "And that's all?"

"No." Purchase ran a hand through his red hair. "He seemed fascinated by medical technology—perhaps because of his own implant. I also showed him the line."

"The line?"

"Yes, the production line. Not directly, of course—it's deep in a class-one-hundred clean room—but I took him to an observation gallery with a video feed."

"BioCertain is one of two areas in the Torus that not only does the technical development, but also the manufacturing of certain products," Asperton explained. "Like MMDs."

Logan gave her a questioning look.

"Mobile medical devices—drug infusion products for people with compromised immune systems. Neurostimulation systems for chronic pain. Therapeutic *and* diagnostic, external or subdermal, worn twenty-four/seven."

"We're constantly improving our medication delivery systems for common conditions like high blood pressure," Purchase said. "Very useful for dementia patients as well, who can't be relied on to take their meds. Bridger's own knee condition makes a good example."

"Tell me more about that, if you wouldn't mind," said Logan.

"Certainly. He suffered from crepitus."

Logan had heard of many exotic ailments, but not this one. The file had mentioned only IBS and a torn knee. "Excuse me?"

"It's a condition of the knee joint where movement causes significant pain and frequent swelling. In Bridger's case, it started ten years ago, when he fell chasing his dog down a muddy embankment. He's done PT to strengthen the muscles surrounding the joint, but with post-traumatic osteoarthritis like his that can only go so far. He tried wearing a knee brace, but disliked it—interfered with his flying, he said. Ambutrexine, one of Carewell's newer meds—fresh out of trials—ultimately did the trick."

"Can you tell me a little more about this med?" Logan asked.

Purchase hemmed and hawed. "I can tell you they used methotrexate as a foundation, given how the other common base drug used for the condition has a higher incidence of adverse side effects."

Logan opened his mouth to ask a question, decided against it.

"Bridger said it practically turned his life around. And when we developed a delivery system a year ago, he was all over it. So to speak." Purchase flashed a small, embarrassed smile.

"What type of delivery system?" Logan asked. This was the second time the man had used the term.

"Subcutaneous implant. One type of MMD. About the size of a small automotive fuse, slipped in behind the lateral collateral ligament. It has a miniaturized receiver that lets him administer dosages, as needed." His smile had now turned into one of satisfaction. "The implant allowed the medication to work much more rapidly and consistently, of course. And the Ambutrexine was so effective that, when I saw him two weeks ago, he said he was down to just a handful of doses per week—and eager for the Mark III to get its FDA approval."

"What is the Mark III?"

"Our newest version, half the size of the Mark II. It can actually sit between the patella and meniscus. The user doesn't even know it's there. Amazing, really: infusion chamber excepted, it's smaller than the movement of a Swiss watch."

Current model, Logan thought. Purchase had gone into full salesman mode. "So does this Mark III come equipped with a Continental tire?" he asked.

Purchase laughed gamely, then both he and Asperton stood up. "Any more questions, Jeremy?" Asperton asked.

"No." Logan turned to the BioCertain exec. "Thanks so much for your time."

"Of course." Purchase hesitated. "Was there some problem? Did Mr. Bridger have any particular feedback?"

"No, nothing like that. This is just routine, as I told you earlier." Asperton thanked him, and Logan followed her out of the office.

As they returned to the reception area, they passed a young woman just entering BioCertain. She smiled at them, and—as she turned to greet the receptionist—Logan noticed a small mole, perfectly centered beneath her chin.

It was, he thought, a rare beauty mark indeed.

10

Logan followed Asperton down the concourse. The lawyer was silent, seemingly lost in thought.

"So Bridger was on medication for a knee injury," Logan said after a moment.

Asperton nodded. "But he'd been on it for over two years. As it happens, I'm familiar with the clinical history of Ambutrexine, both during trials and after it was approved for general use. One of our more popular new medications, with very few contraindications." She paused. "I feel bad about the deception, but if Purchase learned about Bridger's death, he might be . . . well, less forthcoming."

"He's down one Mark III customer."

"I used to think, cynically, high-end medical upgrades were just a new status symbol for aging people of means: having the latest-generation pacemaker, with all the cellular bells and whistles. Until I got one myself."

Logan was surprised. "You?" The lawyer was trim, apparently in good health, and well under fifty.

"BioCertain's finest. My SA node was damaged by myocarditis three years ago—a lasting gift from a vacation I took, paddling down the Amazon. They're amazing things, really—this latest generation of medical implants. Frank wasn't just being a pitchman back there. They have come a long way from the old nickel-cadmium or metallic plutonium batteries. We've got the miniaturization process nailed; tethering, too. Button cells as small as five millimeters that provide cardiac stimulation for twenty years. Telemetry alarm systems so if anything goes wrong, a monitoring station is immediately alerted."

"Do any other board members have medical implants?"

"I know Miles Johnson has the same BioCertain pacemaker I do; we talked about it when I saw him at the board meeting."

"Any others?"

"I'm not sure."

"Isn't that relevant?" Logan asked. "I mean, this implant wasn't mentioned in Bridger's medical dossier."

"Probably too minor a procedure to include. It's not our job to monitor every medication our board members take, far less elective or cosmetic surgeries. If Spearman had decided to have yet another face-lift, for example, I doubt we'd be the wiser."

"Think you can dig a little deeper for me? And speaking of Bridger, I wasn't aware of his Ambutrexine use. I know you say it's a safe drug, but—"

"The ME said there were no traces of unusual drugs: that includes corticosteroids, which would have shown up if Bridger had taken Ambutrexine before or during the flight."

Logan cursed under his breath. The fact the Chrysalis board had met here just two weeks before had seemed such a promising lead. And the fact one of them—one only—had made a detour to a classified research division seemed even more promising. But it was a dead end.

"What next?" Asperton asked, as if reading his mind.

Logan sighed. "I start playing board member. Follow their footsteps of two weeks ago."

Asperton frowned. "If every board member was involved, what could you possibly discover?"

"I won't know until I discover it."

There was a brief pause.

"Well, at least it won't be difficult to do," Asperton said. "After lunch, the board members only visited three divisions. And we're coming up on one of them now."

A visit to Agrinox did nothing but acquaint Logan with several new kinds of fertilizer, and then another five-minute walk through the pleasantly humid air of the Torus brought them to the Arc that housed New Eden. A brisk, businesslike woman met them inside the D security barrier, then led them into a small conference room similar to BioCertain's. New Eden, Logan learned, was a complex AI system that functioned, essentially, as a dating service on steroids: finding perfect matches for candidates and guaranteeing lifetime compatibility. Several years earlier, the original Eden building had suffered a crippling fire—Logan vaguely recalled reading about it—and afterward was purchased and rebuilt, essentially from the ashes, by Chrysalis. It was scheduled to go back on line early next year, and as a result the board members had convened here for an explanation of the updated technology. Logan asked several questions, but when he learned that client interactivity at New Eden was limited to personality inventories, he lost interest. As they thanked the woman and returned once again to the concourse, he began to wonder if perhaps the unspoken thought behind Asperton's frown was correct: this line of inquiry was a waste of time.

"Damn," Asperton said. "Who the hell could this be?"

She was looking down at the tablet in her hand.

"What is it?" Logan asked.

"A call coming in. But nobody in the Torus would route a message through my tablet, because . . ."

Suddenly she went absolutely still. As Logan dropped his own gaze to her tablet, he saw a series of words—white against black—slowly form.

"*Christ!*" he said. "Claire, you need to alert someone—immediately."

His sharp voice snapped the lawyer out of her shock, and suddenly she was in frantic motion. "Dispatch?" she said, now pressing a hand against the Omega device circling her ear. "This is Claire Asperton. I need an emergency link to Marceline Williams. Williams of the Halcyon Publishing Group. She's in London, staying at the Connaught. No, I *don't* know the goddamned number! You need to get her now, *right now,* because . . ."

Asperton's voice receded in Logan's mind as he reread the words on her tablet—and their implication burned into him:

> *Two down.*
> *Are you starting to understand?*
> *If so, you'd better call Marceline.*
> *Call her right away.*

11

Wendy Rothman sat in the marble-draped fastness of the Connaught Hotel's lobby, legs invisible behind a bulwark of baggage. The lobby was perfect, as befitted London's best hotel: elegant, tasteful, with a mix of decorum and solicitude furnishing an air of *gens de notre milieu*. Even the traffic outside, speeding around Carlos Place on its way toward Grosvenor Square, seemed to grow more discreet, slowing and refraining from any presses of the horn. People passed by in groups of twos and threes, occasionally assisted by a member of the staff; if Wendy had been people-watching, she would almost certainly have spotted at least one movie star, fashion designer, head of state, or celebrity philanthropist. But she was not taking in passersby. Her eyes were riveted on the nearby bank of elevators, and the discreet numbers that were set above them.

She'd been told when she took this job—warned, actually—that this would happen. Wendy had paid little attention, believing the opportunity far outweighed any potential crisis. But now, staring at the elevator door that refused to open, she wasn't so sure.

One of the bags at her feet belonged to her. Three others were long black totes made of ballistic nylon, the kind used for large tripods or other photographic equipment. And the other two bags—the Louis Vuitton steamers—belonged to Marceline.

Marceline Williams, president and publisher of Halcyon Group, along with its twelve imprints spread over five divisions. Marceline Williams, who, according to the Wharton academician who'd bestowed an honorary PhD on her the previous week, had "done more to give voice to new writers than anyone else now on earth." Marceline Williams, who—in the role of mentor, confessor, best friend, drill instructor, counselor, champion—had her name behind more best-selling success stories than anyone in New York and Hollywood combined.

Marceline Williams, who—according to an informal count—missed four out of every ten flights she was booked on, and managed to delay two of the remaining six.

Nobody quite understood why this was. Marceline—she insisted on first names—was on time to every meeting, luncheon, awards banquet, and television interview she was booked for. Right now, her bags lay at Wendy's ankles, packed and ready to go. But she always, *always*, had trouble getting to airports. Worst of all, she didn't recognize the problem, and bringing up the subject was the only thing guaranteed to enrage her. And on those rare times she grew angry, she tended to fire someone.

Wendy's own editorial boss had just quit to go to law school—a not uncommon exit ramp in the business—and Wendy had been unsure what her own fate would be: she didn't have enough experience under her belt to become an editor herself, but she was overqualified to be some other editor's assistant. And it was just then that Marceline's invitation had come. Each year, she took a different companion to the world's biggest book fair. More often than not, getting to know Marceline and—especially—having her watch how you dealt with foreign publishers and agents, how you evaluated literary properties, was like strapping an afterburner to your career. She was remarkably modest considering her degree of power, and she was quick to reward those who had a real talent for fostering writers.

Of course, there was the problem with flight times. And now, with this two-day stopover in London complete, the most important flight of all—the one to Frankfurt—was leaving Heathrow in just over ninety minutes.

Wendy's boyfriend, en route to a doctorate in psychology, had a variety of theories for Marceline's condition, most dealing with some kind of chemical imbalance. People at Halcyon liked to speculate endlessly about her mental and emotional health, just like they gossiped about her private life. Right now, however, Wendy wasn't doing any speculating at all. She was looking at the three cell phones held awkwardly in her left hand, and wondering if she dared call Marceline's room and suggest—ever so gently—that they meet in the lobby.

She glanced at Carlos Place. Mayfair was busy this time of the evening, and their limousine—which, like Wendy, had been waiting for twenty minutes—had finally been shooed away by the valets, and was now on the far side of the small triangular square formed by the intersection with Mount Street. One of the phones—her own—buzzed, and a message appeared. It was the driver.

Need to leave NOW traffic on M4 delayed

Need to leave now. *Now.* She glanced at her watch: the driver wasn't exaggerating.

Screw it: missing the flight would be worse than giving the publisher a nudge. Picking up her own phone while balancing the other two, she placed a call to the Somerset Suite, several floors above.

At that moment, several things happened. One of the elevator doors opened and Marceline emerged: glamorous as always, looking bright and fresh and eager to take on the world. At the same time, one of Marceline's two phones—her business number—began to ring. It was a number Wendy didn't recognize, area code

860, but that was a moot point: as Wendy pressed her own phone to end the call, her finger slipped and all three futuristic phones went sailing through the air, landing on the carpeting near the main entrance and bouncing once or twice before coming to a standstill.

"And who says time doesn't fly?" Marceline said with a good-humored laugh as Wendy scrambled to pick up the three cell phones. The fumble, along with Marceline's appearance, had stirred the valets and doormen, and a group of them came over to help with the luggage.

Marceline looked Wendy up and down with a concerned expression. "Are you all right, baby?" She called everyone "baby," even the current vice president of the United States, whose autobiography she was personally editing.

"Oh, yes, thanks, I'm fine." If Marceline had no idea what was wrong, Wendy wasn't going to try explaining.

"It's all good," Marceline said, putting on her sunglasses as she made her way toward the lobby exit, jostling past people as if they weren't there and followed by Wendy and the train of baggage-carriers. "You'll love the book fair. I've been talking to Renauld's agent, and I think we have a chance to sweep up her sequels. *All* of them, lock, stock, and barrel."

They made their way out into the evening, Wendy balancing two bags in one hand while gesturing to the limo across the square with the other.

"Oh, no need to bring him over," Marceline said. "I could use the walk."

Jesus.

Outside the cocoon of the lobby, traffic was much louder: she could hear trucks grinding gears, the low diesel roar of the London transport buses.

The limo driver, spotting them, eased the vehicle forward until he was just across, separated only by the triangle of pavement and its black statues. The retinue altered course accordingly as Wendy silently blessed the chauffeur.

Just then, Marceline's other phone—the private one—rang.

The publisher, hearing its particular tone, stopped. "Who is it?"

Taking a deep, shuddering breath, Wendy put down the suitcases to check. "I'm not sure," she replied. "The same person just tried your business cell. It's an 860 area code."

"Oh. I'd better take that." And Marceline put out her hand.

Take it in the fucking car! But Wendy's scream was as silent as Edvard Munch's, and she handed over the phone.

Marceline put it to her ear, realized it was upside down, smiled at Wendy in mock embarrassment. "Hello?" A London bus was lumbering down Carlos Place—Wendy could make out the driver in his silly uniform, and the sign MARBLE ARCH—PIMLICO bolted just below the roof—and Marceline pressed the phone more tightly to her ear. "Claire! I'm just off to Frankfurt."

Five seconds passed, but it seemed an age, as Marceline listened. Wendy glanced past the statues. The limo driver was staring back, tapping his watch, his face an anguished mask.

"Yes, of course I'm all right, baby! *What?* No, not in the least." Marceline's voice rose with the sound of the oncoming bus. "Well, if it's as important as all that, I—give me a moment, Claire, something's a bit odd."

Now Wendy decided the time had come to take action: she nodded at the valets, then at the limo. Comprehending immediately, they nodded back and moved quickly down toward the zebra crossing.

Wendy looked back, and was shocked to see Marceline staring at her. Slowly, the woman took off her sunglasses. She blinked slowly: once, twice. For a moment, Wendy wondered if the publisher was angry she'd taken the initiative with the bags. But no: as the roar of the traffic grew louder, Marceline gave her a small smile.

And then—with a brisk about-face reminiscent of a Kensington Palace guard—she turned and stepped directly into the path of the oncoming bus.

Wendy, disbelieving and uncomprehending, didn't close her eyes in time to avoid the instant dissolution that followed. Marceline's phone hit Wendy in the forehead, and now she closed her eyes instinctively. And with that blackness came a warm spray across her lips and hair, followed by screams and cries that began to drown out the piercing squeal of brakes.

12

At quarter past nine, Logan was in his modest office suite on the eighth floor of the spire—deep in files both digital and tactile—when a knock sounded on his door and Claire Asperton entered. She was carrying her digital tablet in one hand and bore the expression of someone tasked with cleaning the Augean Stables. She'd taken some personal time the night before, and Logan had needed the precious hours to expand his background research to include Marceline Williams—and the vexing question of whether her horrific death was in any way related to the board's visit to Chrysalis two weeks earlier.

He turned away from his monitor, and the folders—now totaling three—displayed on it.

Asperton tapped briefly on her tablet. "We now have comprehensive autopsy results on all three, and initial toxicology reports on Bridger and Steadman. All three suffered acute physical trauma, especially extreme in Bridger's case. But Marceline Williams wasn't in much better shape. Bottom line: in all cases, lethal assault is not indicated, but it can't totally be ruled out—not yet."

As she was speaking, Logan's Omega unit chimed. "Pythia," he said, "open the door, please."

The door sprang ajar and a man Logan hadn't met stepped in. He was blond, short, and appeared no older than thirty. He nodded at Asperton, then stood looking at Logan, who quickly offered him a chair.

"Hello, Orris," Asperton said. "I knew you'd track me down. This, as you know, is Jeremy Logan. Jeremy, Orris Peyton, head of Operational Logistics here at the Complex."

The man nodded curtly at Logan, then sat in the proffered chair. He was young to be the top cop. Silently, Logan took in the tension in the room. In the last few days, their situation had gone from a tragic accident, to tragic coincidence, to full-blown crisis. Asperton looked stricken, while Peyton's face was an unreadable mask. The air felt full of dynamite: it seemed to Logan the slightest spark would set it off.

"Marceline was the youngest of the three," Asperton said, consulting her tablet, "but she had the longest medical record."

Logan nodded. While enrolled at Wharton Business School, Marceline Williams had an emergency appendectomy. At thirty, she'd undergone a hysterectomy, underlying cause chronic endometriosis. Finally, at thirty-nine she'd had a lumpectomy, a preventive measure due to the breast cancer that ran in her family. But that had been a decade ago, and there were no complications. Her psychiatric profile showed occasional migraines and mild aviophobia—fear of flying—but nothing severe.

"Would you mind running the special blood assays on her that I requested for Spearman and Bridger?" Logan asked.

Asperton looked pained. "Jeremy, we're not going to get the results you *already* requested until next week. What's the point of doing such exotic blood tests when we don't know what we're looking for—and, more to the point, when we've so little time?"

"Is there any harm?"

"Spearman's executors weren't too keen on us reopening the casket for additional fingernail and toenail samples."

"Well, assuming the autopsy file on Williams isn't closed yet, she shouldn't present the same problem." Logan paused. "Come on. I'll buy you an ice cream sundae at that malt stand one level down."

Asperton grimaced, made a notation on her tablet.

Logan changed the subject. "I realize Marceline's assistant was in a state of shock yesterday, but has she provided any further details about what happened, exactly?"

"Wendy Rothman. Yes. There was nothing obviously amiss beyond Marceline being late. They walked to the curb. And then Marceline crumpled forward—underneath a sightseeing bus."

Logan nodded. He'd heard—indirectly, echoing from her Omega—the sound of something loud and awful, just before the connection was lost.

"It was the height of the evening rush hour," Peyton said, speaking for the first time. "Thing is, the limo driver didn't see any groaning or staggering—he swears she was pushed."

"By whom?"

"He doesn't know. Someone in the crowd."

"When I was on the phone with Marceline . . ." Asperton began, then stopped a moment. "She told me . . . she said that something was *odd*."

"Odd?" Peyton echoed. "In what way?"

Asperton shrugged, glanced at him. "You've reached out to the rest of the board, right?"

"We're getting protective details on all of them as quickly and quietly as possible. It's a hell of a job—they're spread across the world. We're telling them about the deaths, without specifics, with warnings to keep it under the radar."

Logan could guess what the others were thinking. *Two down. Are you starting to understand?* Marceline Williams made three. She'd been the publisher of Halcyon Group. When it became a Chrysalis subsidiary during the entertainment expansion, its com-ics division was the first to be coded for Omega readability . . . and Williams had joined the board. Had that acquisition been—in retrospect—her death warrant?

"As far as I can tell, the three who've been targeted had little in common," Logan said. "They weren't outspoken on the same issues; they weren't reviled for any particular positions, political or otherwise."

"What's your point?" Peyton asked. He spoke in staccato tones, practically biting off his words. It was clear he viewed these developments as something like an insult, being overlord of corporate security—and, perhaps, Logan's presence as a personal offense.

"My point is, we currently have two potential lines of investigation: finding commonalities, eliminating motives. These three weren't singled out on principle. And while some internet troll could have falsely claimed one, or even two, deaths for himself, three can't be a bluff. These people were killed because they share seats on the Chrysalis board."

"I don't see how that eliminates any motives," Peyton said after a moment. "But it does highlight a commonality. They shared production-version Voyagers."

"That's true," Asperton said. "During the VR demo, they were all issued the new devices."

"Did they keep them?" Logan asked.

Asperton tapped on her tablet. "It looks like eight left the Center with the upgraded Omega IIs."

"Not that it makes much difference," Peyton said. "Their devices won't go live with the new content until Monday morning, like everyone else's."

"That reminds me." Asperton pulled out an envelope. "Here's the digging you requested. Three members of the board have BioCertain-manufactured MMEs."

Logan took the envelope, removed the sheet within, and scanned it. Miles Johnson, as Asperton mentioned, had the latest pacemaker. Bridger had been given the infusion device for his knee problem, and another whose name Logan didn't recognize had an insulin regulator.

Peyton reached over and Logan handed him the sheet. Peyton scanned it quickly. "What did you request this for?"

"I just told you. Commonalities."

"What kind of commonality is *this*? Three different medical devices, addressing three different conditions?"

"Bridger had a BioCertain implant."

"But Spearman didn't," Peyton said, tossing the sheet onto Logan's desk. "Neither did Williams. And they're just as dead."

"It's an interesting hypothesis," Asperton said quietly. "But there are just too many people out there wearing BioCertain devices—including yours truly—without fatalities."

"Besides," Peyton said, "only three board members have implants, most for several years. On the other hand, *eight* members left here with Voyager VR units two weeks ago."

"Including Spearman," Asperton added quietly.

Logan couldn't argue. "Then let's back up a little. In the unlikely event these three were murdered, how could those acts be accomplished?"

"Given the condition of the bodies, it's hard to be sure with Bridger or Marceline. But the MEs have ruled neither death a homicide. As for Spearman, his fatal lacerations were self-inflicted and unintentional. And remember, both Spearman and Williams were surrounded by witnesses." The lawyer consulted her tablet. "There's something here I didn't know about Spearman, though. He'd been diagnosed with cyclothymia five years ago."

"Cyclothymia?" Peyton repeated. "Just what the hell is that—fear of bicycles?"

"It's a mood disorder," Logan told him. This little nugget had, in fact, been in Spearman's file: he was surprised Asperton hadn't noticed. "Quite rare. Similar to bipolar syndrome in some ways, but not as severe: it doesn't even merit a spot on Cluster B."

"Mood?" Peyton echoed. "As in cranky, irritable, eccentric?"

"Possibly," Logan replied.

"Christ, everybody in the entertainment industry has that *disorder.*"

"And it wouldn't account for the display Spearman put on directly before his death," Asperton said. "According to those present, his actions were closer to psychosis. But again, his blood work came back clean. His dopamine levels were a little high, but his serotonin—which you'd think would be the complicating factor—was within acceptable limits. And there were no illicit drugs in his system—PCP, meth—that would account for his, ah, seizure."

Peyton shifted impatiently in his chair. "Controversial politics, cyclothymia, exotic blood tests—all this speculation in the name of 'commonalities'—when we've already got a *commonality* under our thumb."

Logan turned from Peyton to Asperton. "What's he talking about?"

But Asperton was staring at Peyton. "Are you sure this is the right time?" she asked.

"Three dead, Claire. How much longer are we going to wait?"

Asperton let her gaze drop. Then she nodded. "Very well. But no witnesses. And . . . well, don't *break* anything."

Almost before the lawyer was finished speaking, Peyton was on his feet. Sensing a development, Logan rose as well. Peyton glanced at him; started to say something; then fell silent.

"Where are we going?" Logan asked. When Peyton didn't answer, he turned to Asperton. "And aren't you coming?"

The woman had turned her gaze toward the window. "Call me when the show's over."

As Logan followed the operations manager out the door, Asperton remained motionless, staring out the window, brooding and silent.

13

Compared to the low-key but relatively garrulous Asperton, Peyton made for a vile tour guide. He answered Logan's questions in monosyllables as he led the way through unmarked doors, down yellow-striped concrete stairwells, and along corridors that grew increasingly drab and institutional—a far cry from the beautifully designed and furnished Complex Logan had grown used to.

Within minutes, they were heading down a hallway so long and straight that, Logan realized, it must be one of the four spokes leading from the central spire toward the Torus. The walls were curved slightly like the belly of a ship—implying they were on the lowest level—and there were no windows. Instead, data panels set into the walls winked green, orange, and red, and people in electric carts sped back and forth on nameless errands. Logan noticed that, although they had the standard-issue badges he'd seen throughout the Complex, most workers on this level were wearing formfitting jumpsuits. But Logan had little time to observe; if anything, Peyton walked faster the farther they went. Now and then, he seemed to be talking to himself, but Logan realized he was transmitting orders via his Omega device.

Reaching the far end of the spoke, they turned right and started down another corridor, wider but equally utilitarian. Peyton stopped at a bank of elevators and Logan followed the operations director inside. To his surprise, they were at the top rather than the bottom level. Peyton pressed a button on the control panel.

"What's down here?" Logan asked. "The Chrysalis salt mines?"

"I'm not sure how to take that. My grandfather was a coal miner in West Virginia."

"Take it however you'd like. I just had no idea that part of the Torus was actually underground."

"This isn't the Torus. This is what makes the Torus—and everything else here—run."

The subterranean elevator stopped, and the doors opened onto another industrial corridor. It was warmer down here, and louder: not with music, but the thrum of machinery. The walls were dense with signage, and more people in jumpsuits were scurrying here and there. It seemed as if he'd just stepped out into a lower, institutional deck of an ocean liner.

Peyton opened a door marked simply PRIVATE. Inside was a large office, with a bank of electronics on one wall and a row of privacy blinds opposite. There was a desk; a large conference table surrounded by chairs; and various pieces of equipment on wheeled stainless-steel carts.

"Snow?" Peyton said, seemingly talking to himself again. "Everything in place?"

Logan watched as Peyton nodded at the response. "All right, then. Calm, quick, and by the numbers. I'll be watching." Then he moved to the far side of the desk, pressed a button, and the wall-to-wall privacy blinds were drawn up, like the asbestos safety curtain of a theater stage.

"Jesus," Logan murmured.

A wall of windows looked down over a huge room, perhaps three stories deep, that was something between mission control and an ant farm. He could see row upon row of workstations, each glowing from the illumination of two or even three monitors. At least a hundred people occupied the hangar-like space. He noticed that a number of them were armed.

"What the hell is all that?" Logan asked.

"That, Dorothy, is what's behind the curtain," Peyton said. "Now, come over here. Things are going to happen quickly, and I won't have time to nursemaid you."

"I'm already weaned."

"We'll see about that." Peyton took a seat at the conference table and motioned Logan to do the same. He pulled one of several idle laptops close to them, woke it, then went through a brief syncing process with his Omega device.

"All right, Dr. Logan," he said as the screen displayed the Chrysalis logo. "I've been told to extend you 'every courtesy.' To be honest, I don't know how a publicity hound like you can help."

He swiveled the screen toward Logan. "I'm going to show you a series of short clips. Please watch as I explain: this is your precious 'commonality' in the flesh."

The screen flickered, then arranged itself into three windows. On the left half of the screen was, apparently, a video capture, currently paused. The other, smaller windows were filled with scrolling metadata and other information Logan couldn't parse.

Peyton issued a command via his Omega and the window on the left came to life. It was not a grainy security cam, or the blurred, heat-responsive blobs of an infrared viewer. Rather, the window was alive with tiny black line segments, arranging themselves in such a way as to make distinct images, like iron filings responding to a magnet. The jittering, flickering threads had taken the form of a man in a short-sleeved shirt, unlocking a keyboard case, then bending over the now-exposed keys. He began typing, looking over his shoulder furtively every few seconds. The image jumped around ever so slightly, like an old silent movie whose nitrate stock had been run through too many projectors.

"What the hell kind of new technology is this?" Logan asked. "Is that—camera—peering through walls?"

"Meet Karel Mossby," Peyton said instead of answering a question that was obviously a trade secret. "Systems programmer and Chrysalis employee. He used to be at Infinium, and during the merger Wrigley insisted we bring him over. Loved the guy. Apparently, he'd managed to optimize some codec into two dozen lines of assembly code, half the number anyone else had achieved." He snorted his opinion of this achievement.

As Peyton spoke, a different video began. Now the man— Logan could tell quite clearly, despite the odd medium, it was the same man—was entering a room marked SERVER FARM B2—NO AIR-BREATHING ENTITIES AUTHORIZED! He closed the door behind him, then stepped forward and bent over a rack of thickly twisted cables.

"Wrigley thought Mossby was a genius," Peyton said. "I suppose he is. But he never took to the rules of our little community here in the woods. He missed the freedom of places like Berkeley and Infinium. Despite warnings, he ignored our guidelines. Nothing wrong with a young man being curious—but his was the wrong kind of curiosity."

Logan watched as the figure on the screen deftly switched several cables. Hearing the cherubic Peyton refer to anyone as a "young man" seemed risible.

"At last, things got to the point where his messing around became a danger to operational integrity. Anybody else would have been yanked, given a first-class debriefing, then fired. But that was during our honeymoon with Infinium, so to keep Wrigley happy, Mossby became a white hat with highly restricted access."

"White hat?" Logan repeated. "As in, hackers who find flawed code for the good guys?"

"Right. Performing pen tests, ensuring area denial was as robust as possible." On the screen now was what appeared to be a dormitory. Logan could see the strange, jittery image of Mossby, this time kneeling behind a steel bunk bed and prizing up a piece of flooring with a crowbar. "Mossby was put behind a secure moat. Or so we thought. But as you can see, he continued his unauthorized activities. So: You wanted a commonality? Well, here's one—roaming wild. But he's about to be domesticated."

"And you think he's responsible for those messages?" Logan asked. "For the three deaths?"

Peyton picked up on his skeptical tone. "Dr. Logan, would it surprise you to learn that—with all the 'skunk works' and classified projects being developed here by Chrysalis subsidiaries—this little mountain valley holds more scientific talent than anywhere else on earth?"

"It would," Logan said, quite honestly.

"With so many superior minds, selecting the eager while winnowing out the venal is a task we'll never get a hundred percent right. Scientists and strictures are like oil and vinegar. I'll deny ever telling you this, but right now there are thirty or so hackers, agents provocateurs, pranksters, and—yes—corporate spies here at the Complex that we're surveilling. Some we rein in; others we mislead. But Mossby is in a class by himself. When he was forced out of VR work, we were left with a mind not only brilliant but bored and, it seems, resentful. For a while, Mossby spent his idle hours leeching away ten percent of our processing power for some private project of his own—the second clip you saw. And he spent a lot of time using 'row hammer' attacks on Omega's firewall—I doubt it was homesickness for Infinium. But now here, you're watching him introduce a worm into the internal messaging database, no doubt hoping for access to the Helix—"

As he recounted these arcane feats, Peyton's voice had risen indignantly. But now he caught himself. For a moment he went pale, and Logan sensed both fear and anger as the man realized he'd said too much.

"What's the Helix—?" he began.

With remarkable speed, Peyton leaned in toward Logan, extending a warning finger as he did so. The sudden motion pushed his suit jacket back, and Logan saw the handle of a small-caliber Glock nestled into a belt holster.

"That was my mistake," he said. "So I'll tell you once—nicely. Don't say that word again while you're here. It has nothing to do with your investigation—and it's not something you *ever* want to grow curious about."

Suddenly, the image on the screen flickered again; went black; then came back into focus, this time as a normal, full-colored video feed. It displayed an empty hallway, someone just walking into view. It was Mossby. The laptop speaker, silent until now, crackled into life. Logan temporarily put aside Peyton's odd threat to watch as another two men and a woman appeared out of nowhere to surround Mossby, spin him around, and, with shouted obscenities, push him against the nearest wall, then—guns drawn—cuff and lead him, protesting loudly, through a doorway and off camera. The door closed and the hallway was empty once again.

A second later, Logan heard a chirp from Peyton's Omega. The head of Logistics listened a moment, said, "Excellent," then glanced at Logan.

"Problem solved," he said, leaning back in his chair.

"I'm glad you think so."

Peyton snorted. "O ye of little faith. The man you just saw was angry at Omega for demoting him; he had the ability to send the kind of internal messages Claire Asperton received . . . and he has the ability to plan exactly the kind of exploits that are plaguing us."

"But those images you just showed me—if they are what you say—have no relation to the deaths of the board members."

"This is a tiny fraction of what we have on Mossby. Those thirty rogue workers I mentioned? In terms of capability and motive, he tops the list, by far. We've been watching, assembling evidence, just waiting for Asperton to give us the green light to snag him. If she'd done it a couple of days ago, a few more board members might still be alive." Peyton stood up.

"When will I get a chance to question him?"

"*You?*" Peyton asked, as if this possibility had not occurred to him. "That depends."

"On what?"

"Protocol—among other things. Nobody can talk to him for the moment; not while he's being processed. After that, we'll see." He gestured toward the door. "But I think it's safe to say your 'commonality' is now safely in our hands. I even allowed you to watch his capture. Now, if you'll come with me, I'll find someone to escort you back upstairs and out of this—what did you call it? Oh, yes: salt mine."

14

Five minutes later, Logan was back in the familiar high-ceilinged Torus. He tapped his Omega device. "Pythia," he said, "call Claire Asperton."

There was a moment of silence, then Asperton came on the line. "Enjoy the show?"

"It was confusing. And not very sporting."

"When someone gets fired from the Complex, Peyton usually prefers to give them a running head start—before shooting them in the back."

"Well, this one wasn't fired, and he wasn't released. He's going to be 'processed'—whatever that means." He paused. "Why didn't you tell me about him?"

"Mossby? When did I have time? Besides, he's Peyton's pet conspirator."

"Are you saying you don't think he's involved?"

"He may well be. But . . ."

"But what?"

"I would have preferred he . . . well, be kept under observation longer. There are holes in Peyton's theory, but after Marceline's death, I couldn't in good conscience hold him back."

"You can make up for that dreadful oversight—forgetting to mention Mossby, I mean—by finishing the tour."

There was a brief silence. "I'm sorry?"

"Whether or not this Mossby was involved, we still have no

idea how the killings were carried out, or what the victims had in common besides being board members, or why in particular they were targeted. And before you got that message about Marceline Williams, we were in the middle of tracing the movements the board took on their visit here two weeks ago. Right?"

"Right."

"Well, until we get a complete confession from Mossby, signed in blood, we'd better keep searching. And shadowing the board's movements seems preferable to twiddling our thumbs."

Another brief silence. "Why the hell not? Shouldn't take long to finish, anyway. Where are you now . . . never mind, I see you on my monitor. Stay put; I'll make the necessary preparations and meet you on the concourse in five minutes."

"After New Eden, the board members made only one stop," Claire Asperton told Logan a few minutes later, as they glided along the people mover. "The subsidiary located in Arc E."

"Short afternoon," Logan replied.

"Actually, it's where they spent the most time." The travelator brought them to a large, soaring space, anchored at its center by a sculpture of dark metal cubes, seemingly suspended one above another, through which thin sheets of cascading water slid in liquid curtains.

"Is that a Noguchi?" Logan asked.

Asperton nodded. "Permanent installation. Relaxing, isn't it?"

"It's beautiful."

"Along with the breakout areas, we find these plazas to be excellent catalysts for the exchange of ideas—within security guidelines, of course."

"Security guidelines." Logan shook his head. "After that brief trip to Peyton's lair, it's a little hard to look at all this in quite the same way."

"Even Eden had an archangel for a guard after God evicted Adam and Eve," Asperton replied. "Anyway, those levels excavated below the Torus are almost as much of an engineering feat as what you see here aboveground. They're what supports all this—literally and figuratively. Here we go."

Getting off the moving sidewalk once again, she led the way to the far side of the sculpture, and then—instead of continuing down the concourse—veered off down a narrow, spartan corridor, which continued about fifty yards before making a ninety-degree angle. Ahead, it ended in a single door, bare of decoration save for a palm geometry reader.

"Slumming?" Logan asked.

The lawyer turned to him. "I'm sorry?"

"On the first two stops we entered from the concourse. Through the front door, so to speak—big as life."

"Oh." She nodded. "Well, he prefers it this way."

And before Logan could ask who "he" referred to, Asperton placed her hand on the reader. A red light came on, which turned to green, and the door snapped open. Ahead, instead of a reception area, was an unlighted space. Asperton stepped inside, and after a moment Logan followed. As the door shut behind them, the blackness ahead shifted slightly, and then a faint light began to rise along the walls of the room. As it did so, Logan realized the shifting darkness was a person. The lights rose farther, and as they did Logan suddenly recognized who it was. The slicked-back hair, rimless glasses, pastel polo shirt, faint shadow of a two-day beard, gaunt, almost ascetic face: they could belong only to Matthew Wrigley, founder of Infinium, genius behind Omega and its massive rollout of VR technology that was either going to change the world or bankrupt Chrysalis.

Matthew Wrigley, in the flesh—and looking very angry indeed.

15

The lights came up another notch and Logan's eyes adjusted sufficiently to see they were standing in some kind of screening room, with crimson walls and rows of large, overstuffed chairs, arranged toward a wall of glass looking over another space that remained black and lightless.

Wrigley was at least two inches taller than Logan had expected. He towered over them, arms crossed and an exasperated look on his face. A strange apparatus dangled from around his neck; a closer look showed Logan it was a pair of enhanced bi-ocular night-vision goggles.

"Claire," Wrigley said. "This is bullshit. I thought you were kidding when you left that message. Don't you know we go live in *seventy* hours? I haven't slept in two days, and I doubt I'll sleep over the next three. We've got bandwidth issues with the long-wavelength transcoding, there are problems with the supercapacitor batteries from Taiwan—and those are just the things I've learned about *since* I got your message."

Wrigley spoke in a high yet resonant voice, with just a trace of a Southern accent. Logan noticed that—in addition to his unmistakable appearance—Wrigley was the only person he'd seen on campus without a badge, save Asperton. In fact, Wrigley showed absolutely no deference to Asperton the way everyone else did. Logan had read enough to well believe he combined qualities of Henry Ford and Steve Jobs. Did he occupy a particularly high rank here at Chrysalis, in the wake of the acquisition? Or was he just playing the role of enfant terrible?

Wrigley turned toward Logan, as if seeing him for the first time. "Who is this?" he asked as if Logan wasn't standing directly before him. Recognition flickered faintly in his eyes.

"This is Jeremy Logan," Asperton said. "We've brought him in to help with, ah, the problem I mentioned: ours, and yours."

"Logan," Wrigley murmured. Then he turned back to Asperton. "Is he cleared?"

"To infinity and back. The sooner we get started, the sooner you can get back to putting out your fires."

Wrigley considered this for a second. Then, without another word, he flopped into one of the seats in the front row. Logan and the Chrysalis lawyer followed suit.

"Okay, Claire. Let's hear it. What *is* this mysterious problem I have to drop everything for?"

"Nobody knows this yet," Asperton said. "But three of our board members died under unusual circumstances in the last three days."

Wrigley's eyes widened. "Three board members?"

"Russell, Marceline, and Pierson Bridger."

Wrigley sat forward—something of a feat in the comfy, theater-style chair. "Jesus *Christ*. How?"

"Cause of death was different in each case. Russell suffered some kind of attack, maybe neurological. Bridger died when the plane he was flying crashed abruptly about ninety miles west of here. And Marceline fell in front of a London bus."

"And when did—"

"Russell died first. In a meeting in New York City, Monday morning. Wednesday night, Bridger crashed. And then, last night . . . Marceline."

Wrigley's lips worked briefly, mouthing Marceline's name. Slowly, he settled back. Logan sensed waves of shock—dismay—

confusion—and then, deep anxiety. Suddenly, the man looked at Asperton again. "Why are you looping me in? Look, you've got people to handle—"

"And they're 'handling' it," the lawyer replied. "Dr. Logan, here, has been brought on board independently. Right now, we're looking into everything the three did when they were last together: the board meeting, two weeks ago."

"Why is that important? And what, exactly, does it have to do with our launch?"

"Maybe nothing," Logan interjected. "But Claire has received threatening communications about the deaths, with the strong implication they are neither coincidence nor accident."

"You mean, they were killed? Why?"

"Precisely what we're trying to figure out. Claire has brought me up to speed on just how important your imminent launch is to Chrysalis. It's our feeling that, this close to the Voyager debut, no scenario should be ruled out."

"As in, some competitor trying to sabotage the rollout?" Wrigley raised his voice. "That's corporate warfare 101. Look, I'm really sorry about what's happened, but I can't get involved. I'm managing a dozen critical-path task lines, most of them interdependent. I can't afford to slow, let alone pause, a single one if we're going to make—"

"Obviously not," Asperton interrupted. "That schedule is set in stone. And that's why I'd like you to take a few minutes to personally go over what the board did during their visit here. You're the one who can do it most comprehensively and quickly. Besides, I understand you took lead on that visit yourself."

"I had to," Wrigley said. "Things were still a little brittle and I didn't want to risk letting anyone else give the demo."

"The demo?" Logan echoed, pricking up his ears.

"Well, first I sat them all down at a conference table and waved around some mock-ups. But I mean, they're the people who dictate our future—the ones who keep the funding flowing? Christ, a brief lecture wasn't going to cut it. So I gave them a demo."

Logan had anticipated the mock-ups—but not this. "You mean, of phase two. The Omega Voyager."

"Of phase two *advanced*," Wrigley corrected. "I wanted to show them where we're really going with this technology: not just next week, but next *year*." His eyes flared, as if merely speaking of his pet creation filled him with excitement. "To say they loved it was an understatement. As they were leaving, I told myself the time I'd spent fighting with Agrinox and Carewell for funding was finally over."

"So you gave them a taste of phase three," Logan said.

Wrigley barked a laugh. "If I'd had a time machine, I would have! But that's still two years away—one, if we're lucky. No; I simply showed them what Voyager is *already* capable of doing, once the necessary hardware and data backbone is in place. We can run it now, here, on campus. And after Monday's rollout, it's what we plan to include in the next major release, just before Christmas."

For some unknown reason, a fragment of the nightmare Logan had experienced Tuesday night—lying in bed, in his suite in the Chrysalis spire—came back to him. *Something rotten at the heart of this shimmering marvel.*

"Show me," he said.

Wrigley turned to him. "Sorry?"

"I'd like the same demo the board got."

Wrigley smiled at Logan as one might an irrational child. "That's ridiculous. I'd have to pull half a dozen resources from critical jobs, waste time that we simply don't have—"

"If that's what Jeremy wants," Asperton said, her voice even, "then that's what you'll have to arrange for him. And now, Matthew—not later. *Now.*"

For a moment, Wrigley just stared at the lawyer. He blinked several times, the effect magnified by his owlish glasses. His lower lip trembled. For a brief moment, Logan feared he might leap to his feet, break something irreplaceable, and then storm off into the woody fastness of the Berkshires. But instead—with a brief, withering curse—he tossed the night-vision goggles onto a nearby chair and gave the Omega device behind his right ear a short, savage tap.

"Rosalind?" he spoke into the air. "In sixty seconds, I'll be on my way from Theater One to the production lab. Find me."

Then he flounced back as far as his seat would allow, folded his arms over his chest again, and stared at the blank wall of glass in stubborn silence.

16

In the comfort of his screening room chair, with echoes of the sharp exchange still dying away, Logan snuck a look at the head of VR. Despite what he'd told the anonymous Rosalind, Wrigley showed no signs of moving. He sat quite still, except for his eyes—which glanced here and there at random, seeing but not taking in—and his lips, which moved slightly. Logan realized what the man was doing: he was taking this enormous task he was spearheading— the countless development cycles and beta tests and hardware patches, all the myriad elements that made up the vast rollout due to happen in three days—and mentally rebalancing, making room for this unexpected intrusion.

Abruptly, he jumped to his feet, then beckoned to Logan. "All right," he said. "Come this way." He pressed one of several faintly lit buttons in the forward wall, and suddenly—finally— the space beyond the glass came to light. Logan had a glimpse of what looked like a sprawling soundstage, with DV cameras on dollies, blue screens, body mirrors, clusters of lights, and long lines of marking tape running across the floor. But then he had to hurry, because Wrigley had already walked away and opened a door beside the wall of glass.

"Claire?" he said. "He'll get his demo. But without all that foreplay I gave the board—no PowerPoint deck, no four-color printouts."

"Then I'll see myself out," Asperton replied with a nod. "Jeremy, when you're finished here, please get in touch."

Logan nodded. Then he turned and followed Wrigley as the man trotted out onto the polished wooden floor of the soundstage. As he did so, a door in the far wall—comically small, given the height of the ceiling—opened and a woman in jeans and a white turtleneck stepped through it. She had a tablet with a digital stylus in one hand.

"Matthew," she began as she approached, "what's up—?"

"Roz," he interrupted, "no time for questions. I need you to spin up the demo cage for this guy." And Wrigley jerked a thumb over his shoulder toward Logan.

The woman looked from Wrigley to Logan and back again. "Now? But we're starting the stress test on the—"

"Push it back half an hour. And the final code review, as well. We'll plan to go gold at five instead of four."

"But—" Rosalind cut herself off, realizing silence was the more prudent course.

"I know it's a pain in the ass," Wrigley said. "Just get some people to the cage, so we'll be ready to give Logan here the same tour the board got. But without the Two A stuff: we'll do the dog-and-pony, then hustle him out."

The woman listened, then nodded and turned away.

The head of VR turned back to Logan. "Best right hand I've ever had," he said. "Her ability to absorb technical and creative details is just about limitless. I hired her while she was walking off the graduation platform at MIT. If I croaked, she could run this place."

"Is she better than Karel Mossby?" Logan asked.

Wrigley's eyes narrowed. "What does that have to do with you—or this demo?"

"How long since he left your division?"

"Four, maybe five months." Suddenly, he frowned. "They're still handing out this junk?" And he summarily plucked the Venture from Logan's ear and the bridge of his nose; examined it; then tossed it away as distastefully as if he hadn't designed it himself. "My God. We're about to storm the Normandy beaches, and you've got bows and arrows like it's the Battle of Agincourt."

"There's a pretty good chunk of my life stored in that 'junk,'" Logan said.

"You'll get it all back, stop worrying. Every last bit, byte, and nibble is stored in . . . our subbasement server farms. Everything—even that little conversation with Captain Phasma."

"Claire? She seems pretty pleasant for a bloodthirsty storm trooper."

"It's the quiet ones you have to watch out for. Come on, damn it: we're wasting time." And Wrigley led the way through a sound-proofed door and into what seemed to Logan like barely controlled chaos. Instead of the architecturally neutral work environments he'd seen elsewhere, Logan found himself in a huge space occupied by hundreds of people, separated by labyrinthine partitions, six feet high and in a uniform light gray. The entire space was covered by a low, domed ceiling, like a sports arena. The noise level was somewhere between the floor of the stock exchange and a futures market for cattle. Logan registered keyboards tapping, the mingle of countless conversations and arguments, the glow of lasers rising from invisible offices—and below everything, a low hum, as of a dynamo—before he realized that Wrigley had stopped and was tapping him on the shoulder.

"Do you *mind*?" he asked. And then he turned and started off again, at a pace just short of a jog. Logan concentrated on following him through the confusing maze.

"So they're really dead?" Wrigley said over his shoulder. "All three?"

"Yes."

"In the last couple of days?"

Logan nodded again.

"Jesus. And Claire said Spearman was one of them?"

"Yes."

"Shit." Wrigley shook his head. "I admired that old man. He knew how to kick ass. Someday I hope to be like him."

"I'd say you're off to a good start," Logan replied.

Wrigley stared back at him. "Start at what?"

"Evolving from a wunderkind-with-an-attitude into an old, admirable ass-kicker."

As Logan expected, instead of taking offense Wrigley laughed for the first time since they'd met. "High praise, coming from a"— he searched for a suitable epithet—"a *ghost*buster."

So Wrigley *had* recognized him. "I don't 'bust' ghosts. I find ways to accommodate them. Consider it like a form of arbitration—"

"God*damn* it!" Wrigley erupted suddenly. "You've distracted me again. Come on, we've wasted enough time as it is." And, heading down a final cubicle-lined corridor, they reached a metal door. Wrigley pressed his palm against the security reader, then threw the door open and stepped inside, leaving Logan to catch it before it closed.

He found himself in a long hallway, bathed with indirect illumination, as tranquil as the vast R&D area had been frantic. Logan followed, catching only the briefest glimpses of labs and what appeared to be small classrooms before Wrigley opened a door and ushered him inside.

Logan entered, then stopped. The room had linoleum flooring and plain beige walls. There were diagnostic tools along one wall, and a glassed-in booth with a workstation in an opposite corner. A few wheeled devices that looked to Logan like medical trolleys held monitors and various instruments, trailing cables behind them. But what particularly caught his attention was the cage in the center of the room. "Cage," he decided, was not quite the proper word—it was a grid-like structure of thin strips of non-reflective metal, shaped into a cube-like mesh about eight feet on each side. Small cameras and other lensed devices were fixed to its upper corners. A few action dollies with pneumatic wheels stood here and there, additional video cameras atop them nodding and dark, as if snoozing. For some reason, the room reminded Logan most of a medical lab, where a patient would go to endure a CT scan, angioplasty, or perhaps something worse.

In such an analogy, that made him the patient. It wasn't a pleasant thought.

The woman named Rosalind approached. Logan had not noticed she'd been in the room. Wrigley turned to her. "Set?"

"Repopulating the last few microenvironments. We thought all the demos were finished."

"They were *supposed* to be." Wrigley gestured Logan toward the cage, and a padded, straight-backed chair that sat inside it. "Have a seat."

"Will it hurt?" Logan asked, a little more plaintively than he'd intended.

"That depends." This elicited a laugh from Rosalind and a few other techs manning various control panels.

Logan stepped forward, through a hole in the mesh that served as a door. It was low, and since at six foot one he was rather tall, he had to duck. The chair inside reminded Logan of something that would be used for a lie detector—and he gingerly took a seat.

"Green," said Rosalind.

Wrigley rolled another chair over to the cage, placed it parallel to Logan's outside the mesh, and sat down. "Plug him in."

17

Rosalind came into view again. Logan noticed she had put on a pair of thin latex gloves and was holding a metal tray. She stepped into the cage. Approaching Logan, she took something from the tray resembling the earpiece of his Venture, a little larger but still sleek and streamlined. She next picked up a device like a doctor's otoscope. Stepping closer, she held it up, and a narrow beam of red light streamed from an opening in its front. Bending over Logan, she examined the area around his ear, apparently taking readings of some kind, because she murmured a series of numbers to a tech standing at a monitor a few yards from the cage. Then, putting the device away, she used a tool like a dental pick to make a few modifications to the earpiece. At last, she fitted it gently behind his ear, making a few adjustments for comfort. The final step was to fit a minimalist set of glasses over his nose, not unlike those of the Venture unit Wrigley had so brusquely disposed of. Then she picked up her tools and tray and stepped out of the cage, nodding to the man at the control station. He typed in a series of commands. Logan felt a brief pinch behind his ear, but he shifted and it went away.

Sitting in his chair outside the cage, Wrigley sighed. "Okay," he said. "Since Asperton brought you here, I'm guessing you know what it is we're up to?"

"I have a general idea. You used the first-generation Omega units, Ventures, to get people accustomed to using VR for watching music videos, playing games, searching the internet. Thus ensuring those same people are ready for phase two—which, apparently, takes a little more getting used to."

"Crude, but reasonably accurate. So: How about phase two itself? Voyager?"

"Asperton was a bit more vague about that."

Wrigley snorted. "Well, she did say you had the full whack of security clearances. So it's not my problem. If you learn something you shouldn't in here, she can damn well arrange for your firing squad."

From the corner of his eye, Logan saw Wrigley nod to Rosalind.

"What's with this cage?" Logan asked. "Seems kind of retrogressive, especially after all of the burbling about moving forward."

"Spoken with remarkable ignorance. Phase two of the project requires people to complete a personality profile, so we can tailor the experience to their parameters. Like fitting a virtual pair of skis—only a lot more sophisticated. In your case, barging in here at the last minute demanding a tour, we don't have time to fill out tests and questionnaires or to obtain your medical history. The glasses are a way of compensating. And if you haven't noticed already, I can assure you they won't use glasses anymore. The synaptichron renders them unnecessary."

"The what?"

"A part of the device Roz placed on your ear. The Voyager. Now shut up, will you? My God, you talk more than the board of directors did."

"You—" Logan began, but then fell silent. Something strange was happening. It was as if he were registering events—simultaneous, yet distinct—from every angle of his peripheral vision. There was no pain, or any other sensation, beyond the sheer strangeness of this visual phenomenon.

"Dr. Wrigley," he said, "I'm not sure this—"

And then—quite suddenly—his vision blurred; dimmed; then snapped back smartly. He was seated in a chair. Except it was not the chair within the cage of the VR lab. It wasn't even in the Torus. Instead, it was one of a series of seats in what he quickly realized was the shoe department of a large store. Beyond the shoe department, he saw racks with clothes, signs atop them adorned with traditional Neiman Marcus branding, and other departments in the distance. And yet this was not possible; he knew he was not here—he was seated in the production lab of Arc E, Matthew Wrigley's subdivision of the Torus. But he could *feel* that the shape of the chair had changed. One of his feet was resting upon a shoe-fitting stool. And there was more: he could hear, as well. There were voices in the background that were not from the lab. There was music—or rather, Muzak. Even the air felt different: cooler, overly air-conditioned.

And then, of course, there was the woman. She was about fifty, perched demurely on the far side of the shoe stool, wearing a form-fitting knee-length floral dress, smiling at him. Her nametag read BRENDA, and she looked absolutely real, down to the subtle dimple in her chin. He felt a tug at his foot, and realized it was being withdrawn from a Brannock foot-measuring tool.

The woman seated before him glanced at the device, still smiling. "Looks like eleven D," she told him. Her voice was clear and crisp and without auditory artifacts. "You said you preferred loafers to oxfords?"

She was looking directly at him, clearly waiting for a response. "Yes," he said, feeling it would be rude not to answer.

She nodded. "Tassel, penny, or something traditional like horsebit?"

If he worked hard enough, Logan realized, he could—just barely—see *through* the store; make out ghostly images of the lab that, in real life, surrounded him. But it was difficult, and after a few moments of mental effort he gave up and let himself slip unresisting back into the scenario. "I prefer simple, classic designs," he told Brenda. "Low-slung."

"And color?"

"Cordovan or black."

"Any brand you prefer?"

"Bally. But I have a difficult time finding any that fit."

"Swiss shoes do tend to run a little smaller. But that won't be a problem." She stood up, smile growing even more dazzling. "I'll be right back with a couple pairs."

As Logan watched her move toward a rear section of the store, he heard a cynical voice sound in his ear. "Bally, huh? Good taste. I would have taken you for a Weejuns kind of guy."

It was Wrigley, speaking to him—somehow. Logan looked around, but except for a few other shoppers—at a fair distance, where the illusion of realism grew somewhat compromised—he was alone. "How are you doing this?"

"Quiet. You don't want people in that store to think you're talking to yourself. I'm out here in the lab—hooked into your sensory feed."

"No. What I mean is . . . how the hell is this so real? The sound and sight and touch—"

"Genius, basically—and a *fuck* ton of hard work. Forty million man-hours at last count. Oh, and yes: Voyager, its vestibular implants and synaptichron, and the satellites and server farms that push the data, have something to do with it." A dry laugh.

There was that word again: "synaptichron."

The woman was returning with three boxes in her hands, all Ballys. "I compensated, knowing how European shoes run." She opened the boxes one at a time, showing him the choices.

Feeling just a little silly, Logan said: "I'll try the topmost. Yes, that one, thanks."

She took the pair out of the box and slipped one onto his foot, using only the slightest pressure of a shoehorn. Logan was amazed at how realistically the Omega software, and the neural interface or whatever it was, mimicked the experience of putting on a new, slightly stiff leather shoe.

"What do you think?" the salesperson asked.

"It's beautiful." And it was.

"It's a twelve triple-E."

He looked at her. "Triple-E. Really?"

She nodded as she put on its mate. "Like I said, European shoes run small. Why don't you walk around and see how it feels while I get you one or two others in that size?" And with another smile, she turned and walked off again.

"How real are they?" Logan said into the air.

"As real as it gets," the disembodied voice of Wrigley replied. "Real shoe, real size, real measurement. If your credit was good here, you'd get them in the mail tomorrow. The software takes care of everything."

"And this is part of the rollout? The Voyager device that drops on Monday?"

"You got it. Obviously, it's designed so the *reality* of the environment is the most impressive thing. Fact is, you're interacting with an area no bigger than twenty square feet—if you tried to walk farther, the matrix would collapse—but you have no idea, *no* idea, how difficult implementing those twenty feet were. This isn't some primitive CAVE system. This is total immersion, combined with total interaction. True telepresence—and we're half a dozen years ahead of the competition. More, if we get lucky with some of the patents."

"So on Monday, a hundred thousand people will be able to buy shoes."

Logan didn't mean this to sound snarky, and Wrigley didn't take it that way. "We chose shoes for an initial demo because they're hard to fit properly. Would you ever buy a five-hundred-dollar pair of shoes online? It's not like a hair dryer or a box of lightbulbs. We felt that this best demonstrated how realistic our technology is. It's a way to familiarize the average Joe with VR. But you wait: though the experience will be limited at first, people won't fire up a Voyager just to buy shoes. They'll fire it up *just to sit in that chair.* That's how realistic it is."

Logan gripped the arms of the chair, felt the resistance increase with the pressure. It was true.

"We've partnered with Neiman Marcus to provide a persistent shopping experience that will just keep growing. Monday, it will be the shoe section and a few others. By Christmas, it will be entire departments. Suits, dresses, jewelry—the whole nine yards."

"Jesus," Logan murmured. He watched as somebody else sat down three chairs away—somebody who, he assumed, was just a figment of Omega's imagination. Until next week, anyway. "So what's the 'Two A' stuff, the tour you told Asperton you gave the board?"

"Oh." Wrigley laughed briefly. "We had more time to prepare for their arrival, so their interfaces were more sophisticated than yours. Depth of focus, mostly."

"Depth of focus?"

"Those twenty square feet I was talking about. Take a look out past that workman—to the right, there—and you'll see what I mean."

Logan looked in the indicated direction. The environment was so incredibly detailed he hadn't noticed this angle before. At the entrance to the department store, a workman was standing on a ladder, hammering up some sort of sign. Logan looked at him for a minute. Then he looked *beyond* the man—and abruptly understood.

Outside the entrance to the store lay a wide plaza, and the decorative gallery of what was clearly a shopping mall, stretching into the distance. Beyond the entrance, as elsewhere in this virtual environment, the landscape grew a little pixelated, its details hard to distinguish. Nevertheless, Logan could see other storefronts in the nearer sections of the plaza: Williams-Sonoma, Coach, Pottery Barn. All with OPENING SOON signs on their facades.

"Those storefronts looked a lot sharper and more realistic to the board," Wrigley said. "But you get the idea. The first step is the hardest, actually—and we're taking that step with this rollout. The codecs, the infrastructure . . . it's all in place. Top-level confidential negotiations are going on right now with two dozen more high-end retailers. Half are already on board, agreeing to pay licensing fees for the APIs needed to build the code for their stores on our virtual platform. And those fees are *huge.* Why not? With a beautiful world to shop in, hyperintelligent salespeople, and unlimited inventories—why would a consumer go anywhere else?"

"Why indeed?" Logan asked. Then a thought struck him. "And what happens when the shops are in place? What's phase three?"

Wrigley went silent so long, Logan thought perhaps the man had wandered away. But then he spoke. "Phase three is what happens once the mall is complete. When you can wander anywhere inside, what do you do next? You step *outside,* of course. Jesus, guy, what do you think? If we can create this, once our matrix is fully extensible we can create anything. You want a vacation in Tahiti? Or an appointment with the world's most successful psychoanalyst? I'll bet you could use one of those. How about, instead of taking in a movie, you take in a *fantasy*—captain of a cruise ship, with all that entails. Or a pirate ship." The voice paused, and Logan saw the saleslady walking back toward him with more boxes. "I have a better question for you, Logan: What *isn't* phase three?"

"You're taking the 'virtual' out of virtual reality," Logan said. "Like the open-format games you designed at Infinium—except this won't be just a game."

Suddenly, he realized his own voice sounded different—louder, more direct, with less reverb. Then the world around him wavered, blinked, and went away—and he was back inside the cage. Wrigley, Rosalind, and the tech who had been manning the nearby console were all standing nearby, looking in at him. Their expressions alone made him go cold.

"What happened?" he asked. "Did something go wrong?"

"No. Sorry about the abrupt exit." Wrigley sounded uncharacteristically subdued.

Now Rosalind stepped in and removed the glasses she'd given him earlier. "Here's a new Voyager unit," she said, handing him a thin box. "It's been refreshed with your personal information."

For just a minute, the four of them remained motionless. Then Wrigley spoke. "Don't you think you'd better go?"

Logan frowned as he opened the box and removed the device. "Go? Go where?"

"Oh," Wrigley said. "While you were inside, I just now heard from Asperton. You're needed in the executive suite on the forty-eighth floor. Immediately."

18

"Pythia," Logan said as he stepped back out onto the promenade, "please direct me to the executive suite on tower level forty-eight."

"You're not speaking to Pythia," came a different female voice, low and even more realistic. "I'm Grace."

In the rush of events, Logan had almost forgotten his familiar Venture 7A had been replaced with one of the new devices going live on Monday. It came without glasses: but then it dawned on him—somehow for the first time—that although everyone in the Complex had Omegas, none of them wore glasses. "Sorry, Grace."

With the help of his new Voyager, he managed to find his way back up to the executive suite. Once again, he was shown into the large and elegant boardroom. Except this time, it wasn't empty. Half a dozen people were seated around the table—senior executives, perhaps. Peyton, head of Logistics, was there, as was Asperton. One figure stood out from the others: at the far end of the table, still as a porcelain statue, sat the thin, spectral figure of John Christie IV, his sad brown eyes fastened on Logan, the scar along his jawline red against the sallow skin.

Claire stood up, nodding at Logan and waiting for him to take a seat. Then she closed the door and sat down once again. A different kind of heaviness hung over her now, and Logan tried to interpret what it might mean.

"This is Jeremy Logan," she told the assembled group. "You all know who he is, and why we've brought him on board. Jeremy, I hope you'll forgive me if we skip the introductions for now. Suffice to say everybody here knows the problem that summoned you to Chrysalis—and what's happened since."

She pressed a button on the table, and a section of the opposite wall slid smoothly away, revealing a large, recessed monitor.

"I received a message on my Omega device about twenty minutes ago," she said. "It was encrypted, but just like before, I tried unscrambling it with my private key and—unfortunately—that worked." Asperton spread her hands on the polished table. She looked exhausted. "Whoever sent the message has high-level employee access to the passphrase. It could even be someone at this table."

She pressed another button. The monitor winked into life. A text message appeared on the screen, the now-familiar white letters against a field of unrelieved black.

Hello again.
Yes, we killed all three.
By now you know
This is no coincidence or joke.
But to make absolutely sure,
Tomorrow our demo
Will go outside the family
And kill a civilian or two.
On sunday morning
You will receive wire instructions
For sending one billion dollars in cryptocurrency.
On monday at 8 am precisely
These orders will be confirmed.
If you do not initiate the transfer by noon
If you inform external authorities

If you postpone the rollout
If you try to recall any voyager devices or take them offline
We will use the methods we have already demonstrated
To kill one thousand loyal customers
With a ci of +/- 1.5
Before midnight monday.
Have a pleasant afternoon.

19

For a moment, as the people around the table absorbed the message, there was profound silence. Then a sharp intake of breath, followed by a muttered curse. And then—quite suddenly—an eruption of noise: protests, questions, disbelief.

"Quiet!" The commanding voice came from John Christie. Logan was shocked such a tone could issue from such a frail-looking frame. There was an immediate silence.

"Quiet, please," Christie said again, more softly. Then he glanced at Asperton. "The rending of garments will have to wait. Claire, please go around the table and introduce everyone to Jeremy. Then I want people's thoughts."

In short order, Asperton named everyone in the room. Wilson Pettigrew, in charge of day-to-day business; Flavia Rhinehart, lead for technical integration; Orris Peyton and Peyton's deputy, Daniel Kramer, security at the ARC. Logan nodded at each in turn, committing their faces and titles to memory. A few raised their eyebrows in recognition; others, who had apparently been present during the vote to bring Logan in, looked on impassively.

"Wilson, would you like to start?" Asperton asked.

The president, a very tall, bald Black man with a penetrating gaze, cleared his throat. "The obvious question is: Could this be a bluff of one type or another?"

"What kind of bluff, exactly?" Christie asked.

"The most obvious would be industrial sabotage. A mole, or

moles, inside the Complex that want to gum up the launch of Voyager."

" 'Gum up' the launch?" echoed Peyton.

"That seems clear enough," Pettigrew went on. "We're seventy hours from the Omega II rollout. It's all hands on deck."

"How do you even know this is related to Voyager?" Peyton asked.

"It's right there in front of us." Asperton gestured at the white letters on the black screen. "It says we can't stop the rollout, we can't disable any of the devices that we've already sent out and are coming online. In other words, the note is referring to the initial hundred thousand end users we'll have out there at nine a.m. Monday."

"Those units have gone out in staggered shipments," Rhinehart—dark haired and rail thin—confirmed. "We've gotten close to sixty percent confirmation from the recipients already, and many have already finished the handshaking process." She turned to Pettigrew. "Say we go along with this. What would the impact be?"

"You mean, of stripping a billion dollars from our operating capital? It would mean a serious, serious shortfall. Not mortal, but pretty damned close in the short term. And trying to bury it as a loss would be a nightmare."

"Companies have paid larger fines than that and survived," Rhinehart told him.

"Not by much. Besides, this isn't a fine—it's ransom." This was Kramer, head of Security and—apparently—Peyton's pit bull. It was the first time he'd spoken, and his voice was deep and harsh, like a rasp grater on pig iron. Logan wondered, idly, if he cultivated it that way.

"Nevertheless," Rhinehart pressed Pettigrew, "we could conceivably pay—without interrupting the rollout. If anything interferes with Voyager, it's possible the entire Omega product line might never recover."

"Right," Asperton said. "Especially if a thousand users die while wearing—*using*—our device."

Pettigrew shifted in his chair. "What Flavia says is true. We have so many divisions invested in this rollout . . ." He paused. "If the product imploded, suddenly and publicly, it would have repercussions throughout Chrysalis."

"But this is still only guesswork," Kramer, the security exec, broke in. "We don't know if there's any truth to this at all."

"Three members of the board are dead," Asperton told him.

It was interesting, Logan thought, that not Kramer, nor Peyton, nor even Asperton, made reference to the operation that had captured Mossby less than three hours before. Perhaps there was a strategy behind this silence; he hoped there was.

"We haven't heard anything from our guest, here."

It took Logan, still musing about Mossby, a moment to realize this was addressed to him. He glanced up to see it was Peyton who'd spoken.

"That's right," growled Kramer, as if to emphasize his master's voice. "A billion for your thoughts?"

Logan didn't answer right away. Instead, he glanced around the table. Everyone, including John Christie, was looking back at him.

If nobody else had mentioned Mossby, the rogue employee, Logan didn't think he'd better be the first.

"As you say, I'm a guest," Logan replied, looking at Peyton rather than Kramer. "But I'm happy to offer a few observations. Preliminary, at least."

"Go ahead," Asperton said, as if to parry the hostile front from the security team.

"Some of you are probably betting this is a bluff, but it's

unlikely. Rather, I think some sophisticated game theory is being employed here—and, as Mr. Pettigrew said, from the inside. Ms. Asperton received this message on her personal Omega device, encrypted with a Chrysalis private key. The earlier communications were similarly privileged. This would make carrying out their threats much easier. Also, they're not afraid to back up their threat with the offer of, to put it crudely, a free demonstration."

"And the bottom line?" Asperton asked.

"It would seem you're neatly boxed in. You've said any delay of the Voyager rollout would begin a crippling cascade. On the other hand, a billion dollars might not cripple you—but it would undercut your development capital and hurt for a long, long time. So you don't have much of a hand to play."

"You're saying our only option is to play along?" asked Kramer.

"This bad actor—since we don't know how many or the true agenda, let's just use the term 'opponent'—has set the rules. There's no opportunity to stall for time. You can't ask for proof: he's already offered some, of a most unpleasant kind. You can't negotiate, because he's only making one-way calls. He's timed this to happen while you're busy rolling out phase two—and he's not likely to offer an extension. What's your employee vetting process?"

This last question, aimed at Peyton, was intentionally spoken in the same casual tone. The operations manager had very intentionally started a pissing contest with him, and now Logan planned to douse him in his own ammunition.

It took Peyton a moment to realize the query was aimed at him. "Our background investigations on potential staff are more robust than SCI clearances."

"Any spy agency in the world could make the same boast—yet double agents get hung every day. I hope your people are mobilizing. You've got a lot to do—*without* raising any hue and cry."

Logan held the gazes of both Peyton and Kramer. He already

knew he'd never be friends with either. So he'd do the next best thing: make sure they did what he asked.

"So we agree: the threat is real." It was Christie who spoke. "In that case, Jeremy, what next?"

"First, Mr. Christie, I'd like you to clarify something—if you don't mind."

The elderly man raised a liver-spotted hand for him to proceed.

"When you brought me in to investigate this situation, nobody knew if Spearman's death was a tragic coincidence or something more. Now three are dead—and we can be sure it wasn't coincidence. Our opponent has done my work for me. Given the landscape has changed, do you wish me to stay on?"

Christie nodded.

"From the start, you gave me wide-ranging authority. If I'm to finish this, I'll need total carte blanche: to ask any questions, talk to any personnel, requisition any sort of data—not just from those at this table, but across the entire Complex. And, within reasonable limits, the authority to take necessary action—on your behalf, of course—to bring this matter to a confidential but acceptable conclusion. Will you give me that authority?"

This time, there was a slight pause. Then Christie nodded again.

"Thank you, sir." Logan let his glance settle on Peyton before continuing: *Pissing contest final score, 1–0.* "I'll make my analysis brief because all of us now have a lot to do. I can tell you why that note on the screen means business. Despite the use of the plural tense, I don't believe we can assume this was sent by a team as opposed to an individual. In any case, I've read more than my share of voluntary false confessions—they're rarer than you might think—and I see no self-punishment pathology, delusions of guilt, or anything else to suggest that here. Our opponent freely admits what he, she, or they have done: an admission that, by its very nature, makes it hard to dismiss. And he promises another demonstration, which unfortunately seems very likely to happen: he wouldn't mention it otherwise. He places great emphasis on timing, which—along with the mention of the Voyager devices already distributed—shows he knows what pressure you're under. More troubling, he has no delusions of grandeur. Quite the opposite: he seems rather humble."

"How could you know that?" Asperton asked.

"Because of the line near the bottom: 'with a CI of plus or minus 1.5.' 'CI' is short for confidence interval. This person is referring to the accuracy of a sample distribution. In other words, returning to game theory, our opponent isn't promising a thousand people *exactly* will die—but rather, that it's a tight interval and he's confident the number will be inside one and a half percent. Maybe at most fifteen fewer, or fifteen people more, will die; that's as close as he can make to a promise. That's where the game theory comes in."

This was greeted by another silence. Finally, Kramer said, under his breath: "Jeezus."

"This is all distressingly convincing, Dr. Logan," said Christie. "But my question remains: What next?"

"As I see it, you can do two things, not necessarily mutually exclusive. First, prepare to follow whatever instructions you receive Sunday for paying the ransom. And second—meanwhile—let's get working to prevent whoever's behind this from killing a thousand of your customers."

Another silence blanketed the room. "What if we pay and the killing continues anyway?" Kramer asked. "What guarantees do we have?"

"None whatsoever," Logan replied, staring down Kramer. "But the alternatives are demonstrably worse. Now—since this meeting has taken close to twenty minutes already—I suggest there is no more time to waste."

20

The room cleared slowly until only Claire Asperton, Kramer, and Peyton remained at the table with Logan. Peyton glanced at Kramer, clearly dismissing the security head, and Kramer rose and exited the room. The three of them were left alone.

As soon as the door had closed, Peyton whirled toward Logan. "You son of a bitch."

Logan had expected the outburst. Peyton had already demonstrated his territorial insecurities; they were on a clock, and it was time to headbutt the bully.

"Blame yourself, Peyton," Logan said nonchalantly. "You've done nothing but give me pushback since we met. Shooting holes in plans of action without bothering to explain the flaws. Keeping me ignorant of vital information."

"'Ignorant' is the word," Peyton shot back. "What the hell do you know about the Complex, or its operation, or its history? I've worked here almost a dozen years."

Logan laughed. "Lying. Again. A dozen years ago, you were riding a tricycle."

He had already sensed how self-conscious the logistics director—obsessed as he clearly was with authority—felt about his boyish looks. And this remark had the desired effect of knocking the man off balance: with a curse, Peyton stood up, chair wheeling back.

"Sit down," Logan said. "You heard Mr. Christie: I'm Superman now, so unless you've got some kryptonite around, do us both a favor: shut up, take a deep breath, and let's get to work."

Logan let a brief silence follow before following the stick with a carrot. "I'm not interested in getting in your way. We all want the same thing. And you might just find that my ignorance is a virtue. I can ask the kind of foolish, objective, uninitiated questions you can't . . . or won't. For example, why are you so sure Mossby was involved?"

Peyton stared at Logan for a moment. It was unlikely he'd ever been challenged in this way. Finally, he shifted in his seat and replied in a monotone. "I'll have a summary sent to you, encoded and flagged, of my reasons. Knock yourself out reading it . . . and be prepared to apologize. Oh—and you may be Superman, but let me make one thing clear: if anything I tell you, or *give* you, leaks out of this facility, it's still going to be your ass."

"Let's hope that's all I have to worry about." It was time to deescalate. "So: Why, then, didn't you bring up Mossby? It seemed the ideal time."

"I thought it premature," Peyton replied. "He hasn't been very talkative so far. And as Pettigrew said, there may be more than one mole involved."

"That's true. We don't know how many we're dealing with, or how deeply their hooks are sunk. There could even be someone on the board." At this, Logan glanced at Asperton. "You've effectively arrested Mossby, locked him up. So much for habeas corpus. I'm curious: Exactly how far does your rule of law extend?"

Asperton, who despite being a lawyer clearly disliked drama, looked distressed. "What do you mean, Jeremy?"

"I mean, this place is like a private fiefdom within Windham County. Can you do whatever you please within its walls? Is there a gallows in one of those vaults beneath the Torus?"

Peyton smiled at this question, but Asperton did not.

"That's ridiculous," Asperton replied. "The state gave many

concessions and waived many restrictions that would apply to smaller entities. One of the concessions was to allow Chrysalis to hire credentialed law officers to serve as our internal security team. And as you know, employees sign extensive and comprehensive NDAs, along with other agreements that give us a lot of room for . . . enforcement."

"Including torture?"

She scoffed. "As I said, a great many restrictions have been waived. But no, Jeremy, torture is not a pillar of our corporate philosophy—at least, not to my knowledge."

At this, Peyton smiled again.

Logan considered what he'd just learned. There was now little point in trying to protect other board members, or examining their medical histories: the three already dead had made the opponent's point.

Now he focused in on the crucial issues. "We have a number of unanswered questions. First, how do we think the person we're up against—Mossby, or whoever—will select a thousand random people to target if you don't pay out? Second, how do we identify whether the opponent is internal or on the outside and has just managed to hack past the corporate firewall? And finally—perhaps most important—how were the three board members' deaths carried out . . . and what would be the mechanism to murder a thousand clients if the random deadline isn't met?"

A silence hung in the air for a moment. Then Peyton spoke. "The board members got a tour of the Voyager technology two weeks ago. This message warns, orders, us not to stop the rollout of that same technology."

The silence that followed this was even longer.

Logan glanced down at his watch, changing its display to a timer: sixty-nine hours, forty-two minutes and counting. Counting down. "Should we loop Wrigley in on this?" he asked. "I mean, Omega's his baby."

"I'm not sure what he could add at this point," Asperton replied. "It might just mean one too many cooks."

"Fair enough," Logan said. "Then may I finish with a few recommendations?"

Asperton nodded, followed a moment later by Peyton.

"Given the clock we're on, triage is the only option. That means getting the money ready, and putting all available resources on this mole. Killing a thousand people must require some kind of action—even if it's just pushing a button. Whoever's behind these messages can tell us that . . . or will know the people who can." He glanced again at Peyton. "Maybe Mossby is a lone wolf. Maybe he's part of a group. Maybe he's just a false positive. Whatever the case, you've got some serious resources at your disposal: Can you run *all* HR data, vacation history, bank accounts, psych evals, of Chrysalis employees and contractors through a sieve sort? We can't let Mossby, and whatever sins you say he's committed, blind us to other potential malefactors. Anybody who doesn't act right, feel right, smell right . . . whether you come up with a single name or fifty, it would be a start. That includes the thirty you're already surveilling. Nabbing the mole is our immediate priority."

Peyton nodded. "Done." He seemed relieved to hear Logan suggest a tangible goal that included him.

"And you should assemble a small strike force from whatever cybersecurity team handles your internal intelligence, fends off ransomware attacks: a handful of your sharpest and most trusted. Put them on these goddamned messages Claire has been receiving. Where are they coming from? What mechanism generates them? Even if they find nothing, we need to have sentries posted and ready when new messages come in." He paused. "They should probably be familiar with cryptocurrencies, too. No doubt that's how these bad actors will want to be paid—I doubt they'd be content with shares of stock."

Peyton nodded. "I'll put my best man, Snow, onto it."

Logan turned to Asperton. "I'm guessing you're the person to scrape together one billion. It's Friday afternoon, I know, but can you assemble the liquid assets in time?"

He saw the look on her face. "What is it?"

"Normally it would be feasible, given our market cap. But we're currently restructuring some long-term debt, and a staggering amount of capital has been spread around the divisions in preparation for this rollout."

"What about equivalents? Can't you liquidate an asset, or—if necessary—sell off some underperforming division?"

"Yes. But the note said crypto. That's the difficulty."

"So raising the billion, fast, may end up costing you a premium due to time pressure. But you can do it, right?"

"I think so," came the hesitant response. "I need to make some calls."

"Okay. So, Orris, just one more thing. I'd like to say hello to your guest."

Peyton, unsurprisingly, frowned. "Mossby?"

"He must have had all the 'processing' he needs by now—right? So maybe he'd like a little chat. To take his mind off things."

Peyton didn't answer. He looked at Asperton. Then he looked toward the door through which John Christie had vanished a few minutes before. It didn't take an empath to follow his train of thought.

Peyton stood up. "Come on."

They left the conference room just as Claire Asperton began making her first call.

21

They made their way down through the central spire, then out to the Torus, and finally into the subterranean spaces beneath it. Logan no longer felt surprise at the functional, unadorned corridors Peyton led him through at a rapid clip.

Peyton opened a door, and they entered what was obviously a detention area. They walked past a few administrative offices before arriving at a door with a large window set into it, looking into a darkened room. Peyton unlocked the door with a palm geometry reader, ushered Logan in, then followed, snapping on the lights as he shut the door behind them.

The room wasn't empty. It contained a series of seats along the nearest wall and, in the center, a functional-looking table. On the far side of the table sat Mossby. He blinked a few times as his eyes adjusted to the sudden light.

Saying nothing, Peyton took a seat against the wall. Logan walked toward the table. Mossby eyed him as he drew closer. One of his wrists was chained to the metal chair, which in turn was bolted to the floor. On the near side of the table was another chair, similar save for the accessories. Logan pulled it back slightly and sat down.

Mossby looked furtively at Peyton before letting his gaze settle again on Logan. He had long hair, parted in the middle, with limpid brown eyes. The helixes of his ears were flat—a feature found in less than 5 percent of males. It was remarkable just how familiar the man's face looked, thanks to those strange video clips made from unknown technology.

Logan remained silent a moment, allowing himself to take in, as fully as possible, the man across from him. Then he spoke. "I guess you've had better days."

"I could say the same for you. Like the one when you discovered the twenty lost poems of Sappho."

Other people at the Complex had, of course, recognized Logan. He was used to this. But Mossby's observation told him two things. First, the man was unusually well educated: Logan had found those priceless scraps of verse among the cartonnage in an Egyptian funerary mask; details had been confined to scholarly periodicals. Second, Mossby in particular knowing who he was made his assignment that much more difficult.

"Twenty-two," Logan replied. "And I didn't find them all, I'm afraid." He noticed that Mossby—beyond a disheveled look—had no obvious bruises or marks of rough handling.

"Too bad. But why all this muscle? And what's a ghost hunter doing down here in the Chrysalis dungeons?"

"Fair questions. But first, tell me why you were doing all those naughty things."

"Naughty things?" Mossby repeated. He had a reedy, nasal voice, pitched high; higher, Logan sensed, than normal. He was a decent bluffer, but nevertheless he was extremely frightened.

"Let's not play games, Karel. They caught you red-handed. Someone of your sophistication, too—I'm surprised you were so careless."

"What would you know about it?" came the reply, with a scoff.

"I watched them nab you. Trying to break into something—that seems to be your favorite activity. What were you hoping to do—stub an IP to gain access to some RPC requests?"

Mossby looked at him in a different way.

"I'm not yet sure exactly how deeply you're involved in this."

Logan drew out the last word; let it hang in the air a moment. "But unless you tell us everything, and quickly, we'll have to assume you were all in—and that means pinning some homicides on you, for starters."

Mossby's face essentially shut down. "I want a lawyer," he said.

"Sorry," came Peyton's voice from over Logan's shoulder. "All the lawyers here are on our payroll."

The door opened; Logan saw Claire Asperton come in and quietly take a seat.

"I'm not saying another word," Mossby murmured nervously, "until I've got a lawyer."

"You might be silent for a long time. Look, I'll make it easy. I'll give you some words, and you free-associate their significance. Like a game. That way, it's completely deniable."

Mossby collected himself and went still.

"Spearman," Logan said.

Mossby's left eye spasmed—once, twice.

"Bridger."

This time, no reaction. Logan could hear the man's breathing.

"Marceline Williams."

No reaction.

Now Logan played a hunch. He paused, then asked in a low voice: "The Helix?"

Immediately, a different look came over Mossby's face. Surprise, and a trace of fear: the same emotions Logan noted in Peyton, right after he'd accidentally spoken those same words.

There was a scrambling from behind, and Logan felt himself being lifted by the collar of his suit and escorted from the room. For a small person, Peyton was remarkably strong.

"I ought to wring your neck," Peyton hissed when they were out in the hallway.

"Bad idea," Logan said, freeing himself—none too gently—with a Kote-Hineri twist. "No kryptonite—remember?"

Asperton followed them out, quickly closing the door and then—seeing Logan had no trouble defending himself—keeping silent.

"Get him out of here," Peyton said, rubbing his wrist.

"You really shouldn't antagonize Peyton like that," Claire Asperton said as they ascended the institutional spaces toward the Torus. "He's an asset, you know."

"He's not acting like one." Asperton, nearer the door than Peyton, hadn't heard Logan's final two words to Mossby. Logan wondered what would happen if he uttered them again now. What was this thing that seemed even more secret than Omega?

Instead, he asked: "Will you be able to assemble the money?"

"Yes," Asperton said. She did not look happy.

"Okay. If I don't need to worry about that, and if Mossby won't say anything, then I should take a closer look at the obvious . . . the *only* . . . thing the dead board members have in common with these thousand hostages."

"VR," the lawyer said. "The Voyager rollout."

Logan nodded, thinking. "I know we've been avoiding this, Claire, but we need to tell Wrigley. I can talk to him, if you'd like."

"No," Asperton said. "I'll take care of it." And at the thought, a wince crossed her already unhappy features.

22

In an anonymous room marked E-103, Rosalind Madrigal sat at a computer workstation, staring intently at three monitors. The room she occupied was deep within the Torus, barely large enough to hold the workstation, let alone a chair. But that was by choice. Here, far from her office, tucked just off the operations corridor of the Omega Development Division, she could avoid the constant interruptions and endless noise that inevitably came with "crunch."

She'd been a game developer before moving up to project lead at Infinium, and she was all too familiar with the seemingly unavoidable crunch cycle that came just before a deadline: missed meals, missed weekends, missed life. She'd seen people lose unhealthy amounts of weight, get divorced, even develop neuroses as they went through a crunch. In some ways, the Voyager rollout was the same. Maybe even worse. It had its Gantt charts, its milestones . . . and its crunch. And this was the most important deadline she'd ever faced. Wrigley—everyone called him Wrigley, from the interns to the CTO—had likened it to an evolutionary event: transitioning people from horses to automobiles.

But of course, in many ways this crunch cycle was unique. For one thing, they had practically unlimited resources. For another, the work was far more secretive. But also—and this was what kept her up at night—the deadline was immovable. Most projects had a little wiggle room, but this time there were too many moving parts: too much investment, too much potential collateral damage. This rollout had to happen Monday at 9 a.m. . . . or else.

Come to think of it, there was no "or else."

She murmured a few commands into her Omega device; a series of commands rolled across the central screen, then a status indicator turned from red to green. One more bug squashed.

She murmured into her Omega unit again, striking the task from her list and preparing to move on to the next. As if on cue, a two-note chime sounded in her ear, followed by the voice of Wrigley. "Roz, I need you in Theater One."

She took her fingers from the keyboard. "What's up?"

"Don't even ask. Just get over here, please."

Shit—Wrigley's voice held a nasty harmonic that, she knew, meant something unexpected *and* unpleasant. Quickly, she put the workstation into encrypted hibernation, grabbed her tablet, and hurried out into the corridor.

She made her way through the labyrinthine R&D area and across the soundstage leading to Theater One. As she stepped into the room, she saw Wrigley standing before the first row of seats. His arms were rigidly at his sides, like a Queen's Guard outside Buckingham Palace: another bad sign. Beside him was the man she'd seen just over two hours before—Logan—the visitor who'd requested a last-minute demo. He appeared to be in his early forties, with thick auburn hair brushed back from his forehead. He smiled and nodded his recognition.

"—answer his questions," Wrigley was saying as he gestured toward Logan.

She glanced at him. "Sorry?"

"I *said*, you need to answer this guy's questions. You know the nuts and bolts better than I do by now."

"Questions about what?" The man had already experienced the demo, with all the trimmings.

"I . . ." Wrigley stopped, then shook his head. For the first time she could remember, Roz's boss seemed nonplussed. And he looked worried—more worried than she'd ever seen him. "Just tell him whatever he wants to know."

"Anything?" This was unheard of—but then, she remembered Logan had been accompanied earlier by Asperton, who was a big cheese.

"*Anything!*" Wrigley turned his back, raising a hand in petulant dismissal.

23

Logan waited until Wrigley had shut the door behind him. Then he turned back to the young woman in the white turtleneck and faded jeans who'd given him the demo. "Roz, right?"

"Right. Roz Madrigal."

"Mind taking a seat for a moment?"

They sat down, facing the black wall of glass. Roz looked at him with curiosity.

He paused a moment, calculating how to get her maximal cooperation in the shortest amount of time. "Roz, I'm afraid you have to take what Dr. Wrigley said literally. I have questions, maybe a lot of them, and I need answers to them all."

He could see hesitancy mingling with the curiosity. "What's all this about—?"

"Here's what I can tell you. Chrysalis is under threat—a very dire threat. And it seems to involve your product."

"Omega?"

He nodded. "We don't know how it was accomplished or anything about its mechanics. That's where you come in. You see"— and here he leaned in closer—"during that demo you gave the board of directors, two weeks ago . . . something happened, it's not clear what. But three of those directors have died over the last several days. And Chrysalis has been threatened—unless the corporation pays a staggering ransom, many more people will die, as well."

Roz's mouth hung open as she searched for words. "I don't understand."

"I'm relieved to hear that. But we have very little time to figure this out, and less to do something about it." He considered asking her about Karel Mossby, or whether there'd been recent upticks in unauthorized probes of their firewall, but decided that could wait. "I'll put it as bluntly as possible: somebody—a hacker, an ex-employee with a grudge, maybe even a nation-state—has found a way to leverage your Omega technology as a weapon."

"Omega?" she repeated in disbelief.

"Specifically, the second-generation Voyager. The one you demoed for the board members . . . and that goes live Monday morning."

Very briefly, he described the death of the board members, the threat of killing a thousand clients. Then he steeled himself for questions; he knew she'd been helping spearhead this project for months, maybe years, and such a development could be nothing short of overwhelming.

But it seemed Wrigley had chosen wisely. "How exactly can I help?" Madrigal asked.

"By taking me, step by step, through everything those board members experienced during their time here in your division. It's the only common element they share with the—the hostages."

Roz thought a moment. "It wasn't that different from what you requested this morning. We just had more time to prepare, do a little set dressing."

Not that different. This was a rather alarming thought: in the chaos, it hadn't occurred to Logan that he, too, might in some mysterious way be marked for death. He forced this away.

"Okay, let's go through each step in detail." He paused. "I'm sorry for the trouble, but it's the only common factor we've got."

"Don't be sorry," she replied. "We can do it all from here."

"Pardon?"

"The security cameras capture everything. If I cue up events in the proper order, and from the proper locations, we can view the board's entire visit, and I can answer your questions at the same time."

"The security cameras capture everything?" Logan thought about the beautiful marble shower he'd used that morning.

"Not in the way you mean." For the first time, she smiled. "But they really are all over the Complex—not just Infinium. And not just cameras, either."

"Infinium?"

"I'm sorry. That's what I still call this division sometimes."

"So you've been with Wrigley since before the acquisition?"

She nodded. "Let me just get this set up." She pulled out her tablet and began tapping rapidly on its screen. The wall of black before them turned briefly to glass—Logan had a momentary view out over the soundstage—and then it went dark again, displaying the corporate logo of Chrysalis.

He noticed Madrigal had two Omega units—one, cradled in her hand, that looked like the one he'd been upgraded to, and another, quite different unit in place above one ear: a type worn only by people who worked at the Complex. "Why the two devices?" he asked.

"What? Oh. This one I'm wearing is a Sentinel. It's used internally, by developers, managers, security, and such." She held up the one in her hand. "This is the phase two Voyager. The one that's going live Monday."

"So what exactly happens Monday? Does everyone just put their Voyagers on and it works, like magic?"

"If you can call ten million lines of machine code, countless new patents, and a hundred geosynchronous satellites magic, then: yes."

"What's to stop someone from trying one out early? Get a head start, so to speak?"

"Nothing. In fact, a large number of them are. Already, our people are processing a lot of registrations and sync data from the curious. But they won't see anything different from that old Venture you came in wearing this morning."

"Until you flip the switch on Monday."

"Right."

"And this 'switch' is the same for everyone. There are no special groups or subsets."

"Correct."

"So all the Voyager units are completely identical?"

"The ones sent out in the initial hundred-thousand drop are, yes. It's the code that can be modified."

"In what way?"

She paused. "Omega software includes variables to account for individual users, based on questionnaires and medical forms. And, like most other modern tech, the units have firmware that can be updated as necessary, just like the software."

"Updated how?"

"Pushed out to the individual units, via our two-way links."

"And this will happen to all Voyagers out there in the wild?"

"As long as they have any internet access, yes."

He hesitated. "Roz, could these software or firmware updates be tampered with in such a way as to cause harm?"

She looked at him as if he was insane. "Harm? My God, that's crazy. I mean, there have been endless code reviews, alpha and beta test environments . . . something that sick would be caught long before release. *Everything* gets its firmware updated these days—headphones, televisions, refrigerators . . . and just how could these Voyager units cause harm, anyway?"

"I don't know. Just a thought."

The corporate logo disappeared from the large window-cum-screen in front of them, and she tapped in a few more commands on her tablet. "Here it is. I've tried to stitch together an unbroken narrative. If you have questions, or want me to pause, just say so."

The screen now displayed a well-appointed conference room, with a central table and a lectern at one end. For a security camera, Logan mused, the fidelity was remarkably good. He could see the twelve members of the board sitting around the table, with Wrigley at the lectern, gesturing at a presentation deck displayed on a screen behind him. ". . . Although Voyager works internally with a refresh rate of 144 hertz," he was saying, "we downscale the display to twenty-four frames per second, with a pixel resolution of 3,840 by 2,160 per eye. This gives us the slight blurring effect of motion pictures, undetectable but necessary for the immersive experience that's been our goal."

Logan, recognizing at the table the now-deceased Russell Spearman and Marceline Williams, found himself staring at them. The sound cut out, but Wrigley kept talking, and Logan realized Roz had muted it.

"Do you want to hear more?" she asked.

"Not of that. I assume this is the pep talk that preceded the demo?"

She nodded. "Wrigley met the group at the main concourse, just beyond the security barrier to Arc E. He brought them in for the intro you see here, then moved immediately to the demo itself."

"Can you speed up the playback? I'll let you know if I have any questions."

"Sure." She tapped again. Suddenly, Wrigley's gestures grew frantic. Logan watched as the man darted back and forth briefly, then led the group out of the room. The view cut to another angle of them walking down a hall, Wrigley leading the way like a docent. Another cut, and the directors were filing into a space Logan recognized: the production lab that held the "cage." But instead of a cube-like mesh, the video showed three neat rows of four chairs each, placed in the center of the room. All the various machines had been pushed against the walls.

"Pause it, please." *We just had more time to prepare, do a little set dressing.* "Okay. Start it up again—at, say, four times normal speed."

A few more taps on the tablet, and the board members took seats in the rows of chairs. A small group of technicians rushed in, fawning over them like headwaiters, attaching Voyager-style devices and getting them prepped. The technicians rushed away as quickly as they'd come; the lights dimmed slightly—and then all twelve board members went motionless.

"Pause it again, please," Logan asked after about ten seconds. He turned to her. "What happened?"

"Nothing happened."

"We're still running at four times speed?"

"Yes. They're experiencing the demo."

"But they're not moving at all. Can you zoom in?"

"Of course. I can pan over the group, if you like."

"Really? Normal speed, please."

The camera angle changed again, and—as Madrigal slid a finger over her tablet—the view moved across the faces. Some were smiling broadly, others had their mouths agape in awe . . . and then Logan understood. He'd probably worn a similar silly expression when the technology was demonstrated to him. Wrigley had said it best: *I wanted to show them where we're really going with this technology—not just next week, but next year.*

Now the camera view returned to a bird's-eye perspective: the lights were back up and the board members were standing, looking almost like people exiting a roller coaster—laughing, talking. Logan watched as Marceline Williams embraced some board member he didn't recognize.

And then Wrigley returned and ushered the group back out the way they'd come. They moved out of frame, and Logan glanced at Madrigal. "What next?"

"That's it. Wrigley escorted them to the exit portal, and they headed for embarkation. At least, I think that's where they were headed—it was late afternoon by then."

"You mean—" Logan began, then stopped. He'd been sure something about this demo would leap out at him; there would be some clue to lead him further in his investigation. After all, this was the only common link. . . .

Then he remembered something. "Wrigley said the demo he'd given was not just of phase two—but of phase two *advanced*."

Madrigal nodded. "That's right."

"And is that the same demo I was given?"

"Well, almost. The Voyager devices were the same, but we had to manually re-create some effects that, in phase three, will be automatically—"

"Can you show me?" he interrupted. "These enhancements you gave the board?"

She considered a moment. "I can't duplicate it exactly, but I can offer a reasonable facsimile." She stood. "You'd better follow me."

24

In an office, set along the wall of BioCertain's segmented section, the telephone rang. The young woman at the desk paused at her keyboard and glanced toward it. During her time at Chrysalis, phone communication had grown rarer and rarer—especially once the Omega devices became mandatory accessories. Soon, no doubt, the phone would go the way of 8-track tapes, Vanilla Ice, and the dinosaur.

She cleared her throat, picked up the receiver. "Wing Kaupei."

"Wing?"

Recognizing the voice, she suppressed a frown, then glanced up. The wall of her office that faced the cube farm was part glass, but it was soundproofed—and anyway, her door was closed.

"What?" she said.

"This is your friend in Proprietary Fulfillment—"

"I know who it is."

The man on the far end picked up on the disapproval in her voice. "Look, I'm on a secure line. We made sure—"

"Even if that's true, we have procedures for this kind of thing. Now: What's so urgent?"

"What do you think? I've just learned that B—"

"No initials!" she said sharply. "You know better than that."

"This is urgent. I just found out five minutes ago. Is he really—"

"Yes," she interrupted again. "He is."

"But that was never part of the plan. It's rash. It's unnecessary. And when I agreed to come on board, I made it clear: no deviations."

"This isn't a deviation. It's a reaction to recent events. And if our mutual acquaintance thinks it's important, then we shouldn't disagree."

"Yeah? Well, I'm starting to think it's *himself* he feels is important. I'm part of all this just as much as he is. Just because my assignment's complete is no reason to go behind my back, because I've only got six months until—"

"All right!" she said. "Message received. I'll contact him when I can. Meanwhile, stay under the radar. And no more unauthorized contacts."

She hung up even as she heard the chirp of his voice in the earpiece.

For a moment, the young woman sat motionless at her desk, stroking the small mole beneath her chin as she did habitually when troubled. Then, making a decision, she reached for the phone again.

This might be the first time, she thought as she dialed, the phone would be used not just once in a single day—but twice.

25

Logan followed Roz out of the theater, across the soundstage, and into a room he hadn't seen before. It was relatively empty, save for a bank of controls, a worktable, and—at the far end—the large green-screen wall with embedded lights and red X marks at regular intervals.

A chair was placed in front of the worktable, and Madrigal gestured again. "Sit down, please."

When he did so, she checked that his Voyager unit was adjusted and then moved to the bank of equipment. A minute passed. Then the lights dimmed and he felt the brief, barely noticeable tingling sensation behind his ear he'd experienced during the morning demo. The green screen defocused, then abruptly morphed into the image he'd seen at the close of the demonstration: the storefronts in the wide plaza beyond the shoe department. Except now they were clearer, in realistic focus. He smelled that same cool, refreshing waft of air he had that morning; the distant odor of steak, broiling in a salamander.

Suddenly, on impulse, he grasped the device over his ear and plucked it off. Instantly the plaza, the smells, the indescribable feeling of immersion, vanished and he was once again seated before the green screen, his vision returned to normal. He stared down at the device between his fingertips and thought he caught a glimpse of three tiny fibers retracting into its casing. He blinked and they were gone.

He turned toward Roz, standing by the instrumentation panel, and held the device up almost accusingly. "What were those things?" he asked.

"What things?"

"I felt something tickle me, just behind the ear. It was barely noticeable, but I felt it earlier as well—and I'm sure I didn't imagine it."

She hesitated.

"Remember," he said, "I have the authority to ask any question, see any technology. If you want me to call Asperton to confirm, I'll be happy—"

"No, it's fine." She dragged another chair to the worktable and took a seat herself. Then she sighed. "It's just . . . I feel like I'm giving away the keys to the kingdom."

"This is a request from John Christie himself. Now: please tell me what it is I'm missing."

"It's complicated. And it's exciting."

"So give me the abridged version."

"For years, our competition has been chasing existing technology. Old technology. Higher resolutions; outward-facing boundary cameras; 6DoF *versus* 3DoF."

"DoF?" Already this wasn't sounding abridged.

"Degrees of freedom. Translational and rotational axes. The point is, all they're really doing is sharpening a knife to a finer point, jamming more transistors onto a chip: you can make something sharper or faster, but it's still the same tool. We do share some limitations with everyone else—5G and 6G cell technology, high speed throughput down *and* up. That's why even with the Voyager, to get the fullest experience you need to be 'tethered' to a computer with a fast connection to our servers—obviously, you can't stuff every last image into a module. But we have a leg up, thanks to Wrigley's video codecs."

"That's why my Omega unit seems a lot stupider when I take it on the road as opposed to when I'm home." *Sorry, Grace. Maybe that was just Pythia.*

"Right. And that old Venture of yours especially was limited to a small subset of our satellite network, of course. At home, your device has access to broadband internet. We use fiber optics, client- and server-side, to shave off every possible millisecond of lag: and there's nothing faster than optical except quantum entanglement." She laughed. "Anyway, Wrigley's big idea at Infinium was to leap-frog the bottleneck of existing tech entirely. And it's a big part of why he agreed to become part of Chrysalis: he could work closely with the neurophysiology department."

Neurophysiology. "That 'synaptichron' Wrigley mentioned?"

Madrigal nodded. "It helps make Omega—the Voyager units and beyond, that is—possible."

"How?"

"It involves the CS attenuators. Cortical stimulators—those 'fibers' you noticed on the underside of the unit."

"So they *are* invasive," Logan said.

"Barely." A pause. "You've heard of BioCertain, right?"

"I visited it briefly. The Chrysalis subdivision that develops new pacemakers, insulin pumps, and the like."

"Exactly. But that's not all they do. Like most tech areas here, they have 'skunk works' doing things much more interesting. Like cranial robotics."

"What?"

She hesitated again. "Look, all I do is integrate the technology from Arc B with our own VR software and fiber-optic hardware. It's true that our achievements in physical space modeling are by far the biggest factors. But, yes . . . synthesizing BioCertain's tech with our own makes phase two—Voyager—possible."

"Cranial . . . robotics," Logan repeated slowly.

"One of the research teams in BioCertain is working on embedded products for controlling epilepsy, Parkinson's, even multiple sclerosis. It involves subminiaturized sEEG anchors instead of old-school electrodes. We were able to leverage that same technology."

"The cortical stimulators you mentioned," Logan said. "They're like . . . miniature electrodes?"

"Yes. But they only interact with a very specific part of the brain. Other VR technologies merely push image data. They can barely achieve 1080p without lagging and ruining the illusion. Not to mention the 'vergence-accommodation conflict' when your eyes can't truly focus on anything, thanks to their cheesy misalignment of the real and the virtual. We on the other hand let your imagination, and your visual cortex, do a good part of the work. The brain is a more capable projector than any internet connection. That's how we can achieve perceived reality not just to 4K but—in future releases—6K quality and beyond."

Logan wasn't sure he liked the idea of a company, no matter how large or well respected, manipulating his brain.

"See? The look on your face. That's one reason the details are kept confidential. It's only a transitional step, anyway—phase three will use electrocutaneous stimulation, nothing *remotely* invasive." Madrigal was shifting to full-on proselytizing. "It's no different, really, than the signals you get from your eyes, ears, nerve endings. I mean, perceptions have to come from somewhere. Right? This way there's no outdated interface between your eyes and ears— okay, your *brain*—and how you interact with Omega."

Logan heard everything she said, but he was also thinking fast. Did Asperton know about this? Of course she must. Same with John Christie. They were careful, conservative people: they wouldn't green-light something like this without the most extensive and exacting tests imaginable. Besides, he told himself, how different could cortical stimulators be from BioCertain's other products? Pacemakers, for example, were far more invasive—and, if they malfunctioned, surely more dangerous.

Even so, he couldn't stop thinking of the three who'd died . . . and the much larger number who, at the moment, seemed doomed. Did this revelation—the fact that the new Voyager devices directly stimulated the brain, invasively or not—change the course of his investigation?

"Is there somebody I can talk to about this in more detail?" he asked. "Somebody from this black group at BioCertain that's partnering with you?"

"It seems you've got clearance to talk to anybody you want. I'm sure Wrigley can put you in touch with the right person." She stood up. "What are you interested in, exactly? Because I can assure you that—"

"If you can just get me a name, that would be great." He knew Chrysalis would not have taken any chances if there were even the slightest reservations about this technology. Yet he was troubled nevertheless. The brain was a hugely complex organ, and any neurologist who said he or she truly understood it was lying.

He waited as Roz searched for a contact at BioCertain. What concerned him most—now that this Pandora's box had been opened—was one thing in particular. Spearman had taken a dive through a glass table. Bridger had perished in a plane crash. Williams had slipped and fallen under the wheels of a bus.

Those board members had all died tragically. But there was a possibility all three deaths could . . . *could* . . . have been precipitated *voluntarily*.

Bridger might have pointed his plane toward the ground. Marceline Williams might have intentionally stepped in front of the bus. Was it possible that, despite all the rigorous testing, something had slipped between the cracks while mating BioCertain's technology to Omega's? Because Logan knew that a brain capable of the sensory stimulation offered by such VR was capable of something else, as well.

Induced psychosis. And he feared Omega—and its marvelous new technology—just might cause some of those who experienced it to become suicidal . . . or insane.

26

Two hundred and fifty miles to the south and west, Janelle Deston was pulling into the driveway of her townhome in the Pocono foothills, just outside Stroudsburg. Turning off the engine, she sat in her car for a moment, as was her custom, letting the stress drain away. The mindfulness app on her phone called it "decompression."

It wasn't that her work at Lehigh Valley was uncomfortably stressful—as regional hospitals went—but she wasn't happy with her recent shift change. She'd been rotated to the 4-a.m.-to-noon slot, and it was busier than the 8 p.m. slot she'd become used to. In the late afternoons and evenings, patients were usually preoccupied one way or another: getting adjusted to a step-down unit; being visited by doctors or relatives; eating dinner; getting their nightly dose of meds. The morning was a different animal. Everything was wearing off by the time they all woke up—pain meds, anxiolytics, benzos—and they were cranky or, worse, cranky *and* hungry. It wasn't that she no longer enjoyed caring for people, she most definitely did . . . it was just that, since Paul had left her, she had problems of her own to deal with—and she'd started to prefer her patients asleep rather than awake.

She closed her eyes, then took twelve deep breaths, ending her routine. Possibly the worst thing about this new shift was that she never seemed to get out on time. Today, for instance: she hadn't left the hospital until one thirty, and with the lunchtime traffic it was now nearly three. And she still had shopping to take care of at Pocono Commons.

She glanced in the rearview mirror, confirmed that her hair did indeed look like the Bride of Frankenstein's, got out, and walked to the front door. She reached for a key, noticed it was unlocked. She frowned: Courtney knew better.

Opening the door, she was greeted by a blast of pop music. "Hey, Court!" she yelled over the din. "I'm home!"

A minute later, the volume dwindled to a tolerable level. "Hi, Mom!"

Janelle hung her jacket in the front hall, then began climbing to the second floor. "What are you doing?"

"Just sending out applications."

Janelle didn't reply. She knew it was pretty common nowadays to have a grown kid living at home. Courtney had been stubborn, insisting on computer science courses at the local community college. Now she had a freshly minted associate degree . . . but it seemed all the decent-paying employers wanted students from a four-year college. So far, the only offers she'd gotten were from places like Rochester, Minnesota, or some little town in Texas. Janelle had explained to her daughter years before that nursing was a perfectly good profession. It gave you a lot of options, too. You could go straight for an RN, or you could get an ADN degree, find a job, and then take evening classes through an online program. That's what she'd done. The hospital had paid for most of it. Now she had the equivalent of a bachelor's degree, and the salary that went with it. If Courtney played her cards right, she might end up in a private hospital—where there'd be less chaos.

Janelle walked into her bathroom, washed up—even though she'd already done so when ending her shift—then glanced at her hair again. God. What was it about her job that made it so disheveled? She combed it in long, violent strokes as she stood before the mirror, only to see it frizz out. Now she looked like the Bride just after her daily electrocution.

She glanced again at the time. Three thirty. She'd wanted to get her shopping done and be home before the schools let out—never mind the Friday afternoon traffic.

Janelle pulled open a drawer for a hair tie. None. Damn it, that was one of the things on her list. Slamming the drawer closed with a thrust of one hip, she walked out of her bathroom, through her bedroom, and into the hall. "Court?" she called as she entered her daughter's room. "I'm going to borrow a hair tie. Okay?"

It took Courtney a moment to answer. "What? Oh no, Mom—wait! *Don't!*"

But it was too late: atop the dresser was a relatively small box of heavy, coated cardboard, like a jeweler might use. She turned it over in her hands and noticed it was unmarked save for a small logo, stamped in gold on the top.

For a moment, she stared. Then: "Oh my *God*!"

Courtney had bounded up to the second floor. Now she burst into the room, intent on preventing her mother, but stopped abruptly when she saw she was too late.

"It came!" Janelle said, turning toward her. "And you didn't tell me!"

"It was supposed to be a surprise," her daughter said.

"But I've been worried sick. You know how I've been following the posts. Half the world's already gotten theirs—and according to the tracking number, this arrived *three days ago*!" She shook the box in emphasis—then opened it. Inside, beneath a linen-colored protective shield, was something from another world: iridescent, beautifully curved, with J. DESTON stamped in tiny letters along one edge.

She stared at it for a minute, drinking it in. Then she looked up at Courtney. "Where's the rest?" she demanded.

Courtney walked back out of her room, returning a moment

later with another, larger box. Janelle grabbed it, then rushed downstairs to the dining room, where she spread everything out carefully on the table: user manual, app guide, adjustment chart, accessories. She carefully removed the Venture she'd been wearing, glanced over the "Getting Started" brochure, then seated the new Omega II Voyager unit in its place.

"It fits perfectly!" she exclaimed. "Just like they said!"

Courtney slumped down in a nearby chair, visibly deflated. "*This* is why I didn't give it to you," she said. "You're not supposed to mess with it yet."

"Why not?" Janelle grabbed her phone, tapped it. "Look? The app sees it—it's updating already."

Courtney let out an exaggerated sigh. "Why do I have to have the only mother in Pennsylvania who's not only a tech nerd, but an early adopter?"

"I'm *not* an early adopter."

"You shouldn't be putting that on, let alone activating it. I read the emails, too. And they said the enhancements won't go live until nine a.m. Monday."

"I know that. They *said* the device would operate as an ordinary Venture if you tried using it before that. But can you imagine the rush at nine a.m., when all those people try to fire theirs up? The servers will probably go down." She took a small mirror from her purse, held it up to her ear. "See? That little light turned orange. It's activated. And now it's green—online." There was a pause.

"Well?" her daughter asked, curious despite herself.

Janelle looked around. "I see all the menus—the television, thermostat, refrigerator, alarm. Wonder how they do it without the glasses. Oh!"

"What is it? Your stim?"

"No. I felt a tickle or something—let me adjust this a little more." She fiddled with the device.

"I'll bet they can see you're already online. You'll be lucky if they don't ban you for a month. Maybe a year."

"Don't you think a billion other people are doing the same thing? In fact, most of them did it already." She stood up, grabbing her purse, then swiveled her head back and forth. Like Courtney said: no joy until 9 a.m. Monday. At least she'd have the weekend to get used to it.

"I'm headed to the Commons," Janelle said. "Want to come?"

"No. I'm good."

"Okay. See you in an hour or so."

She shrugged into her coat again, went out the front door, trotted down to the steps, and got into the car. An unintrusive bar along the upper edge of her vision told her the ambient temperature and her heart rate, and when she started the car a small map came up. Just as it had with the Venture—except without the annoying glasses. *Incredible.*

As she backed her car down the driveway, it was odd how everything—from the clouds overhead to the trees lining the street, to the school bus across the intersection—began to seem sharper, more real, than they actually were. That was just projection, of course: a manifestation of her eagerness, like the thrill of excitement spreading like a strange heat to her nerve endings. *Monday can't come soon enough.*

27

Logan was halfway to BioCertain when his Omega unit chimed.

He answered with a quick blink. "Logan."

"Jeremy? It's Claire. You need to get over here."

There was a tone in her voice that—even given the recent tension—Logan had not heard before. "Where is 'here'?"

"I'm in D606. We can all get there fastest."

There was the faintest crackle as Asperton ended the connection.

As Logan's pulse accelerated, a vague feeling of dread washed over him.

Within ten minutes, he'd located Asperton's unmarked office in the spire. He knocked and the door was immediately opened by Orris Peyton. The logistics chief nodded for Logan to enter, then shut the door behind him.

Also in the room was Kramer, Peyton's head of Security. Kramer glanced at Logan with black, expressionless eyes, and might have nodded a greeting. Then again, he might not have; Logan wasn't sure.

To his surprise, Wrigley was there, as well. He was looking around uncomfortably, like someone at a chummy cocktail party who didn't know any of the other guests.

Asperton was behind her desk, alternately typing on a keyboard and tapping gently on what Logan now recognized as an Omega Sentinel.

"I received another communication," Asperton said without looking up. "Fourteen minutes ago."

"Same source and method?" Peyton asked.

Asperton nodded. "Encrypted message to my private account. I'll bring it up."

One of the flat-panel screens awoke and a message—its text white on black, as spare as before—appeared.

Hello again.
You deserve a treat
For all the money you're assembling
And just in case you still think it's a bluff.
So we've moved up tomorrow's entertainment.
In fact it is currently under way
But you can enjoy the aftermath.
Link to the address we will send you in precisely 15 minutes
Do not bother to trace
That will only end unpleasantly
Sit back and enjoy the show.

For a moment, paralyzed oblivion—then everyone began to speak at once.

"You're positive it's the same source?" said Kramer.

"Where is this link?" Peyton asked.

"I've routed it to this screen." Asperton pointed to a darkened monitor. "We've got thirty seconds."

"Dan," Peyton told Kramer, "fire up all the monitoring and tracing tools we have. Route data directly to the Helix. I want to know how he's communicating, and what his location is."

The Helix, Logan thought. "He just warned us against tracing him."

"We're using passive tools only," Peyton replied.

Now the second screen came to life. It contained nothing but an unusual-looking hyperlink. The room went silent again.

Taking a deep breath, Claire clicked a button, activating the link.

This got Kramer moving, as well: stepping behind the desk, he pulled Asperton's keyboard toward him, removed his own Sentinel, and placed it nearby. Some kind of handshake took place and the Sentinel chirped a series of tones.

Now a full-color image came onto the second screen. It was blurred at first, then came slowly into focus. Logan realized it was the view of an intersection. He could see a green traffic light, but a line of cars waiting in all directions. There was no audio.

"Anything?" Peyton asked Kramer.

"Nothing. It's coming in through some kind of anonymizer."

"Shit. Well, scrape all the data you can. We'll have Snow comb through it later." Peyton paused. "That's a traffic camera, right?"

"Either that, or a pole cam installed by the feds."

"It could be a dummy," said Wrigley. "Doesn't seem to have any listening wand."

"Can you get a location at least?" Peyton said to Kramer.

"Yes." A beat. "Latitude 40.94 north, longitude 74.98 west."

"Christ, that doesn't tell me anything."

"It's . . . in Pennsylvania. Stroudsburg, wherever that is."

"North of Philadelphia," said Logan.

"It's moving," Asperton murmured.

At this all eyes returned to the screen. Sure enough: the camera was panning slowly away from the intersection and along the street. As Logan watched, he realized what he was seeing wasn't a blurred image: it was smoke, obscuring the view as it drifted past.

The smoke grew thicker. Through it, Logan made out the flash of light bars—police vehicles, ambulances—and then other, larger shapes. A school bus, its rear end ablaze—and a small SUV, perpendicular to the street, engine seemingly buried in the flank of the bus.

"Sweet Jesus," murmured Asperton.

Through the billows, Logan could see emergency workers swarming ant-like around the scene. The camera stabilized, then moved in almost languidly on the wreckage of the SUV. Its front end was crumpled beyond recognition.

"Who's controlling that camera?" Kramer said.

No one answered.

Logan glanced briefly back at the words on the other screen: WE'VE MOVED UP TOMORROW'S ENTERTAINMENT. *My God. Is this one of the people they promised to kill tomorrow?*

"How many customers for the Voyager rollout live in that area?" Logan asked.

"Thirty-one Voyager units were sent out to people in a five-mile radius," Kramer said.

"Have any of them been activated?"

"Let me see. Yes. Twelve."

"The new programming," Wrigley began, "won't be effective until—"

"Check the logs," Logan interrupted. "See if any of those activated units recently went off-line."

There was a short pause. "Just one," Kramer said. "Janelle Deston, forty-three. Ridgeline Road, West Stroudsburg. Her device went off-line six minutes ago."

And then, as if on cue, the camera moved again, focusing tighter on the SUV. Logan saw that firemen had pried open the driver's door and cut away the airbag. Two paramedics were gingerly pulling a broken body from behind the wheel. The camera lens zoomed in still tighter, but for Logan this wasn't necessary: through the smoke, he'd already seen the dirty blond hair, the singed face covered in a mask of blood . . . and a brand-new Voyager unit, snugly in place behind Janelle Deston's right ear.

28

The smoke grew thicker, and then the image froze in place. A shocked silence fell over the office. Everyone stood still, agape as the monitor reflected its image of death across the conference room.

Logan felt the same shock. For the first time, he'd actually seen their opponent, the puppeteer behind this sadistic conspiracy, pull his strings . . . and kill someone in real time.

His eyes fell from the image to the others in the room. Now they were all staring back at him.

They don't know what to do, he thought. This drama had been orchestrated to perfection. With each move more control had been leeched away. And now, these people had no agency left. They were like deer in the headlights.

Suddenly, Logan's shock turned to anger. Anger at the days they'd wasted—floating one theory after another, arguing over threat credibility. Anger at the perpetrators of this cruel, needless demonstration of violence. Anger at the specialists and power brokers running this palace of technology, now looking to him for the way out of this nightmare. And anger at himself—for having no answer to give them.

Now was the time to let that anger do some of the work.

Stepping between Peyton and Kramer, moving behind the desk, he jabbed the monitor's power button with such force it fell backward against the wall. Then he glanced at his watch.

"We've got sixty-six hours left," he said. "Somebody take notes."

Asperton reached into her desk, pulled out a pad. Kramer raised a hand to his Sentinel.

"Put the campus on lockdown. Nobody in, nobody out. You must have scenarios for that—choose one that's credible so nobody panics."

Nods all around—except for Wrigley. This had all been secondhand, corporate gossip-mongering for him . . . until now. But here, he'd witnessed the violence with his own eyes, and he seemed to be stunned.

"Wrigley," Logan said to him. No response.

"Wrigley. *Hey!*"

Now the VR visionary looked over.

"We can't stop Monday's rollout. But we can slow-walk ongoing development and fabrication—*everything* related to the project. Can you see to it?"

"Yes," Wrigley said after a moment, in a quiet voice.

Logan turned to Peyton. "That cyber-forensic team I asked you to pull together. Any hits so far?"

"No joy."

"Well, now we've got more meat to throw at them. Have you put the screws on Mossby yet?"

Peyton shook his head.

"Then start turning them now, please. We need to know whether to rule him out or put a gun to his head." He glanced at Kramer. "I suppose that's your department."

Without waiting for a response Logan continued. "Our opponents have made it pretty clear where we need to focus. Wrigley's VR empire." He looked around the room. "Anyone disagree?"

Silence—Wrigley included.

"Let's not stop our vetting at Omega's coders and developers. We have to check the whole logistical chain these new devices took to get from the blackboard to assembly to end users. Wrigley, I'm counting on you to help Peyton fast-track his investigation."

"Don't worry about my 'empire'—just make sure all this wasn't for nothing."

Logan turned to Asperton. "Claire, I know I already asked for some preliminary searches of the public and private sides of the board members. But now we need to get a whole server farm chugging away on what *else* those three had in common. Maybe it was a mistake to stop looking once we got the ransom note." He paused. "And what about those special blood assays?"

"As I told you, it would take—"

"At least ten days. Well, assign somebody on your staff to call for updates. Once an hour. If we're uncomfortable, let's make somebody else uncomfortable, too."

He stopped to take a breath. He was surprised by how fast his heart was beating. He looked from one person to the next, calming himself, letting some but not all of the anger drain away. "How many assignments did I just dole out—six?"

"Seven," Kramer and Wrigley said in chorus.

"Can I leave you to sort them out among yourselves?"

Both men nodded.

"Good." Logan turned to leave.

"Where are you going?" asked Asperton.

"I'm late for a date with a neurologist." Then he opened the door, heading for the skyway that would lead him back to Bio-Certain Medical.

29

Twenty minutes later, Logan found himself in what looked like—and probably was—a medical lecture hall. He was standing by the lectern, next to a long metal cart on wheels that held an array of tools, a Voyager unit, and several unmarked boxes sealed in plastic.

Logan had not yet allowed his upwelling of anger and frustration to fully recede. On the way here, he'd decided to stop briefly at his office and glance through his digital in-box. Peyton had followed through on sending evidence of Karel Mossby's suspect behavior. Although much of it was technical, what Logan understood did seem damning enough to warrant Mossby's apprehension: over the last four months, surveillance spyware had caught him attempting—and on two occasions, succeeding in—a hack of the supposedly air-gapped firewall around the Omega project. Exactly what he'd done, the surveillance worm couldn't pick up without alerting Mossby, but a large amount of data had evidently been transmitted in both directions. In addition to the sins already cited by Peyton, Mossby had also created numerous back channels in the Omega packet distribution system, and it appeared he'd spoofed some clueless ex-Infinium employee into giving him his private cryptographic key. This, coupled with the public keys of the Complex, allowed him to reverse engineer decoding algorithms for almost any information encrypted by Chrysalis. And send messages just like those they'd been receiving.

. . .

Now he looked across the gleaming table at the three others in the room. Logan had finished briefing the three doctors in the room, a man and two women, explaining the true reason for his presence at the Complex as well as the desperate nature of their situation. There was Dr. Purchase, the BioCertain implants chief whom he'd spoken with the day before, and two medical doctors, Ransom and Gupta. They were both thin women with dark hair, dressed in clinical whites, although Ransom was old enough to have been Gupta's mother.

Dr. Gupta was the first to get over her surprise. "And these people were murdered how, exactly?"

"We're not certain. All died from different causes, and for different reasons. That's the point—we're trying to find what they *do* have in common. Right now, it obviously seems bound up with the VR project—specifically, Voyager—and its synaptichron unit, which I understand was the product of your R&D."

The three glanced at one another. "We developed the synaptichron," said the elder woman, Dr. Ransom. "I was chief neurologist consulting on the project. What does it have to do with these deaths?"

Logan pointed at the Voyager on the metal table. "This newest model. It contains a synaptichron—right?"

"A variant, yes—"

"And it, in turn, makes the cortex receptive to virtual reality: illusory sights and sounds. Specific images that aren't actually there at all." He paused. "Or perhaps it can even alter behavior? If the synaptichron technology was altered, could it provoke actions that might seem strange? Even psychotic?"

A chorus of "no" from all three.

Logan wasn't surprised. This was an inventor's maternal

instinct. "All right. Tell me what I'm getting wrong. Because if a 'cortical stimulator' can't cause suicidal or psychotic ideation—then what can?"

Dr. Ransom picked up the Voyager unit. "This embedded synaptichron, despite its use of next-generation fiber optics, has limited functionality. It can stimulate certain neocortical neurons, yes, but since it's designed for minimal invasiveness—the Voyager model, particularly—it's extremely limited in the spectrum of electrical activity it can influence."

Logan looked at the younger woman, Dr. Gupta. "May I ask what your role is in this?"

"Very minor. I concentrate primarily on the more invasive implants: 'smart' vascular stents, palliative cancer treatments."

"But you agree with what Dr. Ransom says? That a synaptichron, no matter how obviously manipulated, is incapable of causing irrational or insane behavior in the wearer?"

"Not even with the most drastic modifications." She turned over the Voyager in her hands, picked up a tiny tool from the table. "If you'll allow me to demonstrate—"

"Just one moment, please." Logan glanced over the cart, his eyes falling on the small boxes sealed in plastic. "What are those?"

"Voyagers," said Purchase.

"Like the ones sent out this week?"

Purchase nodded. He looked at Logan questioningly. "I just grabbed a few, in case we—"

Logan chose one at random, pulled off the stylish covering. Inside the box was a brand-new Voyager, with a clear seal and a registration card, currently blank. Breaking the seal, he pulled it from its box. "Would you mind using this one to demonstrate?"

Ransom looked at him. "Why that one, in particular?"

In response, Logan placed the unit on the cart, picked up one of the medical tools—a small metal mallet—and struck it against the Voyager.

The little unit was tougher than he expected, and he hit it again. This time, a small crack appeared across the otherwise smooth surface. He picked it up and handed it to Ransom. "This one, please."

The three looked at him in surprise and displeasure. "Did you enjoy breaking things as a child?" Ransom asked.

"I want you to demonstrate on a random production model." He took a deep breath. "Look. We have very little time, and I don't know who to trust. Humor me."

After a silence, Ransom lowered her eyes from his and used her small tool to make minute adjustments to the damaged Voyager, poking and pressing some almost invisible detents. A small red light winked on, then turned orange.

"It appears to work," she said. "Remarkable, considering the manhandling." More poking. And then three tiny metallic fibers, almost whisker-like, slid out from invisible ports in the unit's underside.

So Logan *had* felt something, after all.

"Extend them farther," he said.

Dr. Ransom picked up a different tool and deftly used the crack to split the device down the middle. She tossed both halves across the table to Logan. Catching them, he could see that—while the miniaturized guts were incredibly complex, particularly the threads of fiber-optic cabling that seemed to encase everything like a spiderweb—the three metallic whiskers were already at full extension.

"I don't suppose you know any more about chemical absorption than you do about handling delicate objects." It was Gupta, the implant specialist, who spoke: it was almost amusing how they seemed more worked up about his breaking a perfectly good unit than the larger problem at hand. "Getting the API, active pharmaceutical ingredient, to its designated target—heart, brain, wherever— in a safe and timely fashion is a huge medical issue. That's especially true for chemo and other caustic drugs, which require a port-a-cath and a central line: if you try injecting such drugs into a surface vein, it'll just collapse. They require a highway, like the internal jugular or subclavian, to reach their destination inside our allotted time. Other drugs—Valium, ketamine—unaffected by slower absorption can be administered IM. Our frontline job here is getting lifesaving drugs where they need to be, more quickly and safely."

"Okay," Logan said. "Your point?"

"My point is that the *least* invasive way to administer a drug, short of snorting it, is also the *slowest* way—subcutaneously. Of course, we have numerous such implants in our product line now, so that diabetics don't need to jab themselves in the stomach anymore. But subcutaneous . . ." She stopped.

"Subcutaneous," Ransom, the neurologist, picked up the thread, "is the holy grail. If we can find a way to get the body's microcirculation—capillaries—to absorb and transport meds to the brain quickly enough, we could improve the quality of life for countless millions of people now dealing with PICCs, biocompatibility, dosage errors. And we're making real progress. But the synaptichron you're holding is sadly not that holy grail. It's only the first step. And it certainly can't induce behavioral change, much less psychosis."

"Why not?" Logan asked.

Ransom, although displaying no outward indication of a sense of humor, nevertheless laughed at this—in disbelief. "Why *not*? Why do you think it's worn behind the ear—and thus so close to the brain? Look at those sEEGs: What can those tiny things deliver? Nothing but micro-impulses of electrical energy to certain sensory and associative neurons that increase the user's receptivity to artificial sensations—and that's where Omega's virtual technology comes in."

Logan processed this. *Artificial sensations.* "You mean, the synaptichron has no significant effect on brain function?"

"Only in a preparatory sense. Like warming up before a workout. It readies the mind to receive and process a simulated reality ... but it's Wrigley's work that does the heavy lifting. *That*"—she pointed to the broken pieces in Logan's hands—"is a prototype model in our search for less invasive medical treatments. But that's all."

Over the last several minutes, Logan's anger had disappeared, leaving disappointment in its wake. He tried once more. "So there's no way, *no way*, this device could be modified to cause hallucinations, temporary insanity?"

"That would require a serotonergic drug, or perhaps a poisonous compound," Ransom said. "And a synaptichron has no ability to *inject* anything. The worst thing you could do is up its voltage ... which might tingle a bit, but nothing else."

Now Purchase spoke up. "I'm actually rather grateful to Wrigley. Under normal circumstances, the synaptichron would have outlived its useful life span for BioCertain a year ago. But instead it remains on our balance sheet as a hybrid component, developed for—and billable to—the virtual reality division."

Logan looked at each of them in turn. "Shit."

From her desk just inside BioCertain's segmented area, Wing Kaupei watched Dr. Purchase walking along a far wall toward the main concourse. A man was walking beside him, eyes downcast, silent. He looked like someone who'd just received some very bad news.

Wing lowered her head, smiling to herself.

Just then, a tone sounded overhead, and a calm, feminine voice—apparently speaking throughout the entire Complex—spoke. "If I could please have your attention. Due to a large rockslide across the central access road several minutes ago, there will be no arrivals to or departures from the Advanced Research Center until the area has been cleared and the damage repaired. We anticipate this condition lasting no longer than forty-eight hours. If you have any questions or concerns, please contact your resident manager. We will provide updates as they become available. Thank you for letting us put your safety first."

Wing listened with interest. This "condition"—lockdown, actually—was not unexpected. In fact, it might prove useful . . . assuming one very important condition had been met.

To make sure of this, she turned away and, with a casual movement, raised her fingertips to the stylish Sentinel device fitted over her right ear.

30

The man waited for the hotel valet to leave, then closed the hallway door and walked across the carpeting to the bank of windows. He had asked for a room on a high floor, and was glad he had: the view of the wild escarpment of the mountain and surrounding valley, with the gleaming bulk of the Torus curving around its base far below, provided a most interesting study in contrast in the evening light.

Turning from the view, he took off his jacket, hung it over a chair, then placed his suitcase on the rack at the foot of his bed. He had completed the security check-in, registered, and was just riding the escalator to this room when the announcement of a temporary lockdown came.

His timing, as usual, was excellent. Fifteen minutes later, and he would have needed to make other arrangements far less convenient—or comfortable.

Opening his suitcase a crack, he removed what appeared to be a leather toilet kit, pulled a chair into the middle of the room, and placed the kit on the seat. He reached in and snapped on a device. There was a faint humming. After fifteen seconds—once he was confident all monitoring equipment in and around the room was disabled—he telescoped the surveillance baffle up out of the leather case to its full height.

He had registered as Reginald Bryant, architectural engineer and planner, here to finalize a proposal for modifying points along the main concourse to accept cantilevered stained glass. The real Reginald Bryant was at this moment stuffed inside a metal drum, his molecular bonds loosening in a cocktail of lye and sulfuric acid. In any case, the man's work was low priority and low security; in the unlikely chance a surveillance camera were to examine his room, it would find an anomaly with the wireless video link, which would require addressing from a central data hub . . . in due time, of course.

Potential prying eyes dealt with, he now opened his suitcase wide. Inside was a beautiful suit of blue silk, a close-fitting tactical outfit in black, and a few Chrysalis uniforms in various hues. There were several accessories, as well: an all-access badge with seals; a 9x19 Parabellum with silencer; several coils of piano wire; a 100 mV taser; and other more exotic devices. Beside all these was an Omega Sentinel, registration-free, with all clearances and channels unlocked. Now that he was inside the Torus, he fixed the Sentinel above his ear, allowing it to run its bootstrap loader. As it finished, he heard three beeps in rapid succession: it seemed Wing was already trying to contact him.

He responded with a "go" signal, then closed the suitcase again and—returning to the windows—allowed his gaze to settle once more over the remarkable view.

31

Orris Peyton, head of Operational Logistics, sat in a low-ceilinged room with his chief security specialist—an ex-Mossad asset named Dafna—beside him. The room had no table, but what it lacked in furniture it made up for in electronics. Controls and displays— enough to land a lunar orbiter—bracketed both sides of a large window set into the far wall.

Peyton prided himself on knowing every last nook and cranny in the twelve million square feet of the Complex. He liked to boast that he'd personally checked every hotel room and staff dormitory for security breaches. But he wasn't especially familiar with this particular space. It was deep inside Carewell; as deep as that division got, in fact: about thirty feet ahead of them lay the outer skin of the Torus, and beyond that there was only the dressed rock of Hurricane Mountain. But two of the three subjects on his interview schedule had particularly requested this location, and it seemed prudent to oblige.

The man they were currently interviewing—Simon Cawdor, fabrication lead—was one of the two. He was sweating a little beneath his white lab coat.

"So let me understand," Peyton said. He'd placed Cawdor several seats away, to make it obvious he was being scrutinized. "You're stating for the record that it's physically impossible for somebody to sabotage the Voyager units during assembly. To, say, put some kind of skin-acting poison on the surface or in some other way render it harmful."

"Yes." Cawdor tugged on the knot of his tie. "The line is fully automated, from the initial extrusion to the final laser that creates a hermetic seal. Everything is performed in a clean room, partly for sanitation and quality control, and partly to make sure the scenario you're suggesting couldn't happen." As he spoke, he pointed toward the window set between the electronics.

Peyton held Cawdor's glance a moment while Dafna took notes, then looked toward the window. Beyond, he could see the "Line"—a series of thick rubber belts, threading their way through large machines on which digital inventory numbers constantly incremented. Here and there, robots could be seen hovering over the belts, attaching miniaturized pieces or making spot welds with tiny showers of sparks. There were no people in sight, of course: in fact, there was no floor to speak of, just equipment caches that were refilled automatically and the robots themselves. As the entire process moved like a silicon-and-steel battalion beyond the soundproofed glass, Peyton could see Voyagers—in essence—being born: entering from the left as unassembled components and heading out of sight to the right as complete units.

He felt he should ask more questions, just to please that bastard Jeremy Logan, but he couldn't think of any. "What about a nerve agent, or radioactive polonium? It takes just the smallest drop."

At this, Cawdor appeared to suppress a smile. "The devices—even just the initial components—are under constant surveillance. Same is true for the final tests once fabrication is complete: thermal cycling, solvent resistance, seal terminal strength. And there are fluoroscopes that scan everything before *and* afterward."

The smile irritated Peyton. And he knew all about the surveillance. "Thanks," he said, with a dismissive gesture. "Please send in the next."

Cawdor left, and moments later another man in a white coat approached nervously. He was heavyset and young, younger than Peyton—but then, most of the staff at the Complex were under forty. Peyton conferred with his Sentinel unit just long enough to assure himself this was Scott Prawn, who led one of the Proprietary Fulfillment teams handling the final steps—inspection, boxing, loading—before the Voyager units left the Complex.

"Have a seat," Peyton said, indicating the spot, six chairs away, so recently occupied by Cawdor. He heard a brief tap behind him as Dafna prepared to log a new entry. "As I mentioned to you when we first spoke, we're selecting staff members for random procedural reviews. We conduct such reviews now and then to ensure safety, security, and optimization. As you know, Chrysalis hates redundancy."

Peyton was confident he'd already done two things: put Prawn on guard by mentioning safety procedures, and made him fear for his job with the dreaded word "redundancy." Sure enough, the chubby technician's eyes widened slightly, and he glanced around, as if looking for a cattle prod.

Peyton went through the formalities and initial questions, Dafna prompting him once or twice. Soon, Prawn was sweating as much as Cawdor, if not more. "I know the assembly process is lights-out, completely automated," Peyton said. "What about Fulfillment?"

"It's automated, too. Not all that different from Fabrication, down there." Prawn pointed through the observation window at the robots assembling the Voyagers.

"I note your staff is rather small," Peyton said. "What—two, three dozen people?"

"Well, ah, only a small percentage of fabrication takes place on-site, here in the Torus. Just sensitive things like high-end medical implants and now those Omega units. Robots do most of the work, under careful supervision. Human interaction only occurs during the loading phase."

"And I assume security is heightened accordingly at that step?"

"Yes. Three people must be on hand as observers during load-ing and sealing. The chain of integrity is maintained at all times."

Peyton nodded. He understood the basic process well enough: once the units were ready for shipping, they exited through a series of secure airlocks to a loading bay, cut into the side of the moun-tain, where unmarked trucks took them through a tunnel that hugged the outer side of the Torus and then down a back road leading out into the real world.

A voice murmured in his Sentinel unit: Dafna, who had just done some background checking, had a suggested line of inquiry. "I understand you're in charge of the fulfillment team for medical implants."

The man blinked, nodded.

"But two weeks ago, you also took over fulfillment of the Voy-ager units."

At this, Prawn became noticeably more nervous. "For one day, yes."

"Why was that?"

"The tech lead for Omega Fulfillment reported in sick. Word came down they were in the middle of an important loadout and didn't want to pause."

"Did that cause any problems? For you, or Fulfillment as a unit?"

Prawn shook his head vigorously. "Oh, no. As I said, it was only one day. And the boxing, loading, and sealing processes were simi-lar to what I'm used to with BioCertain implants. It was a question of supervising two lines instead of one." His eyes widened again as he realized that downplaying his role might raise the fearful spec-ter of redundancy. "Of course, I had to up my game substantially for that one shift. I was practically dead when it was over. But we had procedures in place to ensure there were no hiccups. Short-term procedures, you understand."

"How many Voyager units were distributed that day?"

Prawn chewed his lip. "I don't have the exact number at my fingertips. Probably four, five hundred."

"Six hundred ninety-one," Dafna said after a moment.

Peyton raised his eyebrows at the man's humility. "Very good, Mr. Prawn. You may go. For now. Please ask the person outside to step in."

Seconds later, it seemed, the third and last interviewee of the session was standing before him: standing rather too near, in fact, practically violating Peyton's personal space. Peyton waved him back, indicating the seat the others had taken. The man retreated, but his attitude remained, hovering front and center. He couldn't have been more different in appearance or demeanor than the first two Peyton had questioned: bald, fifty, with a huge red handlebar mustache. His lab coat was unbuttoned, displaying a flannel work shirt of red and black plaid. He stood for a moment—silhouetted by the window overlooking the robots that were mindlessly working the line—then settled into the chair.

"You're . . . Seamus McBride?" Peyton asked, nearly faltering. This had to be a mistake—nobody outside of a dirty Irish joke had a name like that.

"Yes," the mustached man replied. He looked Peyton in the eye, silently adding: *Got a problem with that?*

Peyton skipped the pleasantries and usual mind games and launched directly into his questions. "You're in charge of distribution and tracking?"

McBride nodded.

"We're performing a logistics audit, making sure everything fabricated at the Complex shows a clean line end to end. This is because, in addition to medical devices, Omega Division units began being assembled and distributed."

McBride nodded again.

"Have you encountered any difficulties?"

"No." McBride shifted in his chair. It was clear he considered this interview a waste of time. Peyton wasn't used to such truculence, and via his Sentinel unit he indicated to Dafna they should take a closer look into McBride's background, psychological as well as professional.

"I'm glad to hear that. Could you be more specific?"

"We spent a lot of time developing a system to transport our medical products to their destinations in a safe and timely manner. It's been refined and battle-tested. It was simple enough to modify this process to handle Omega products."

"Really? I would think it completely different."

McBride shook his head. "We use the same principle for Omega devices as we do for medical implants: a data ledger that tracks transport of goods from point A to point B. Each device shipped from the Complex is geotagged with its metadata: when it was fabricated, where it's going, and twenty other things you don't want to know about. When that device leaves Fulfillment, its metadata is entered into the ledger."

Peyton began to feel very tired. He interrupted this explanation, which showed no signs of ending, by raising his hand. "Thank you. Basically, what you're saying is this . . . data ledger . . . ensures there can be no tampering between here and the delivery point."

"That's exactly what I'm saying."

"What about *from* the delivery point?"

McBride frowned. "Excuse me?"

"What mechanisms protect our product once it reaches its destination?"

"With all respect, that's like asking what somebody does with a bottle of painkillers—or a bazooka—after they take possession. The medical devices arrive at hospitals, or central depositories, and from there surgeons attach or implant them into patients."

"Surgeons," Peyton repeated.

"Surgeons," McBride echoed. "Many, many surgeons."

"What about the Omegas?"

"They're securely transported and delivered, the same way—in this case, to the customers that ordered them." He paused. "We aren't responsible for what Fulfillment gives us. Our job is to get an item safely to its destination. And whether it's Omegas or pacemakers, we have a perfect record at doing so."

Peyton realized Dafna was no longer making notations. So: Delivery had a perfect record handing off Chrysalis-manufactured devices, Omega or otherwise. And he'd just finished hearing that those devices couldn't be tampered with—before, during, or after fabrication. Both out-QA and out-QC tight as a drum.

Christ, what a pain in the ass.

"Thanks, Mr. McBride," he said, rising and massaging his posterior, which had fallen asleep. "We'll contact you if we have any more questions."

And as he watched the bald man make his way to the exit, he noticed the person he'd interviewed previously—Prawn—was still loitering in the back, near the door. Why was that? Was McBride a friend? Peyton had made it clear he was dismissed. But there was no point in saying anything now, because the moment Prawn saw he'd been noticed, he slipped out the door—and in so doing let it swing back into the face of Seamus McBride, who unleashed a verbal data ledger of his own, consisting entirely of what—to Peyton—sounded like Gaelic curses.

32

"I'll stop a car . . . and I *won't use my thumb*!"

In front of Logan, two hundred–odd people broke into laughter as Claudette Colbert instructed a dubious Clark Gable in the art of hitchhiking: raising her skirt four or five inches above one very attractive knee.

Unable to sleep, Logan had paced aimlessly around his suite. From his vantage point, the view from the window revealed just a segment of the vast Torus, curving around the inner rim of the valley. As always, countless lights winked on its various levels as the third shift got up to speed. Then, something on the Western Skyway caught his eye. The lights flashing from one section of its upper level—some kind of retro ballroom, he'd assumed—tonight were all scales of gray. Then he suddenly realized what it was and, quickly dressing and grabbing his ID and Voyager, set off to get a closer look.

A section of the spoke's topmost level was given over to a cinema. Tonight, he learned, was the start of Screwball Comedy Week, kicking off with the pre-Code classic *It Happened One Night*. Logan knew the film well, and he slipped into the rear row of the theater just as Gable finished assembling the Walls of Jericho.

The theater was a real find: lavishly appointed with Art Deco decor, sporting buttery leather chairs. Looking up at the ceiling, he saw the arched roof of glass far above had been opened to the sky, and—it being a pleasant evening—night air was streaming in from the dome of stars, the scent of evergreens mixing with fresh buttered popcorn.

It was peaceful here in the dark, surrounded by so many others, enjoying the sophisticated comedy. For Logan, the surroundings had another benefit: they got him out of his inner space, helped achieve some objective distance.

Because he was faced with a monumental decision.

Quickly, he ran down a mental checklist. The software and hardware behind the Voyagers, while proprietary and cutting edge, couldn't be weaponized. As for the synaptichron itself, a device he'd felt almost certain was responsible, the scientists at BioCertain had set him straight. *What can those tiny things deliver? Micro-impulses of electrical energy. The worst you could do is up its voltage . . . which might tingle a bit, but nothing else.* Even Dr. Purchase, the closest likeness to a flesh-and-blood Walter Mitty Logan had ever met, agreed vigorously on this point.

So if the devices couldn't be made harmful from the inside, so to speak, could they be tampered with after the fact? Peyton and his minions had spent the day looking into that possibility, conducting numerous interviews and spot checks. It seemed units were constantly surveilled until they left the Complex, after which they were monitored by some tamperproof system Logan hadn't even tried to understand.

And now it was Saturday night. Tomorrow, their opponents would deliver their wire instructions for the billion dollars. And the day after that, if anything went wrong with the payment—still in the delicate process of being assembled—a thousand customers would die.

On-screen, Claudette Colbert had quickly managed to get them a ride—only to discover the driver had a loud and dreadful singing voice that he nevertheless insisted on exercising. "Aren't you afraid you'll burn out a tonsil?" the irritated Gable finally asked, to another laugh from the appreciative crowd.

The only bright spot, if it could be called that, was—as far as Logan knew—there had been no "demonstrations" that day. *Tomorrow I'll kill a civilian or two*, the last note had threatened. Janelle Deston had died on Friday afternoon—and Saturday was apparently a reprieve.

. . . Was there some reason for this? Was there some mechanism, or set of circumstances, that required this madman to move up his demonstration?

The question wasn't answerable. It was time to look at the answers they *did* have. Because his watch had ticked down to thirty-nine hours. And if nothing was done, this particular Chrysalis would soon metamorphose into something out of a nightmare.

He had assumed—everyone had assumed—the Voyager units were the instruments of death. The upgrade had been flawed or corrupted by a rogue program or the marriage with BioCertain's synaptichron. *Or* there was a killer on the inside, working in the VR department. But they had examined all these possibilities and many more . . . and come up empty.

A new thought hit him, and he sat upright in his theater seat.

It suddenly occurred to Logan that the entity behind all this might, essentially, have led them up a blind alley. *If you postpone the rollout . . . If you try to recall any Voyager devices or take them off-line . . .* Was that a giant smoke screen: a finger pointing them directly at Wrigley's own division?

Logan bolted from his seat and made for the theater lobby. A wave of laughter rolled over his shoulders, but he didn't look back. His thoughts had already leaped ahead to a new and chilling question.

If he now believed—and, as far as it was possible, he did—the Voyager units and their rollout weren't behind this threat . . .

. . . Then what the hell was?

33

Numerous other entertainments were also under way at the Complex. The eight basketball courts in the Tower recreation complex had been converted into a vast dance floor, where a swing competition was currently under way. Nautilus—the large, popular seafood restaurant whose balcony deck overlooked the northern side of the valley—was offering all-you-can-eat lobster, shelled tableside. Sprinkled elsewhere throughout the Complex were the usual smaller diversions common on Saturday night, including an informal jazz concert being held in the public plaza where the Western Skyway joined the Torus. A band was belting out "Muskrat Ramble" in true Dixieland style, always threatening, but never quite, collapsing in confusion.

Wing Kaupei stood in the center of the gathered throng, swaying gently in time with the music, when a short, somewhat overweight man approached her out of the crowd.

"Here you are," he said. "I didn't expect we'd have to meet in—"

"Don't look at me," she said. "Look at the band. And keep your voice down."

"If I do that, you won't be able to hear me."

"I can hear you fine. You've got two minutes before I wander off into the crowd. Now: What's so urgent that we had to break protocol and meet like this?"

"You wouldn't respond to my messages."

"Doing that would be a greater breach of protocol. You know the conditions: no communication once the operation begins."

"Tell that to Peyton."

Hearing this, Wing almost paused in her swaying.

"What about Peyton?"

"He grilled me today for, like, half an hour. About why I spent a day supervising the Omega line in addition to my usual job."

"So? You knew that was always a possibility."

"I think he suspects something."

Applause started up as the tune ended, and Wing joined in enthusiastically. This plaza, like all public and most private spaces in the Complex, was infested with cameras and microphones, but she knew even the best sonic algorithms could not extract meaningful conversation if it was buried amid enough overlapping chatter.

"Did he say anything specific? About the Omega units?"

"No."

"Had he detected any anomalies?"

A pause. "No."

"In other words, he was just trying to intimidate you. That's his job in a situation like this. And if you run to me like a scared rabbit, then you're doing his job for him. Just calm down. Two days, and you'll get the rest of your money."

"That's the other thing. I don't think I'm being compensated enough."

"You're being compensated exactly what was agreed on—a hundred K up front, and two upon completion."

"I know. But this isn't what I expected. This is turning out to be a lot bigger—and riskier—than you promised. I inserted the payload with hardly a moment's notice. And I'm starting to feel—"

"Listen to me. You've *already* done what you had to do. Now all you need to do is your normal job: the same thing you've done every day for the last two years. Except later this week, you'll be a whole lot richer."

"But I'll still have to come back to work. Every day."

"For six months. As agreed. When the dust settles, you can quietly take a job elsewhere."

"But—"

"There's no more to discuss. For you, the hard part's already done. Nobody's going to link you to anything—unless you keep breaking protocol like you did, calling for a crash meeting."

And with that, she moved away slowly, as if she'd never met, or conversed, with the overweight young man. She swayed with the band as they segued into "Cakewalking Babies from Home." She did not look in the man's direction, but in less than a minute she knew that he'd left the assembled throng and was gone.

". . . So what did that fat fuck Prawn want?"

The new voice in her ear was so unexpected, it was all Wing could do not to turn toward it. But long training came to her aid, and she stepped forward slightly so the gangly, bearded man speaking to her was behind her rather than beside her.

Doing so gave her a moment to think quickly.

"Standard procedure," she said after a brief interval. "I had to meet with him one last time before op completion."

"Why? I thought it was hands-off from now on."

This one, at least, knew enough not to look at her; pretend not to know her . . . even though he, too, had broken protocol—and in perhaps a worse way, by coming upon her unexpectedly. "Why are you here?"

"Because something's starting to stink about all this."

She clapped, swayed. "Spit it out."

"I was looking over the internal feeds this morning. I came across one that implied the messages you've been sending weren't what we agreed on . . . and, worse, that the board member, Bridger, didn't just 'get a little sick.' He crashed."

It took all her effort to stay relaxed. "First of all, you agreed to keep off the feeds."

"Easy for you to say. I gave you the keys to the kingdom, performed risky single-client interventions, and you've left me in the dark—"

"Don't you remember this is a lot bigger than you? Than *me*? Everything is unfolding as I promised it would."

"You never promised me anything about a message threatening to—"

"Because *it's not part of your brief.* Okay? You play your role; I play mine. Just like Prawn's played his. At the end of the day, everyone gets fat and happy."

"What about Bridger? The feed said he *died* in that plane."

"You're just parading your gullibility. Those feeds that you *aren't* supposed to look at might be bait. Don't you think they've guessed that a hacker's involved here—maybe one on the inside? Of course they'd send phony information across that internal network, looking for a reaction. That's why you're supposed to keep hands-off. Unless you want to expose us both."

"What about your message telling them—"

"I told you: we've each been given a part to play. You weren't told everything in advance, because the planners probably guessed you'd do something foolish like this if you got ahold of wrong information. We're compartmentalized for a reason. Do you think Prawn knows what you've done? What do you think he'd say if he did?"

For a moment, just music. Then the bearded young man spoke again. "That makes sense."

"I'm glad. Because rehearsal's behind us and it's showtime. And in a couple of days, that will be behind us. Now, Ben, you've got to leave."

She felt his hand brush the small of her back. "I've *got* to?" His voice turned silky. "I'm off shift. What if I come by your suite? It's been how many weeks now since—"

"Work first. Play after. Okay?"

After a moment, the answer came. "Okay."

Applause rose as the piece ended, and she used it to end the conversation. "When it's time, I'll be in touch."

And then she began to applaud with the rest of the crowd as she moved slowly toward the rear. This double meeting—one expected, the other not—had been disagreeable. However, it was over now—and for the best. Both men, she felt, could be expected to keep up their ends . . . at least until they were no longer necessary.

As it happened, all this might, in fact, have an unexpected benefit. She turned away from the crowd. To her left was New Eden; to her right, Arc C and Carewell.

And in a small breakout area between them, sitting in a lounge chair, was the man who had registered yesterday as Reginald Bryant. He was relaxing, letting the music float over him. She did not stop as she walked past, but their eyes met briefly and she lazily tapped her chin: once, twice.

He blinked slowly in return, like a lizard.

He'd seen both men. That was good: it would make things easier later on.

And as Wing walked on, past Carewell and toward BioCertain security, she decided the interlude had been valuable, after all.

34

Logan stared out of his office window. Soon, he'd probably start counting trees . . . and from there it was only a matter of time until straitjackets and Thorazine.

At precisely eight thirty that morning, Claire Asperton had received another message. It was longer than the others by a factor of ten, and technical in nature. It laid out the payment method: one billion dollars paid in five different cryptocurrencies, to be dispersed into a total of twenty digital wallets. The QR codes for the e-wallets would be sent to Asperton's public-facing Chrysalis email as confirmation at 8:00 EST Monday morning. Chrysalis would have eight minutes to convert a billion dollars into the cryptocurrencies and transmit the assets.

Logan hadn't bothered parsing the long list of financial codes and routing numbers in the message, but the final sentence remained with him:

> *This will be the last communication*
> *Until our final acknowledgment*
> *That the transaction is complete*
> *And the infection of your system has been cleansed.*

Peyton's team of crypto-detectives hadn't had any more luck tracking this message than the earlier ones. And their opponents offered no guarantees. Logan knew from experience this was common enough in such negotiations: it was the chance they'd have to take. But he was struck by the choice of words: *the infection of your system has been cleansed.*

He abruptly swiveled away from the window.

The night before, he'd decided that spending more time investigating Voyager and the Omega project was a luxury he couldn't afford. He'd taken the phase two demo himself without ill effect. Besides, whatever was killing people clearly had nothing to do with that demonstration: Janelle Deston was living proof of that.

"Living proof" was a poor choice of words.

He sighed and asked himself the same question he had the night before: If it wasn't the Voyager devices . . . what else did that leave?

There was a tone in his ear. "Jeremy," came the silken voice.

"Yes, Grace."

"Summary two of your request is now available."

Logan sighed as his own words to Asperton came back to him, like a curse: *Get a whole server farm chugging away on what else those three had in common.* The lawyer had followed through, requisitioning every tiny commonality between Spearman, Bridger, Marceline Williams. Some of the data dealt with travel times, locations, or appointments that embodied the faintest correlation. Other information was far more granular—television shows, documentaries, movies, operas, plays, books, and concerts the three board members had individually taken in over the last two years. Clothing brands, food choices, luxury items ordered . . . the list was exhaustive and Logan didn't want to know how Chrysalis obtained such information.

"Switch to summary display, please, Grace."

A moment later, a virtual printout—letters forming words in

the air, semi-transparent, scrolling upward as if spooling out of a printer—appeared before his eyes.

```
Request B-523zz
Initiator: Asperton, C.
Recipient: Logan, J.
Status: in progress (2 / 5)
Priority: Alpha-1
Clearance: CIS-8
Scrape level: full
Distribution: wide
HEADER FOLLOWS
```

"Grace," Logan said, "slower, please."

"Certainly. Scroll rate reduced to .75."

Logan blinked. Reading holographic documents, especially complex ones, was something he had yet to grow comfortable with.

```
chrysql> create database dump2;
chrysql> use dump2;
chrysql> create table hash_sort (
    -> incept_date int primary key,
    -> recsize int,
    -> recdata varchar (80),
    -> is_two logical,
    -> is_three logical,
    -> );
SUMMARY DATA SEQUENCE FOLLOWS
chrysql> select * from dump2;
    -> for .not. limit;
```

"Grace!" Logan said again.

"Yes, Jeremy?"

"Please route the output to my screen."

"As you wish." The rows of phantom information disappeared; his screen winked into life; and the display picked up where it had left off.

Logan put his elbows on the desk and began to examine the data that crawled up the screen. Now and then he told Grace to flag a particular line or two, but mostly he just watched.

Suddenly, he stopped.

"Grace," he said yet again. "Halt output."

He stared a moment. "Go forward one screen."

He continued staring. *Wait a minute.* . . . "Upload those last fifty lines to memory, and commit."

"Very well, Jeremy."

"And alert Dr. Purchase in BioCertain—right away. Tell him I'll be waiting where we were first introduced." He stood up, cleared the screen. "And forward him a listing of those same fifty lines, please. That should save time in explanations."

"My pleasure, Jeremy."

"Grace, you're a peach." Logan stood to leave.

"No, Jeremy, I am a virtual assistant."

35

Logan sat in the small conference room where he'd met Dr. Purchase three days before. The man's piercing blue eyes looked anxious, and now and then he tugged on a lock of his carrot-colored hair. He had brought Logan's printout with him and placed it on the conference table before he took a seat. Now and then he instinctively began to reach for it, then drew his hand back sharply, like a child toying with a garter snake.

Logan waited until Claire Asperton joined them. Then he went around the conference room, closing the automated louvers over the glass walls. He met the lawyer's glance and raised his eyebrows. She silently nodded a go-ahead.

He cleared his throat. "Dr. Purchase, this is what we're going to do: I'm going to speak briefly; then you will answer. And once you're done, all the uncertainty Ms. Asperton and I currently feel will be resolved. Agreed?"

Purchase swallowed, nodded.

"You've been very forthcoming about certain things, such as Piers Bridger and his interest in the prototype of your new diagnostic device." He leaned forward. "I understand you didn't know exactly why I was asking so many questions at the time. But surely you understand I would have had great interest in *this*." He pointed at the sheets in front of Purchase. "So please explain why you neglected to mention your *fourteen* phone calls—the shortest five minutes, the longest twenty-five—with Russell Spearman over the last eighteen months."

"The dead board member," Asperton said, taking the ball.

As Purchase opened his mouth, Logan interrupted. "We're in a hurry, so no need for rationalizations or handwringing. Just tell us completely and succinctly what those fourteen conversations were about."

Purchase paused, took a handkerchief from his pocket, mopped his brow, tucked it away. "Spearman had an implant," he said.

"To control his cyclothemia?" Logan asked.

Purchase looked surprised, but nodded. "Normally, mood shifts associated with that condition aren't extreme enough to require mitigation. But in his manic states, he was closer to bipolar one disorder. Of course, that wasn't my diagnosis to make."

"Of course," said Asperton.

"It was his doctor's," Purchase added quickly.

"And who was that?" Logan asked.

Purchase drew in a breath. "A clinician at Columbia's Vagelos College of Physicians. I'll get his name for you."

Logan nodded.

"He'd tried lithium, but didn't tolerate it well. The specialist at Columbia suggested Carewell's own new formulation, Thanturil. We'd locked the clinical database on the drug, gotten sign-offs from the PIs, months before. It had just come out of trials, and—since it combines a mood stabilizer with an anxiolytic—seemed a perfect fit."

"Why the implant?" Asperton asked.

"Two reasons, really. Mr. Spearman was almost pathologically forgetful. He had encountered problems repeatedly by forgetting to take his medication, so a small implant in his shoulder, preprogrammed, made that moot. And second . . . well, I guess you'd call it vanity."

"Vanity?" Logan echoed.

"It's not as surprising as you might think. As more true implants have become available—intrathecal spinal pumps, ICDs, so on—wealthy people have begun to see bespoke implants, tailored to their conditions, as a status symbol. Not unlike cosmetic surgery."

Someone had mentioned this peculiar vanity to Logan before. "What do you mean, 'true implants'?"

"Just that. Not 'depot' injections that only last until their polymer coatings wear off—but 'smart' implants that can be replaced, updated. That can transmit information to a hospital or a doctor. That can send a warning in case of an emergency. Whose dosage schedule can be adjusted remotely. Whose firmware can be updated from home clinics almost anywhere in the world."

Despite the relative gravity of his recent offense—lying to superiors in order to appease a member of the board—Purchase couldn't keep a note of pride out of his voice.

"Firmware," Logan repeated. "In pacemakers, too?"

"Of course."

"And if there's a bug in the update? If somebody starts stroking out because their pacemaker turns flaky, there's not exactly a lot of time to program a patch."

"There are procedures in place for any exigency."

Claire Asperton shook these speculations away—perhaps because they struck close to home. "We're getting off track. Besides, our facility here isn't in the business of implanting devices, made-to-measure or otherwise."

"Normally, that's true," Purchase replied in a quiet voice.

Both looked at him.

"Spearman put a lot of pressure on me. So did his doctor."

"When was the device implanted?" Asperton asked.

Purchase thought. "Twelve—no, thirteen months ago."

"Done where?"

"Here," Purchase said, even more quietly.

"What?! *Secretly?*" Asperton was suddenly more agitated than Logan had ever seen her.

"He said he'd have me fired. Me and the BioCertain surgeon both. Said he'd go to Christie directly." Purchase paused. "He made a lot of threats."

For a moment, the conference room was silent.

"I guess that explains the dopamine levels in Spearman's blood," Logan murmured.

"What was the procedure?" Asperton snapped at Purchase.

"He wanted a PCA pump to control the dosage himself. Both his doctor and I disagreed, but I gave his physician discretion over the release schedule. That was the one condition under which we'd do the implant."

"But you didn't see him during the board meeting two weeks ago?" Asperton asked.

Purchase shook his head.

"When did you last see him?" asked Logan.

"About four months ago."

"Here?"

"Yes."

"Why?"

"That's the way Spearman was. He always demanded the latest and greatest."

Asperton cursed under his breath.

"So how many implants did you arrange for him, in total?" asked Logan.

"Just two. We were finishing trials on a new module in June—"

"That can wait. For now." Asperton put an ominous spin on the last two words. "What about the medication itself? How was the implant refreshed?"

"His doctor at Columbia did that. We sent him the medication directly. Thanturil's been available in solution since they first approached me."

"Let me make sure I understand," Logan said. "His doctor has been refreshing his implant's medication—upgrading the device along the way—for over a year?"

Purchase nodded.

"And the doctor himself is the only one in charge of dosage control? Not Spearman himself?"

"Besides us, technically—yes."

"Do you usually send out refill medications for implants to individual doctors?"

"No. But in addition to everything else, Spearman was a hypochondriac. I had to personally watch each time his recharge dose was drawn. Then it was identified with a UV stamp and shipped directly to his doctor, rather than the normal bulk route to a hospital or medical supply house."

"When was the last time you sent this doctor a fresh supply of Thanturil?" Logan interrupted.

"Around three months ago. The same time I sent him half a dozen trial implants."

"Trial implants?" Asperton echoed.

Purchase nodded. "That's what I'm trying to tell you. The new implant, the one Spearman wore when he was here for the board meeting, now has FDA approval for use with nearly a *dozen* medications . . . in addition to Thanturil."

This was greeted by silence.

"In a way, I'm glad Spearman didn't stop by after the board meeting," Purchase said into the quiet of the office. "I'd hate to have told him his special implant was now available to anyone."

Logan abruptly stood up. Asperton did the same.

"Be sure to get the name of Spearman's doctor to me," Logan told Purchase.

"Of course, of course. Right away. Anything else?" He cocked his head like a scolded dog, anxious to please.

"No. Actually, yes. I want you to assemble all the synthesis data on new drugs for the last eighteen months. Be especially thorough with Thanturil. And please: note anything out of the ordinary. *Anything.*"

Purchase nodded.

36

Back in the noisy concourse, with the cool humid breeze wafting over them, Logan stepped onto the travelator.

"What's going to happen to him?" he asked Asperton.

"He, and that unnamed surgeon, broke just about every rule we've got. Performing procedures on-site. Offering prototype medical devices to clients rather than test groups. And, of course, deliberately concealing all this from us." Asperton sighed. "Think he held anything back?"

"I have a feeling we got everything."

"So do I." They stepped off the travelator and made their way through the plaza leading to the Northern Spoke. "So both Spearman and Bridger had medical implants."

"But completely different types."

"And the number of types BioCertain has developed would fill a catalog. But Marceline had none—we know that for sure, because her body was autopsied." A brief silence. "Do you think Spearman might have found a way to mess with his? Dose himself without an inhibitor? It seems like it might fit his character profile."

Logan considered this. "It would have shown up on the device's output. Remember, those things now send and receive messages. Besides, if it was as simple as a mere overdose, Spearman could obviously have gotten his hands on more Thanturil—in pill form, if not suspension."

Asperton nodded, then lowered her voice. "So where does that leave us?"

Where, indeed? Logan thought a moment before answering.

When he learned Spearman had been conversing regularly with Purchase, he felt sure he'd made an important connection. But connection to what? They'd tried feverishly for days to figure out how Omega devices could be hacked or converted into killing machines . . . without success. Now, here was a Chrysalis subsidiary that did manufacture devices that *could,* if abused or malfunctioning, potentially kill. But countless different types were available, many in successful operation for years, and the supply chains that delivered them—at least, those built by BioCertain— were bulletproof.

"I don't know about you," he said after a moment. "But I'm going to have a nice, long chat with a certain psychiatrist at the Vagelos College of Physicians."

As he spoke, Logan saw Asperton touch the Sentinel unit cradled over her right ear. "Yes?" she said. And then: "Yes."

She looked around, quickly taking in the surrounding plaza. "Give me two minutes."

Then she ended the conversation and grabbed Logan by the elbow. "Come on."

37

"Where are we going?" Logan said as he followed Asperton—who was now, for the first time since Logan had met her, running—back across the sky lobby, past an inviting-looking pub called the Crosskeys, toward the wall of smoked glass sealing off Arc A and Agrinox. Logan could see its security station ahead, the green-and-gold logo shining in welcome. But before they reached it, Asperton stopped at what appeared to be a structural joint, glanced around, then touched her Sentinel unit again while pressing the glass-and-steel wall. A coffin-size rectangle of wall sprang inward slightly with a *pop* of air pressure. Beyond was darkness. Asperton pushed the hidden door wider and stepped in, followed quickly by Logan. She pushed the rectangle of glass door shut again, and the darkness became complete.

"I give up," Logan said. "What's going on? A game of sardines?"

Asperton snapped on a light switch, revealing a closet-size room with a narrow, U-shaped staircase leading upward. Logan followed her up the steps into a small eyrie overlooking the main concourse, equipped with a desk, chair, small leather couch, and a CPU.

Asperton took the chair, and Logan the couch. His left shoulder was pressed against the glass wall, and he looked straight down at the groups of people walking past. If anyone had seen them just duck through what looked like a featureless wall, they didn't seem surprised.

Asperton had pulled the CPU's keyboard over and was giving commands to her Sentinel unit at the same time.

"Is this an executive love nest?" Logan asked. "You should have put in a larger sofa."

"Sometimes we 'executives' need to speak in a hurry," Asperton said. "In private."

"We're in such a hurry we couldn't go back to your forward office?"

"The person who called me is on a tight schedule."

As Logan wondered how many other micro-offices, surveillance crannies, or sniper nests might be concealed in the vast bulk of the Torus, a microphone came to life with a squeal of static. "Two minutes are up," a voice said.

"We're ready," Asperton replied.

There was a brief pause. "King to protect rook, Kf2."

"I only play backgammon," Asperton said. "With a doubling cube."

There was another pause, even briefer. "Okay, Claire," the male voice said, apparently satisfied. "Who's 'we'?"

"Jeremy Logan is with me."

"His clearance?"

"TS/SCI."

"Logan. Hmmm." A tapping of keys sounded over the speaker. "*That* Jeremy Logan?"

"Yes."

A chuckle. "Well, it's your party. Seems he's got the clearance, all right. While we're together like this, mind asking him if he could exorcise my mother-in-law?"

"You're the one on a clock, Gerald," said Asperton.

"So I am, so I am. All right: What was the subject's name again?"

"Marceline Williams."

"Right. Here she is. And you have two private labs running full-spectrum assays on her, you said?"

"As of this morning, they still couldn't give me a precise date when they'd be finished."

"Well, just let the results stroll in on their own. They'll come in clean. But they'll be wrong. Because she was poisoned."

Asperton and Logan exchanged glances.

"Those labs won't find it. We almost missed it ourselves—except we're already on needles-up status for certain synthetic markers. Our friends in Lubyanka Square have been so busy recently—Novichok, polonium-210—they're keeping us on our toes. Anyway, this agent used on Ms. Williams was just unusual enough to raise a red flag." A tapping of keys. "How old was she?"

"Forty-nine, I think."

"Did she have gout?"

"Not that I know of."

"Early-onset arthritis? Still's disease?"

"I don't know anything about 'Still,' let alone his disease."

"Philistine." The person called Gerald sighed audibly. "Any joint problems of any kind?"

"No," Asperton answered. "Wait! She suffered occasionally from bursitis. It had something to do with her insistence on over-exercising with a damned rowing machine."

"There you go. The pathologist would have had her medical history, so a trace presence of C. autumnale wouldn't be surprising."

When Asperton didn't answer, the voice from the speaker continued. "Too bad I don't have time to give you and your ghost-hunting friend a botany lesson. The plant known as the autumn crocus is particularly fascinating. It's not a member of the crocus family, but a species of lily. Two things about it are relevant from a pharmacological standpoint. It's rather poisonous. And it's that rare 'natural' herb approved for medical dispensation by the FDA."

"I thought you just said it was poisonous," Logan interjected.

"Is that you, Dr. Logan? I did say that. Colchicine, the alkaloid extracted from said crocus, has a very narrow 'therapeutic index'—the dosage within which it's safe, rather than toxic. Yet for some conditions—gout, certain joint afflictions—it's almost a miracle drug. It's been used as a remedy as far back as the sixteenth century, at least."

"Are you saying she was poisoned by a prescription drug?" Asperton asked. "That would have been flagged right away."

"It's not quite as simple as that. The colchicine was bound to something else. It's only because we were *already* on high alert that we saw this. Some bad, bad person bound a small amount of colchicine to an even smaller amount of carfentanyl. Was she wearing glasses when she died?"

This perverse question, coming out of left field, took them both by surprise. Asperton thought a moment. "The security tapes at her hotel caught her putting on sunglasses as she left."

"*Ecce signum!* That's where the lethal agent was planted. It would have moved from her glasses, to her eyelashes, to her eyes. Colchicine is absorbed particularly quickly through the sclera. It's rather elegant: fentanyl is fifty times more powerful than morphine, and the synthetic descendant carfentanyl is ten *thousand* times more powerful. The stages of clinical toxicity would have gone by almost too quickly to notice; she would have been dead within minutes of putting on her sunglasses."

"If the bus hadn't gotten her first," Asperton said grimly.

"Well, even bad guys deserve a break now and then, don't they? You must have taken the seizure of someone lethally poisoned as just a badly timed footstep. Or a push." A chuckle. "As for the pathologist, the carfentanyl dose was so minute, and its synthesis so complete, all he or she would have noticed was a small amount of colchicine in the blood—which Williams's history of bursitis would have explained away quite naturally."

During this explanation, the voice of Gerald had taken on an increasingly satisfied air. "So there you have it, Claire. Naturally, I can't put any of this in writing, and you wouldn't be foolish enough to record our conversation. But Marceline Williams *was* poisoned—and, given the nature of the poison, by somebody who knew what they were doing." A pause. "And that brings me to our final topic of discussion."

"Yes?" Asperton asked.

"We've given you the answer. Without it, you'd have remained as you are, stumbling about in the dark. It's only fair to give us the compound."

"Give it to you?" Asperton asked in confusion. "But you already have the blood sample."

"That's not what I mean. *Give* it to us. Forget these bothersome details. She was poisoned: that's all you'll say, and that's all you'll remember. Same goes for you, Dr. Logan—if you want to keep clear of Leavenworth, that is."

Asperton shook her head. "I feel like I ought to go to confession."

"Except you're not Catholic. At least, not according to your dossier. Now, much as I'd like to continue chatting, I have to go. Enjoy the rest of your day. And Dr. Logan, please reconsider the request about my mother-in-law. I'll make it worth your while."

Quite abruptly, the voice was gone.

A few moments passed as Logan stared at Asperton, then finally broke the silence. "Claire, I'm both enlightened . . . and bewildered. Who the hell were we just speaking to?"

"My friend Gerald works in the CIA's Directorate of Science. He's always rushed—but he still enjoys listening to his own voice."

"He gave us a crucial piece of information."

Asperton nodded. "Marceline's death was clearly intended to make us suspect Omega, so we'd keep barking up the wrong tree."

"And in exchange for that information, you just gave him the delivery vehicle for a brand-new, effectively untraceable poison. . . ."

"You were the one riding me about those blood assays. When it was clear those labs wouldn't get us results in time, I went to the one entity that could."

"They're a client of yours too, I suppose?"

An odd look came over her face for a moment. "That's not important. Just let me remind you *they* discovered the poison. I 'gave' Gerald nothing." She paused. "I don't mean to sound defensive. I just never get used to dealing with the devil. So: Still want to call that physician at Columbia?"

From his seat on the couch, Logan looked down onto the bustling concourse—and the nearby pub—for a moment. "I suppose. But I'd like some single-malt scotch, served neat, a whole lot more."

38

At noon, Asperton convened a war-room meeting. Rather than her own private eyrie in the Chrysalis Tower, she chose Peyton's subterranean office beneath the Torus, from which Logan had watched Karel Mossby being apprehended.

Peyton and Asperton were at the conference table, along with Kramer and a man Logan hadn't seen before: short, very thin, with smooth features and tightly curled black hair, cut in an almost military fade. The privacy shades were up, and Logan noticed the worker drones in the huge room beyond were even busier than when he'd first seen them.

"We have twenty-four hours left," Asperton told the assembled group. "Most of the funds should be in our hands this evening, once the Asian markets open. The rest—God willing—we'll have by ten a.m. Monday, at the latest." She glanced at Peyton. "You'll be ready? On the crypto side of things?"

Peyton nodded.

"Shouldn't Wrigley be here?" Logan asked.

"He refused to come. Said there wasn't any point anymore; nabbing Mossby was foolish; that his time would be better spent cleaning up the mess 'the security goons' had made of his department."

Guess he's finally been shaken back to reality, Logan thought to himself. Learning that Omega, and VR, might be off the table as suspects had probably helped. But why would he dismiss Mossby's apprehension? He'd fired Mossby, after all—and the guy had spent a lot of time afterward trying to break back into Omega.

"Wrigley," Peyton muttered. "What a fucking prima donna."

Asperton glanced from him to the stranger sitting at the far side of the table. "So, Virgil Snow. Did this morning's communiqué yield any new information?"

The man, wearing a suit so somber it would make the secret service envious, shook his head. "Same delivery mechanism as the other four. Spoofed internal VPN, run through an anonymizer. Impossible to trace."

Instead of trying to understand, Logan instead watched the speaker. Virgil Snow—at least twice, Peyton had spoken via his Omega to someone he'd addressed as Snow. Logan guessed this was the person in charge of the cyber strike force.

Kramer, head of Security, turned toward Snow. "What about that sieve sort Logan here asked for? Any bad apples other than Mossby turn up?"

"We identified six employees even remotely capable of doing— or *wanting* to do—something like this," Snow replied. He had a strange accent: Flatbush or elsewhere in Brooklyn, filtered through Beacon Hill. "But they were already on our radar. We ran additional back-tracing on every last one." He shook his head. "Nothing."

There was a brief pause around the table.

"So here's where we stand," Claire said, straightening her shoulders. "We know Spearman secretly had one of our implants installed. Bridger had one, too . . . completely different, of course. And Marceline was killed by an exotic, nation-state-grade poison."

Peyton turned to Logan. "How does that mesh with your 'commonalities'?" he asked with a tinge of sarcasm.

"Actually, it's the first real connection we've made."

"What connection?"

"All along, these aggressors have been encouraging us to look in the wrong place: the tech behind Voyager. The board members who died all took the VR tour. We were told not to hamper tomorrow's rollout in any way. We've been pushed again and again in the wrong direction. But the fact is, Voyager devices have no way of harming people. The new version that drops tomorrow isn't dangerous."

"You're sure of that?" Peyton asked.

"Yes."

"Then what the hell's going on?" asked Kramer. "You take away that, and you leave us with nothing."

"Not necessarily," Logan said. "If they've been leading us on a false trail, they clearly wanted to mask the true one. Look at Marceline Williams. She was poisoned by something so unusual, it even aroused the CIA's curiosity. There's no way in hell our antagonists would have done that *unless they had to hide the fact she died by poison.*" He looked at each face at the table. "So the question is, are we sure—really sure—what killed Spearman and Bridger? And what about Janelle Deston?"

And then, something occurred to him.

He turned to Asperton. "You know our overly modest friend in BioCertain?"

"Purchase? Modestly doing a little moonlighting with Spearman and his prerelease implant?"

"He's Omega-cleared, right? I mean, he's the one who explained to me how the synaptichron was originally a BioCertain product."

Asperton nodded. "As much as any of the line leaders are."

"And he knows the details of our, ah, little problem." Logan turned away from the table and—after thirty seconds of fumbling with Grace—managed to use the device to contact Purchase.

"Dr. Logan?" came the voice, sounding both anxious and excited. "I've been working nonstop on that synthesis you asked for, cross-checking all new Carewell drugs for overlooked contraindications, and—"

"Dr. Purchase?" Logan interrupted.

The voice stopped midstream. "Yes?"

"I'm very glad to hear that. But I'm afraid I have another request. One with priority."

"Yes?"

"I'd like you to discreetly put together two client lists: those receiving the new Voyager devices, and those with medical implants. Then do a comparison for matches."

"You mean, like 'doubles'? Early adopters of the Omega Two rollout, but who also have—"

"Pacemakers. Insulin infusers. Active, passive. IVRs, 'matchsticks,' *anything*."

"Somebody's been doing his research," Kramer whispered, listening in.

"Okay . . ." Purchase sounded dubious.

"Is that a problem? Too complex, maybe?"

"No, not at all. I have the security level to access databases from both BioCertain and Carewell; it shouldn't take more than thirty minutes. It's just that—"

"Good. Please contact me as soon as you have the results."

Asperton was staring at him. "What possible connection could there be between Omega's virtual reality and people with diabetes or osteoporosis?"

"We'll find out." Logan had asked himself the same question the night before, as he sat in the dark watching Gable and Colbert.

"We're market leaders in both fields, Jeremy. He'll probably find thousands upon thousands of matches. Wouldn't it make more sense to get in touch with Spearman's doctor, as discussed?"

"I left a message with his answering service."

"Well, I hope you left it smoking, because if we're going back to square one, we—" Abruptly, Asperton went silent. In the instinctual way Logan had noticed before at the Complex, the lawyer lifted her hand toward her Sentinel unit: not to hear better, of course—but because what she was hearing was clearly important.

39

Asperton dropped her hand and looked around the table. "Another message is coming in."

"Now?" Kramer asked as everyone exchanged glances.

Asperton nodded. "In real time."

"Shit!" In unison, Peyton and his cyber-warrior, Snow, rose from their seats and ran to separate workstations. As Logan watched, he saw Peyton routing the incoming message to a screen so they could all read it. Snow was up to something else—and whatever it was, he was typing furiously and it occupied his entire attention.

A screen came to life with the kind of white-on-black message Logan was all too familiar with. There was one difference: it was still scrolling up the screen, like the opening credits of a movie—clearly, still being transmitted. But what remained did not take long to come into view.

You will receive a way
To neutralize the threat
By using it's private key
Monday pm
When you do
Remember you got this msg
From a friend

For a moment, silence. Then, suddenly, everyone was speaking at once.

"What the hell?" Kramer thundered.

"Full capture!" cried Peyton in a tone close to exultation.

"This wasn't an authorized communication," Asperton said almost to herself as she stood up.

Wasn't authorized, Logan thought. Only a lawyer would think of it that way. But she was right: earlier that same morning, they'd been clearly told that there would be no further communication until after payment had been transacted.

That was not the only unusual thing about this message. It was written in the first person. It had no punctuation, except for the mistaken apostrophe in a possessive pronoun. The tone was different, too: it had less authority. If Logan understood it correctly, it was offering a way to defuse whatever "bomb" had been placed—an offer conspicuously absent from all previous missives. It sounded almost as if the sender was . . .

He was jolted from these speculations by the sound of an argument nearby. The man named Snow was still at the workstation where he'd taken up position, and now Asperton and Peyton stood on both sides of him, practically yelling at each other.

"There's a precedent!" Peyton was saying. "A precedent that can't be broken—under any conditions. We all agreed!"

"This supersedes any agreement!" Asperton *was* actually yelling. "The conglomerate's at stake. *Lives* are at stake!"

"We don't have a lot of time here, people!" said Snow, as loudly as either of them. His fingers were on the workstation keys. "For some reason, they were a little sloppy this one time. Our sniffer caught a couple of stray packets. If we freeze the feed—the whole damn feed—there's a chance we can grab this thread, see where it leads. But if we don't do it now, *right* now, the cache is going to flush."

"But that could crash the entire architecture!" Peyton said. "It's never been tried. You'd be yanking a hatch off a jet in midflight. And besides—*he's* here."

Peyton turned toward Logan. And as he did, Logan realized what they were talking about. It was the only thing they *could* be talking about: the unknown entity whose mere name—the time he'd heard it, and then later when he'd mentioned it—seemed to carry the force of a tactical nuke.

"You're talking about the Helix," Logan said.

Peyton's face, already red, flushed deeper. And in the momentary silence, Asperton seized her opportunity.

"Freeze it," she ordered Snow. "Freeze it *right the fuck now.*"

40

At the same moment Logan uttered the unutterable, Ben Cardiff—principal software engineer level II, BioCertain Research—was approximately a quarter mile south and four hundred feet above, standing at the railing of one of the large parapets that sprouted like mushrooms from the bulk of the Chrysalis Tower. An al fresco lunch was currently being served, and he'd left the table he'd been sitting at with friends and walked over to the railing, Bloody Mary in hand, to take in the view. Working in Arc B of the Torus all day, and most evenings, he didn't often get a chance to admire the surroundings while the sun was at its zenith. It was a sight that never grew old. He took a sip of his drink, relishing how the sharpness of the vodka offset the Worcestershire and Tabasco, harmonizing perfectly with the sour tang of tomato.

Located on the thirty-second floor, this cafeteria was as high as he'd ever been in the Chrysalis Tower, and as high as he was ever likely to get. While he drank in the sensation he felt a rustle at his side, and then Wing Kaupei was standing beside him. She placed her slender fingers on the railing as she looked over the expansive vista.

Cardiff noticed her knuckles were turning slightly white. "Don't like heights?"

"It isn't the height so much as the openness. I suppose there's a clinical term for the condition."

"You should learn to enjoy it. Best view I'll ever get for free."

"And you should learn to do as you're told."

"Care to elaborate?" Cardiff drained what was his second Bloody Mary. He knew his tongue was a bit looser than was wise, but he didn't care. It felt good to unwind the mainspring in his chest a little.

"You know what I mean. You just took it upon yourself to send a transmission. That's my job."

"I know, I know: you're surprised. But remember—it's a job I made possible, and then taught you how to do."

Wing ignored this. "Worse, you didn't even run the contents past me, or our superiors. How do you think they'll take that?"

"If they're smart, they'll take it as a statement of independence. You keep saying we all have our own parts to play in this; that we're all happy, equal little cogs. But that's not really true, is it? I mean, you dictate what gets transmitted and what doesn't."

"I'm just the conduit."

"Whatever. But the fact is, you'd never have been able to do any of this without me. This whole mission, or whatever you want to call it, couldn't have happened."

"You overestimate your importance."

"Now you sound like an apparatchik. Who else could have arranged untraceable communication with someone like Asperton, *and* engineered the Line, *and* taken care of the video array so Prawn could do his thing?" He tried to take another slug of his drink, realized it was nothing but ice, and put it down again.

"None of that justifies stepping outside your prescribed role. Everything we're doing is scripted. There's a good reason for that: it keeps us all safe. And in case you've forgotten, at the end of the day it puts a million dollars in your bank account."

Cardiff swirled the ice in his glass ruminatively. "You know, you really should have come up to my room last night."

"Is that what this is—payback? Sour grapes?"

"No. I'm not that petty. But, see, it left me with time on my hands. Time to look at a few more of those feeds you told me to stay away from."

Wing frowned and looked away, muttering something in an unfamiliar language.

"You've been keeping secrets from me. It seems people *have* been hurt—and a lot more seriously than you let on. You said I'd targeted those three as some kind of proof of concept for our superiors: but it was a lot more. For me, that changes the playing field. And I asked myself: If you could talk so dismissively to me about Prawn, that fat little worker bee—who knows what you think or say about me? Could it even be that thing we had, all those months together, was just an act?"

Now Wing looked back at him. "You're being a fool."

"No. No, I'm not. I told you: I was just thinking independently. But I also know there's a line I shouldn't cross. I wouldn't want these 'superiors'—as you call them—to get upset, maybe garnish some of my million bucks. So, yes: I sent a message of my own. But all it did was assure our superiors *here* at Chrysalis that we're going to play by the rules. That they'll get what they're paying for: and we'll turn it all off. This way, they won't get so worked up that they do something rash—something that, say, might get one of us in trouble down the line."

Wing said nothing.

Cardiff glanced at her, raising his eyebrows. Then he chuckled. "But you know what? I don't think anyone's going to be upset by my tiny act of insubordination. Everything's still going exactly as planned. And, Wing, I shouldn't need to remind you: unlike Prawn, I still have a critical role to play. I'm the only one who can activate the kill switch."

When Wing remained silent, Cardiff pushed himself away from the railing. "Have one of these," he said, shaking his empty glass. "It'll cheer you up. Twenty-four hours from now, it will be mission accomplished. But today being a Sunday, I'm probably going to stay in this evening. Just thought I'd let you know, should you change your mind—for old times' sake." And with that, he turned and walked across the expanse of balcony, passed through the archway into the cafeteria proper, and was lost from view.

Wing watched him go. Most of what he'd said was vainglorious nonsense, typical of a certain type of man who rises only so far yet remains convinced he deserves more than his true worth. But he was right about one thing: his bit of "independence," as he'd called it, had come as a surprise to her. Now at last she smiled, secure in the knowledge she wasn't the only one who'd find this to be a day for surprises. Benjamin R. Cardiff, for example, had no idea how little a million dollars meant to those behind this operation.

And he certainly had no idea she cared even less about his "kill switch"—or, for that matter, about turning anything off.

41

Logan occupied himself by counting the seconds of frantic activity. He'd just reached 190 when Snow popped his head up from the workstation.

"Prep's done," he said. "At least, everything I can do from here. If we're going to minimize possible damage, we have to do the rest from I/O control."

"You mean . . . *touch* it?" Asperton asked, as if they were discussing El Greco's *Laocoön*.

"Hell yes, touch it. We don't have much time. As it is, we're weighing our chance at catching this bitch against the harm a cold interrupt might do the Helix."

"What about Omega?" The decisiveness she'd shown moments before seemed now to be mingled with lawyerly reservations.

"It's indirectly integrated—I can put a moat around the virtual environment. Beyond that, though, no guarantees."

Asperton hesitated, in an agony of indecision.

"What's it going to be?" Peyton asked angrily. "I'm not making this call."

"Go," Asperton said.

Almost before the word was spoken, Snow was out of his chair and headed for the door. Peyton told Kramer to stay and monitor developments, then followed, Asperton and Logan on his heels.

The four trotted along the corridor, then Snow stopped to unlock and open yet another unmarked door. Following the others, Logan ducked into a utilitarian concrete stairwell, painted battleship gray, which they began descending quickly. The thrum of machinery grew briefly louder, then faded as they continued, floor after floor. Then, from the far side of the cement wall, Logan heard the distinct grinding of a diesel engine. He glanced at Asperton, rounding the stairwell landing below him.

"Delivery trucks," she said, noticing the glance. "Heading up from the Fabrication loading docks to the exit portal."

They kept descending until the stairwell ended at a door marked NO ENTRY UNDER ANY CONDITIONS. Peyton used a palm-print analyzer and the door opened into a narrow corridor with security cameras and—to Logan's surprise—two guards armed with automatic weapons manning a hatch at the far end.

"Sir?" one of the guards said, looking from Peyton to Asperton and back again.

"Open it," said Peyton.

Now both guards looked at Asperton, who nodded.

The guards took up position flanking the hatch and fished out digital keys, hanging from lanyards around their necks. They simultaneously inserted and turned the keys in identical mechanisms.

"It's like Fort Knox," Logan said.

"You're closer than you realize," Claire Asperton replied.

Beyond lay a wide corridor, dimly lit and cold enough for Logan to see his breath. From its lazy arc, he guessed this corridor matched, more or less, the circumference of the Torus, its base now perhaps a dozen floors above them. On the closer wall there were stenciled numbers and small control panels. Parked against it in a neat line were half a dozen sleek electric warehouse vehicles, like futuristic golf carts.

The far wall drew Logan's eye and made him do a double take. It consisted of black metal racks framing identical CPUs mounted vertically, each arrayed in columns half a dozen rows high. The series of racks followed one after another along the curve of the corridor until they disappeared around the curve and out of Logan's vision. Each blade server was winking with a variety of green and red lights; so many, he realized, they rendered additional illumination unnecessary. Thin strands of fiber-optic webbing were everywhere: similar to what he'd seen within the synaptichron, but in logarithmically greater abundance. A scattering of people in black jumpsuits, digital tools snugged into utility belts, were moving around the racks like worker bees. One after another, they stopped and looked at the new arrivals in surprise.

"How did they get down here?" Logan asked nobody in particular. "Surely not the same way we did."

"No," Asperton said. "A much slower route. They live as well as work here, rotating on and off at monthly intervals."

The dazzling array of computing horsepower had occupied Logan's full attention. Now he turned to look the other way, where the broad corridor ended in a confused tangle of equipment surrounding another hatch, marked simply i/o, manned by another pair of armed guards. Snow and Peyton were just now stepping through it.

As it closed with an echoing slam, Logan looked back toward Asperton. "Maybe now would be a good time to tell me what all this is."

Asperton looked at her watch. "Why not?" she said.

She appeared to have made peace with the mysterious decision she'd made in Peyton's office. She crossed her arms and leaned against the near wall as the workers returned to their duties. "I suppose you've heard of blockchains?"

"The things used to keep track of digital currency?"

"That's what they're commonly known for, yes. And, actually, a chain of blocks is a pretty good metaphor. In banking, every transaction involving cryptocurrency—purchases, sales, transfers—is stored in a block. When that block is packed full of data, a new block is created and linked—'chained'—to the previous block by a unique algorithm, derived *from that first block's contents.* More transactions start pouring into the new, empty block . . . and when that is full as well, a 'hash' is derived from its contents and sent to yet another newly created block. And so on and so on. This way block five, say, knows the contents of block four because they share a consensus algorithm. If somebody messes with the contents of block four, its hash will no longer match block five's and alarms will go off. Then the suspect block four will be replaced with a backup."

"And that's why people trust cryptocurrencies? They're tamper-proof?"

"It's a big reason. Another is the fact blockchains are immutable: no data is ever lost. Old blocks are never deleted—new blocks just keep getting added to the end of the chain. This gives you a complete, uninterrupted history." She paused. "Companies are only beginning to wake up to the potential of blockchain technology, and digital currency is the tip of the iceberg. Investments, intellectual property, medicine—imagine a hospital where every patient's data is available instantly, and can be added to or referenced at any time: meds scanned for contraindications or surgical X-rays from twenty years ago always at your fingertips, via a distributed network where everything is transparent. And why stop at one hospital? With the decentralization blockchains allow, why not a chain of hospitals? Why not *all* hospitals? The possibilities for leveraging vertical markets are endless."

"And I suppose all this"—Logan waved his hand at the endless procession of CPUs—"is Chrysalis doing just that, ahead of the curve as usual."

Asperton nodded. "These nodes you're looking at form a complete circle, in the bedrock here beneath the Torus."

"My God." Logan started to mentally calculate how many individual computer servers that added up to. Roughly ten CPUs per row, half a dozen rows high, meant sixty nodes per rack. . . .

"Of course, only a fraction of the potential servers are in place and currently operational," she said, interrupting his thoughts. "We need room for future growth. Actually, that's one of the downsides of blockchains."

"So there *is* a downside," Logan said.

"For all their benefits, they're inefficient. And costly. All those distributed CPUs gulp energy. And despite the rosy picture I've painted, the consensus algorithms used for security make them a little hard to scale up."

"But we clearly wouldn't be down here if Chrysalis hadn't found a solution," Logan said. "And this, ah, Helix wouldn't be so critical to the conglomerate, so deadly secret, if you weren't planning to go to market."

Asperton didn't answer immediately. "Are all ghost hunters so cynical?" she asked.

Logan smiled, letting the low whir of CPU fans answer for him.

"I doubt Thomas Edison had GE in mind when he perfected a filament for the incandescent lightbulb," Asperton told him. "The Helix was originally—like so many other things here—an experiment. Proof of concept, undertaken by X."

"X?"

"What began as a modest internal investment five years ago has turned into the biggest—and most classified—project at the Complex. We've been using *ourselves* as test subjects, recording every transaction, every video stream . . . every damned thing going on in this valley that can be captured as data. And in the process we've solved some of those downsides I was telling you about."

"How?"

"Photonic computing."

Logan winced. "Don't tell me."

"I won't. I don't understand it myself. All I know is that what we're doing at this particular moment is a big risk. Hence, Peyton getting so hot and bothered."

Logan glanced down the corridor, at the hatch through which Peyton and Snow had disappeared. "Why?"

"Because, despite all the hardware, this is still something of a seat-of-the-pants design. Imagine building an engine and starting it up, only to realize you forgot to include a clean way for turning it off without crashing. You'll fix that the next time, of course . . . but what about now, while that first engine is running you down the road at full speed?"

Logan whistled.

"That's essentially what happened here. Oh, there are protocols for shutting it down—but they're time-consuming and have only been modeled. With all the data streaming into the Helix, from everywhere in the Complex simultaneously: think terabytes per minute, all needing to be processed by the registry system and stored in real time . . . there's no mechanism in place for *pausing.*"

"Hence, Peyton's example of yanking open an airplane hatch midflight."

Asperton nodded.

"But why, exactly, would that be so dangerous? You called it a test subject."

"I did. But already, it's proven so valuable that many sectors of our everyday processing have begun to rely on it. How do you think the Omega virtual machine can store, and access, so much imagery, let alone the usage logs of a hundred thousand clients? It's all stored in the Helix. Luckily, Snow said he was able to sequester that data. Otherwise, if the Helix crashes and we can't go live tomorrow . . ." She fell silent.

"Okay. But there's still one thing I don't understand. If this huge info-ring of yours records everything, why can't you just comb through it and find out who's been naughty? You said every data point here at the Complex feeds into the Helix."

"Every *data* point. But if somebody has garbled, stenographized, or otherwise corrupted that data *before* it's transmitted, then we've got nothing. That's why this moment is unique: for some reason, this one time, the antagonist who just sent me that message forgot a single step in anonymizing himself. So if we can stop the most recent blockchain buffers from purging, there's a chance we can find out who sent the message."

"And possibly crash the Helix in the process."

Now it was Asperton's turn to wince.

Suddenly, the hatch at the end of the corridor opened and Peyton emerged, followed by Snow. They walked quickly past the guards. Peyton had a look on his face that Logan could only compare to a doctor having delivered his own stillborn child.

The two men each got into electric vehicles, turned on the power, then drove slowly out into the corridor like two golf carts heading for the next tee. As they approached, Peyton slowed; Asperton jumped in; and then the two sped off down the passage at remarkable speed. Logan looked over at Snow, behind the wheel of the second cart.

"Shotgun?" Logan asked.

"Be my guest."

He got in, and the personnel carrier—with surprising acceleration—followed Peyton down the long, lazy arc of the subterranean tunnel.

42

They continued so long that, for Logan, the racks speeding past became a blur. He estimated they'd traveled almost half a mile before he asked Snow: "So, you're one of Peyton's computer security experts?"

"I wear two hats," Snow replied from behind the wheel. "I help with the more problematic security breaches—such as this, which to date is the mother of them all. But I'm technically part of Department X."

"X?" Logan echoed, for the second time.

Snow laughed. "I know. Sounds like an old spy movie, right?" Then he glanced over, saw the look on Logan's face. "Shit. You don't know about it."

"No details, no."

"I was told you had complete clearance. All the trimmings."

"I do." Before Snow could say anything more, he went on: "So what is it?"

"It doesn't have a name. We do the more advanced computing work—crypto counterespionage, AI, a little of the heavy lifting for Omega's coders . . . and, of course, maintain the Helix."

A secret within a secret within a secret. Hoping to get the worried look off Snow's face, Logan changed the subject. "Asperton was telling me you used photonic computing to solve some of the problems of enterprise-scale blockchains."

"She did?"

"She did. One question, though: Did you buy the photons from Star Trek, or Star Wars?"

Snow chuckled and appeared relieved. "It's also known as optical fiber computing. Maybe that sounds less intimidating. Conventional computers and storage devices use electrons. The Helix uses photons. Not everywhere yet, of course: we're simply grafting photonics onto our blockchain platform, to help solve its biggest downside."

"You mean, speed?"

"Precisely. Give us five years: instead of just data pipes, we'll have developed CPUs of nonlinear optical crystals."

Abruptly, the brake lights went on in Peyton's cart. A moment later, both Peyton and Asperton jumped out. Three people in regulation jumpsuits were waiting for them.

"Showtime," Snow said, pulling in behind. "We initiated the freeze. Now we have to complete the circuit, so to speak, and temporarily pinch off any new data blocks from being added while we find the metadata of that message. Otherwise the Band-Aid won't hold . . . and you'll be witness to the first, and last, cascade shutdown in history."

Logan looked out. The line of rack servers stretched on ahead of them, as unchanging as the hundreds or thousands they'd passed already. "I thought we had to go to the newest data block if we were going to track that rogue message."

Snow turned to reply, but Logan raised a hand. "Never mind. You've got more important things to do." He'd recalled what Asperton told him: *Only a fraction of the possible servers are in place and currently operational. We need room for future growth.* That "future growth" was obviously the line of computers stretching still farther down the curve of the corridor, ready and waiting to be populated with fresh blocks. . . .

. . . That is, if the Helix could be unfrozen—and restarted.

He stood back as the workers in black jumpsuits surrounded

Snow. To Logan they now looked less like worker bees and more like surgeons, in worried consultation over an operation that was going poorly. He heard fragments of meaningless sentences, spoken in tense voices. All he knew for sure was whoever sent them this last message—he felt sure it wasn't the same person as before—had rushed things slightly, and this sloppiness allowed Chrysalis a chance to put a name to some text, get an ID . . . at great potential risk to this vast, secret dynamo.

The workers had now gingerly navigated countless fiber-optic linkages and disappeared behind the racks of servers. It was obvious that manhandling the data flow of this vast machine, using fingers instead of keyboards, was an almost unheard-of scenario. Voices rose and fell: first eager, then deflated, then eager again. One worker stood not far from the carts, looking intently back down the endless array of blinking lights, radio raised and at the ready. Logan wondered what on earth he was staring at . . . until he realized the man wasn't staring so much as being the lookout for disaster. The Helix activity had to be frozen . . . but that meant idling in cryogenic sleep, *not* shutting down. If something went wrong now, while they initiated something that had never been modeled—if Snow's feared "cascade shutdown" occurred and all those endless blinking lights *went out* . . .

Then, as Logan stared down the corridor with the same intensity as the nearby worker, he saw all the countless tiny lights abruptly pause. Even though he was only a bystander, his heart seemed to pause along with them. He felt a shudder, real or imagined, course through his frame. And then the lights once again began winking on and off as before. And then Snow appeared from behind the webbing, relief practically etched on his face.

"Looks like the Helix tolerated the data pause," he said as he made his way back to them. "And we've got an ID for you. That message was sent by employee 4281292."

Peyton activated his Sentinel. "Cardiff, Benjamin R." He took a moment to pass this information along to Kramer, waiting in the office. Then he turned to Snow. "Return to I/O control and roll back the freeze. Blaze it up. *Now.*"

Snow nodded, jumped back into his cart, negotiated a smart three-point turn, and shot back down the corridor, while more jumpsuited workers—Department X, Logan assumed—rushed behind the servers as if to suture up the patient.

Three minutes later, Ben Cardiff—principal software engineer, level II—was walking along a well-appointed passage on the nineteenth floor of the Chrysalis Tower. His buzz from the Bloody Marys was wearing off, and he now wondered a little anxiously if the message he'd impulsively sent—meant to save his own skin if things went south—might have been as rash as Wing intimated. He had left BioCertain early, before his shift ended, and was heading back to his room to sleep it off.

As he approached the door to his quarters, however, he saw a woman and a man standing before it. Noticing him, they turned in his direction.

Without needing to be told, Cardiff sensed immediately: *security.*

He prepared to bolt, only to see two men he hadn't known were behind him now advancing. Both were armed.

"Mr. Cardiff?" the woman said. "Would you mind coming with us, please? We have a few questions."

Instinctively, he tensed to run, but the woman reached out with jaw-dropping speed and grasped his arm. Her grip was vise-like. "It'll be much easier if you come with us," she said.

For a moment, Cardiff hesitated. Then he seemed to go limp. One of the men took his other arm, and the little group continued past Cardiff's doorway and down the hall.

The corridor remained empty for ten seconds or so. Then a

figure emerged from a secondary corridor and walked up to where security had stood a minute earlier.

The guest registered as Reginald Bryant took a few more steps until he reached the door to Cardiff's quarters.

This was an unexpected development. Unexpected, indeed.

43

"They nabbed Cardiff," Kramer told the group that had reassembled in Peyton's bunker. "He's on his way to detention now."

"Good," said Peyton. "Now Mossby will have some company."

"What was his job description?" Logan asked.

"He was a software engineer in BioCertain." Peyton reached for a keyboard, typed briefly. "Excellent performance reviews—until just recently. He seemed to develop an attitude over the last half year or so. Thinking he'd outgrown the job, apparently—not uncommon with coders as they start to age out."

"But no red flags?"

"Nothing obvious. Let me check the tangential data, bar tabs and off-hour activities, that sort of thing." After a moment, he sat back in his chair. "Shit."

"What is it?" Asperton asked.

"As I feared. The Helix—it's slow coming back online. This SQL query I just ran on Cardiff keeps coming back with flaky results."

As Snow moved over to help, Logan turned to Asperton. "He's checking on this Cardiff's 'tangential data.' In other words, the guy's been watched the entire time he's worked here at the Complex. All of us have. And the data from all that surveillance captured *tangentially* in the immutable, unerasable Helix."

Asperton said nothing.

"Why didn't you tell me about Arc X before?"

"Why didn't you guess?"

Logan frowned in surprise.

"How many sections did I tell you the Torus was divided into?"

"Eight."

"And their designations? The ones you called boring?"

"Arcs A through G . . ." Logan counted on his fingers. "Shit."

Asperton smiled a little smugly.

"Here's a theory I'm developing that may wipe that smile off your face," he said. "Down in the bowels of the earth, you were telling me about all the wonderful things this next-gen blockchain will do for humanity. Eliminate hackers from the financial sector. Bring world peace."

Asperton rolled her eyes.

"But what you left unsaid are all the other uses it might have. For example, I think an autocratic government might find a persistent, omnipresent tech platform like this—that sees everything, forgets nothing, makes data-mining its citizens a breeze—useful indeed. Same for law enforcement or intelligence services."

"Jeremy, you're exceeding your brief," Asperton said, only half joking.

"They'd pay a pretty penny for a Helix of their own—once all the kinks were worked out." A new thought occurred to him. "Is that perhaps why your friend at the Agency, Gerald, is being so helpful?"

Asperton frowned, touched a finger to his lips. "I told you: the Helix began as internal research, to see if the true potential of blockchains could be leveraged."

"And look where we are five years later: with the world's biggest server farm under our feet—your very own database supercollider—and a secret Department X . . . and a potential source of revenue even greater than Omega someday. If we can get through the next twenty-four hours."

Asperton started to object, then just shook her head.

Grace's silky voice abruptly spoke in his ear. "Jeremy, Dr. Purchase wishes to speak to you."

"Okay."

Purchase came on, sounding a little breathless. "I've finished that comparison you requested. Running the names of the first Voyager recipients against people with BioCertain implants."

"And?"

"There are roughly thirty-five hundred hits."

Logan sat forward. "No *shit*."

"Of course, we're talking a dozen different kinds of medical implants, but . . ." His voice trailed off for a second. "There's one person you'll want to know about in particular."

"Go on."

"It's Janelle Deston."

"The woman who—" Logan stopped. "The early adopter?"

"Yes. She had a vagus nerve stim, with the usual shoulder implant. It's one of our newer products, but they've taken hold very quickly, because people with Parkinson's or clinical depression often have difficulty sticking to a treatment schedule—"

"Hold on." Turning to the others in room, Logan called out: "Janelle Deston had a medical implant."

Peyton was slower to raise his eyes than the others but was the first to speak. "So?"

"Don't be an ass. We've established that Voyager units can't kill people. But we've never established that medical implants can't."

"We haven't established it because, obviously, medical implants *can*," said Asperton.

"She's right," said Peyton impatiently. "A pacemaker could fail. Or, if you really want to be paranoid, imagine some terrorist with the right connections, pushing out a firmware patch to a particular model—firmware that would make it intentionally malfunction, cause ventricular fibrillation—and kill everyone implanted with one."

Now that was a disturbing thought indeed. Logan recalled that the same tech that made Omega devices work—background updates, two-way communication—was also used in many advanced medical implants.

But, having reeled this nightmare scenario out, Peyton now reeled it back in. "That's one of countless doomsday scenarios keeping us up at night. So naturally we have safeguards in place. Now: Where's your beloved 'commonality'?"

"Over three thousand early adopters, going live with Voyager tomorrow, also have Chrysalis-branded medical implants."

This stopped Peyton—but only for a moment. "Okay, I'll admit it: that's a comparison I never thought to make. But where are you going with this? BioCertain makes dozens of different devices—implanted and maintained by doctors worldwide, with no affiliation to us. That market is on fire, closing in on two hundred billion dollars a year."

"Our opponents are threatening to kill a thousand Voyager clients. We know Voyager itself is harmless. Yet four people have been killed. One of them was poisoned . . . and it turns out the other three had medical implants designed right here."

"Three *unrelated* implants," said Peyton. "Are you seriously implying sabotage? Of different devices? After all the workers we've questioned? We don't even know for sure if any of those particular three malfunctioned."

This was true, and Logan couldn't argue. Still, his sixth sense told him this was the right path . . . the *only* path left.

"You're right," he said. "Countless doctors, outside your control, implant those devices. And the Voyager units, which I'm banking aren't involved here, basically implant themselves. Obviously, all those surgeons aren't involved in a massive conspiracy to blackmail Chrysalis. That means we have to look at the implants themselves—the ones fabricated *here*, before they enter the supply chain—if we're to have a chance of finding any sabotage."

Peyton sighed. "I told you, we did that already. Yesterday, we interviewed everyone in charge of the fabrication and fulfillment teams—for both medical implants *and* Voyagers. They came up clean."

"Then we need to look again. We've obviously missed something, just like we missed the commonalities the first time," Logan retorted.

"There was that one guy," Kramer piped up. "Prawn. For one shift, he had to man both the implant line and the Voyager line . . . remember?"

"Sure," Peyton said. "But we saw the video. There was nothing."

"It's an anomaly," Logan said. "And it's one of the very few we've found. Isn't it worth checking out?"

Kramer shrugged, turned, and walked toward the windows overlooking the security hive. As he did he spoke into his Sentinel unit, ordering a team to bring Prawn down for some follow-up questions.

Peyton meanwhile turned back to the workstation where Snow was tending to the troubled Helix. He frowned with obvious frustration. "I'm going down to watch Cardiff's interrogation," he told Kramer. "You should come along."

44

As the two headed for the exit, Logan suddenly remembered Dr. Purchase was still on hold. He tapped his Voyager. "Terribly sorry, Dr. Purchase. Thanks for letting me know about Janelle Deston. Could you please send a list of all those 'doubles'—as you call them—to me, Ms. Asperton, and Peyton?"

"I'll take care of it myself."

"Thanks." Logan paused. "You said there was something else you wanted to tell me earlier?"

"That's right." A brief clearing of the throat. "I've been doing some of that . . . well, that research you asked for. Checking candidate compounds, preclinicals and so forth, for any interactions that might somehow have gone unnoticed. And two things came to my attention I thought you should know about."

Two things. Logan took a moment to try wiping his mind clear of everything else. "Go ahead," he said, praying this would be quick.

Purchase must have picked up something in Logan's tone, because he seemed to snap to attention. "You'll recall we were talking about Bridger's implant. The one he was planning to have upgraded."

"Yes," Logan said. "The Mark Two. With the Continental tire."

"Um. Right. I told you it supplied doses of Ambutrexine for his osteoarthritis. I also noticed, tangentially, no corticosteroids were present in his blood—which they would have been had he taken Ambutrexine before the flight."

"Tangentially." It seemed that was the word management liked to use whenever they accessed the Helix for data.

"The ME did find traces of silodosin in Bridger's blood. That's a drug used to treat enlarged prostates—pilots take it sometimes so they won't need to urinate as frequently, so its presence in his blood was no surprise."

"Go on," Logan prodded.

"Well, knowing as I did what happened to Mr. Bridger, I looked further into the matter. Theoretically, if Bridger was administered one *very specific* drug at the same time as the Ambutrexine implant was active, it could have caused a highly dangerous interaction."

"What drug is this?"

"An anticonvulsant, oxcarbazepine. Not only would the interaction cause extreme vertigo, dizziness, syncope . . . but the anticonvulsant could disguise itself as silodosin in Bridger's bloodstream. Especially given the amount of time that passed before any bloodwork was done . . . and especially if the pathologist wasn't actively looking for foul play, or an ADR. Adverse drug reaction."

But now, at last, you are, Logan thought. "Fascinating. So it's possible Bridger's implant might—indirectly, at least—have been responsible for his death."

"If combined with that anticonvulsant, yes. And it would be undetectable unless, as I said, you were looking for just such a thing."

"How exactly did you discover this?"

A hesitation. "Given your other requests, it seemed like a practical line of research to undertake."

"Thank you, Doctor. I appreciate the initiative. And this finding might be of great importance."

So it *wasn't* certain Bridger's death was accidental. But neither, it seemed, could they prove otherwise—not in the time left them. As the weight of the conundrum grew more onerous, Logan's mind drifted to the pub he had noticed earlier, the Crosskeys, and he concluded he was now well overdue for that glass of single-malt scotch.

"There's one other thing, Dr. Logan. I stumbled upon it while doing the research you requested. It's something of an anomaly."

Hearing this, Logan's sixth sense came alive again. A faint warning bell went off in his head.

"I'll tell you what," he told the BioCertain manager. "How about if I come by your office in five or ten minutes?"

"Of course."

"Thanks." Logan disconnected and turned toward Asperton, who'd been waiting for his talk with Purchase to end.

"I'm going to follow Peyton, watch them interrogate this Benjamin Cardiff," she said. "Care to join the show?"

"Under other circumstances, yes. But I'm off to talk with Dr. Purchase." He waved to her and left the room.

Whether Purchase had to wait five minutes or ten depended on if the Crosskeys had a bottle of sixteen-year-old Lagavulin on hand.

45

Bill Cortez waited for the service elevator doors to open, then led his team out onto the fourteenth floor of the Tower. He told his Sentinel unit to double-check the target info.

"Scott Prawn, Fulfillment lead two," he told the team. "Staff Quarters 1477."

Nods all around. Target retrieval was a common enough assignment: usually somebody who'd drunk too much the night before and made a scene. Given the population here at the Complex, it wasn't all that different from the five years he'd put in as a cop in a small Vermont city. Except, of course, every now and then this job offered him the opportunity to nab a corporate spy.

From the dossier, Cortez didn't think Prawn was one of those. Still, things had been a little strange over the last few days—heightened security, lockdown, somebody placed in the max detainment facility—and so he'd decided to take a team of three instead of the usual two for the escort down to the security wing. Peyton seemed eager to talk to this guy.

They walked along the hall, Cortez glancing at door numbers. It was funny, how you could tell what kind of a job somebody had at Chrysalis just from the decor of the floor they lived on. The managers and high-level propeller heads had wide corridors and plush carpeting. Grunts like him had more spartan accommodations, a step or two up from an army barracks but with more privacy. And this Prawn guy was somewhere in between: the common hallway of floor fourteen had nice enough carpeting, but painted walls instead of wallpaper, and framed pictures instead of flowers. Fewer lounges, too. Midlevel habitation for a midlevel drone.

He stopped. This was it: 1477.

His skeleton passcard unlocked the door, and they stepped into a shared living space also familiar to Cortez. It was a standard four-and-one: two double bedrooms, kitchen and common area, and then a private room at the far end—with a window—for a fifth person, a few notches higher on the pay scale.

Cortez walked through the living room—past the messy couches and tables covered with game controllers, the emergency door topped with an obligatory red EXIT sign—then stopped to glance into the shared bedrooms. Both equally messy, as expected; both empty, also expected. Cortez knew that four of the people occupying the dorm space were currently at work. He also knew that Prawn, who had the bedroom of honor at the far end, was home. That door was closed, however, and Cortez could hear nothing but background hum, part human and machine, that made up the heartbeat of the Chrysalis spire.

"Mr. Prawn?" he called out. "Scott Prawn? I'm Bill Cortez, from Logistics. Sorry to intrude. Would you mind stepping out, please?"

Nothing.

Cortez walked deeper into the staff quarters, passing the kitchen, which was full of half-eaten, individual-size boxes of cereal, crackers, and—disgustingly—ramen. Put five bachelors together and the surroundings quickly devolved into those of a dorm room. The bathroom, he could see, was open: Prawn was not in it.

Cortez glanced at his team, then approached the door to Prawn's room. This time, he knocked. "Scott Prawn? I'm sorry, but I've been asked to escort you to security for a few questions."

Still, silence. Cortez stared at the door, which was plain,

unadorned by posters, holograms, or anything else. "Mr. Prawn, if you don't open the door I'm going to be forced to do it myself."

He waited another fifteen seconds, just in case the guy was jacking off or something else Cortez preferred not to see. Then, again using his skeleton card, he turned the door and pushed it open.

The room beyond had about as much personality as its bare door promised. Inside was a bed, neatly made, with two rec tablets lying on it; a long worktable—constructed, Cortez noted, of better wood than the one in his own single—the suite's emergency door with its exit sign; bookshelves; a guitar with one broken string; the usual closets and overhead compartments; and the coveted window, polarized a light blue.

This was odd. Prawn was off duty, and he should be home. His ID, which employees at the Complex were required to keep on their persons, indicated he was here. But he obviously was not.

There were other, more obscure ways of tracking him, but they took time and weren't always reliable. Nevertheless, Cortez pulled the radio from his belt. "Cortez to Forward Twelve."

"This is Forward."

"Subject 3877209, Prawn, Scott L., is not in his quarters. Requesting a video confirm."

"One moment." There was a brief silence. "Got him—hall camera shows Prawn entering his room fifty-two minutes ago."

"What about afterward? Did he leave again?"

A longer silence. "Sorry, Bill, that's a problem. We lost access to most of our tangential feed half an hour ago."

Tell me about it. That was the latest odd rumor: that Central Storage, maintained by the spooks in Department X, had just crashed. For the time being, there was no way of knowing whether Prawn had left his room again.

"Forward, copy that. Cortez out—" Cortez began to lower the radio, his thumb still on the transmit button. Something was wrong. The exit sign across the room was red, as usual—but a darker shade than normal. And wet. As he stared at it, a single crimson drop gathered at one corner, then slid slowly down the wall.

"What the fuck?" said a team member behind him.

Grabbing a chair from the worktable, Cortez dragged it over to the emergency door, then stood on it, peering into the cube-shaped box behind the sign.

Two eyes, bulging and glassy, stared back out at him.

Cortez had already begun to guess what he might find; nevertheless, he narrowly escaped falling off the chair in his instinctive jerk backward. Regaining his balance, he took a screwdriver from his belt and removed the screws holding the sign in place. It fell away with a scraping sound and a sudden release of fluid; what was hidden behind it rolled out, as well. Cortez put his hands out reflexively to catch it, then thought better of the idea and jumped out of the way as it fell onto the chair and bounced to the floor.

"Jesus on a *stick*!" came a voice from the doorway.

Cortez raised the radio, thumb still frozen on the transmit button. "Cortez to Forward Twelve."

"Cortez, why is this channel still open?"

"Send an incident team to Suite 1477, code orange. Tell them to bring body bags. Tarps, too."

"Did you say code *orange*?"

"Make it fast. Cortez, out." This time, he removed his thumb as he put away his radio and glanced back at the three shocked faces.

"They'll be here in five minutes," he said. "We might as well pass the time by finding the rest of him."

46

Logan decided to hold off on the single malt.

"I'm sorry to trouble you," Purchase said as he led Logan through the BioCertain cube farm. "But I couldn't help keeping your concerns in mind as I checked the new drugs we've developed over the last year and a half." He swallowed a little painfully. "Well, I finished the correlation. There was rather a lot of data, as you might imagine." He drew a deep breath. "You have to understand, I worked briefly in Carewell research before being promoted to BioCertain. That gives me a unique perspective. It's rare that Chrysalis allows that kind of . . . cross-pollination, as it were. Anyway, what I stumbled on, most unusually, affects both departments."

Logan nodded with what he hoped was encouragement. *I know: you're in the doghouse. But just get to the anomaly, damn it.*

"Carewell funds numerous field expeditions—gathering unknown plants, learning indigenous medical techniques, and so forth. We—I mean, they—are always searching for compounds from which to synthesize new medications. You know, aspirin originally discovered in willow bark, things like that. About eight months ago, Carewell sent a small research expedition to the Arctic. The year before, ground-penetrating radar at that location had revealed what appeared to be a Neanderthal gravesite. The two scientists Carewell sent had various tasks on the new expedition, but a primary one was to extract core samples that, hopefully, contained Neanderthal DNA. If it was indeed a mass grave, we might learn something useful from what killed them, if only prophylactically. Permafrost is an ideal preserver of microbes: frozen, lightless, starved of oxygen. Of course, the greatest likelihood was they died from starvation or in a territorial dispute, but we thought it worth—"

"Of course you did," Logan interrupted. *Twenty-one hours. Shit.* "What did they find?"

"That's where the, ah, anomaly begins. The senior member of the team, Dr. Randall Pike, sent back a single message, almost jubilant, about what they'd found. But that was the team's only communication beyond the regular coded pings, and we don't normally allow dispatches from the field. In any case, Dr. Pike met a tragic end—he fell into a crevasse on the final day of the expedition—and the other scientist returned with a number of ice cores and the unfortunate news that what Pike initially thought to be a breakthrough was actually just a set of mistaken readings. The ice cores were set aside in frozen storage—merely as a formality, since they contained nothing of value—and were destroyed in an accidental fire a month or two later, effectively ending the project. I mean, with the lead scientist dead, the samples valueless . . . it was one loss too many. Future field research at the site was canceled, and the other scientist was reassigned. But as I began to examine the correlations of our new drugs—per your request—an unindexed artifact appeared."

"What?"

"A piece of data just hanging there, with no associated reference or index point."

"And why is that important?"

"Because the system enforces referential integrity for all information. Orphaned data simply can't exist—except on purpose."

"You mean, as in hiding something?"

"I can't think of any other possibility. Everything that takes place here is recorded, by"—his voice dropped—"well, you know, Arc X. There's no way you can stop that . . . but if someone's clever enough, they could damage a record so it wouldn't show up in a normal search. It would just be floating out there in the ether. I would never have noticed it had I not undertaken such an unorthodox search."

So Purchase *was* aware of the Helix, as well. Logan began to think that—even if they didn't know its name—a lot of people at the Complex found it increasingly necessary in their everyday duties.

"Can you tell me more about this data artifact?" he asked.

"There was enough intact to make a partial reconstruction. It came from the ice cores that had been brought back from that Arctic expedition."

"I thought they were all melted in the fire."

"Supposedly they were. But nevertheless, the metadata indicated at least one section of core survived the fire. Not only that, but it had been moved to a different subdivision of Carewell."

"What subdivision?"

Purchase swallowed again. "DNA Synthetics and PCR Replication."

Logan went abruptly still. He had a good imagination, and all of a sudden, it began to suggest a lot of unpleasant possibilities.

"Dr. Purchase," he said, "do you have a name and photo of the other scientist who went on that failed expedition?"

"Yes, Wing Kaupei." Purchase spoke to his Sentinel unit, and then a hologram appeared on the table between them. Logan recognized the woman—down to the mole centered on her long, slender throat.

"Send her entire dossier to my private account, please," he told Purchase.

"Her tracking logs, as well? Everything?"

"I want to know if she likes her eggs sunny side up."

There was a pause. "Done," said the scientist after another brief consult with his Sentinel earpiece.

Jesus Christ. Purchase had just uncovered a nest of fire ants—and he knew it, too. What neither of them could guess yet was just how deep, or nasty, that nest was. "Thank you. Sorry I kept you waiting. I think I'd better inform Asperton." And Logan began to rise.

"There's something else," Purchase said.

Logan sat down.

"While I was waiting for you just now, I went over my findings again. And . . . well, something must be going wrong with our data farm, because not only was I unable to input any new information, but a lot of unrelated dead data began to spew out. I've never seen anything like it."

Peyton must be having a fit, Logan thought. It seemed that their "freeze" had caused more damage to the Helix than even he'd expected.

"What do you mean—'dead' data?" he asked.

"Useless stuff that the system deems need not be retained. Obsolete system logs, for example."

Logan thought fast. The Helix, he knew, was a work in progress—they were improving it as they built it—and he'd been told it stored data from every node at the entire Center. It determined what to retain, whether you wanted something retained or not—look at the lengths Wing Kaupei had taken to redact data. So if the Helix kept everything—if it was as immutable as Asperton bragged—wouldn't it keep everything that it *deleted*, too? Maybe a final, production version wouldn't. But it seemed to Logan that if the Helix, abruptly halted in its busywork, was going temporarily haywire—it might start displaying *all* records, marked as deleted or not, until such time as it regained sanity and began filtering those out again?

"I realize you didn't expect to see this dead data filling up your screen," Logan said. "But once you determined what it was—were you able to make sense of it? Could you, say, follow a breadcrumb trail through it?"

Purchase took a deep breath, exhaled slowly. "I didn't hire her, you know."

So they'd come to it at last—the root of why Purchase was acting so twitchy. "What did you find, exactly?"

"Randall Pike's personal log from the Arctic expedition. Along with a partial series of tests that took place . . . here, in PRC Replication."

"May I have it, please?"

Purchase hesitated. "It's about three gigs in all."

Logan stood up again. "There's a tablet in my quarters. Can you transfer it to that? Three gigabytes—I don't think even Grace can read that fast." And, without waiting for an answer, he thanked Purchase and left the office.

"Jeremy?" came the voice in his ear. "Just so you know: I can assimilate three gigabytes of data in less than a second."

"Sorry, Grace," he told his Voyager unit as he made his way back to the main concourse. "I meant reading *aloud*."

"Aloud? As in a bedtime story?"

"Something like that."

47

Orris Peyton sat at a large table in a large, uncluttered space. It was, in fact, the biggest of the three interrogation rooms within the security center, located—like the middle bun of a double hamburger—below the Torus and above the Helix, this latter currently on the cybernetic equivalent of life support.

The staff referred to the room, rather morbidly, as "the arena." It was rarely used—none of the interrogation rooms were used, any more frequently than were the detention cells—but efforts had been made to disguise this. There were cracks and chips in the cinder-block walls, long rubber skid marks on the tiled floor— decorations designed to fuel speculation, in the person facing inquisition, that heads had once been banged here, chairs dragged along while their occupants struggled . . . perhaps on the way to waterboarding or some form of electrical persuasion.

Peyton glanced behind him at the two rows of security staff near the far wall. Those in the first row sat at desks, monitoring video cameras and a lie detector. Behind them stood a trio of guards in security cammo: Athos, Porthos, and Aramis with machine guns. He knew the goon on the left: Fenton, whom he'd hired himself years before. The other two he didn't recognize— a tall, heavyset woman with short-cropped dark hair, and a thin but vaguely military-looking man. Christ, as head of Logistics he really ought to spend more time rubbing shoulders with the hoi polloi.

At a middle distance, set apart as if to remove herself from the distasteful work of "wet" security, sat Asperton, silent, arms folded across her blouse. To Peyton's left sat Kramer, and to his right Dafna, his go-to security asset in difficult moments. She glanced back at him, her attractive almond-shaped eyes shutting, then opening, like a camera shutter at its slowest speed. That was her signal that everything was ready, and they were waiting for him to start.

Peyton looked across the table at the man handcuffed to a chair. The lie detector leads ran away from his chest and left arm. The man looked back with a placid, almost supercilious countenance that surprised Peyton. Here he'd staged such a show—the big room, the guards, all the trappings of some East German kangaroo court . . . to apparently little effect. With Hurricane Mountain and the surrounding land almost a private municipality, Peyton had a great deal of leeway when it came to incarceration and interrogation. He could, of course, have the man—Benjamin Cardiff—taken away and let Kramer smack him around for a while; it had been a tense, frustrating few days, and the security chief would probably welcome the chance to work up more of a sweat than he'd been allowed with Mossby. But Peyton had been trained in tactical psychology, and he'd studied all the seminal mind-control, psychochemical, and brainwashing studies, from Project Dork to MKUltra to the Milgram experiments. He had a sense Cardiff felt entitled for some reason, and applying muscle might be counterproductive.

Besides, there was a wild card: the unexpected murder of Scott Prawn, the drone he and Dafna had interrogated about the Omega fabrication line. Running him down had been Jeremy Logan's brainstorm, and Peyton didn't know yet exactly how he fit in to this huge clusterfuck. Cardiff couldn't have killed Prawn, of course: he was being processed just down the hall when the murder took place.

Time to get busy. He took a deep breath, stared at the subject. "Mr. Cardiff."

The man nodded.

"You sent an encrypted message to Ms. Asperton, here, roughly three hours ago."

"I did."

Once again, Peyton found himself surprised. He'd expected vehement denial, not calm assent. Asperton, too, looked surprised.

"Would you care to explain?"

"I thought it was clear enough. Why ask?"

Peyton knew better than to let a subject ask questions, but there were rare occasions when such questions could open up unexpected avenues of investigation. "Certain people believe that was the first message sent by you," he replied, choosing his words carefully.

At this, the coder sat up with something like eagerness. His handcuff jangled as it slid up the arm of the chair. "That's good. That makes things easier."

"I don't follow."

Cardiff sat back. He was obviously making an effort to project a serene, confident air. Peyton—recalling a few of Dafna's war stories—wondered how long that confidence would last if he put Cardiff in a room with her instead of Kramer.

"Well, it means you know someone else sent the other messages."

Peyton waited, neither affirming nor denying.

"And, if you know that, you must also note my message contained a very different offer."

"It seemed similar enough to me," Peyton said, casting out a fly.

"You can't be serious," Cardiff replied, rising to the bait. "Those other messages were nothing but threats. *My* message offered a way to verify your money was well spent."

"You mean, verify that . . . unwanted events would not take place if that money was paid." Peyton cast once again, and once again he was rewarded.

Cardiff nodded. "Right. I'm the critical link in this whole thing. That's why I let you catch me."

Peyton didn't believe Cardiff's fuckup was intentional, but he let this pass. "Explain."

"This whole—exercise, if you will—was built on certain rules. Nobody gets caught; nobody gets hurt; we get paid . . . and everyone lives happily ever after."

"Except the four people you killed," said Dafna in a low, toneless voice.

"That was *not* me! I told you: there were rules. There wasn't *supposed* to be any killing. And when we got the money, you were supposed to get the key."

An alarm went off in Peyton's head. "What key are you talking about?"

"What key do you think? The one that determines whether those people live or die."

"Don't play games!" Peyton shouted suddenly. "Tell me what's going on. You're the one under lock and key . . . or hadn't you noticed?"

"I'm *not* playing games!" Cardiff said, composure beginning to slip. "Look. They changed the rules on me. Nobody was supposed to be endangered, let alone killed. I did my part, opened communication channels, looped the Fulfillment cameras . . . and then found out I'd been played. They don't give a shit how many die, one or one thousand or a million. But *I* do." He swallowed. "That's why I sent you the note. The others, the control group, they'll walk off and let everyone die. See, I know how to stop that. I built the key; I can use it to unlock all this. But you need to guarantee me five million dollars, drop all charges, and keep me—"

"What have you been smoking?" Peyton interrupted. "You're

guilty of extortion, murder, corporate espionage—and you talk of being exonerated? *Paid?* You're crazy if you—"

Abruptly, he stopped. He'd almost forgotten he had another fly in his tackle box. And given Cardiff's attitude, now might be a good time to just stay cool and try another cast.

"There's been a death in the Chrysalis Tower," he said.

The BioCertain programmer looked at him.

"A murder, actually. Someone named Scott Prawn. Fulfillment lead. You probably knew him. In fact, since you mentioned Fulfillment just now, I'm sure you did."

Cardiff's eyes widened involuntarily, and his nostrils flared.

"We know it was a murder because a bone saw was involved. Very messy."

Cardiff tried to stand, was pulled back into his seat by the cuffs. "Put me in a protective cell. Now."

Peyton wasn't sure he'd heard correctly. "What?"

Cardiff was talking fast now, trying to stand again, looking anxiously around the room. "If they killed Prawn, it means they're rolling up the carpet a little early. So you'd better fucking keep me safe, because they might come for me next. And if I'm dead, you're done. And so are all those innocent people. Guarantee my protection *and* the five million."

Peyton started to respond, but Cardiff raised his voice and spoke over him. "Without me, those clients of yours are going to die! Sure, I want to save my own skin. And they double-crossed me. That's why I sent that message . . . to let you know I'm cooperating. The trigger mechanism *defaults to on, not off.* I'm the only one with the key to disarm it. I thought that made me bulletproof—but they don't care *who* dies! I'll bet they're just covering their tracks and walking away. But I can still fix this. I'm your letter of transit. Otherwise, it's only a matter of hours until—"

Peyton was listening so attentively it took a second to notice the stuttering noise behind him. It was unusual, but instantly familiar: automatic weapons fire.

As he swiveled in his chair, Dafna was already out of hers and pulling her M1911 pistol. As if in a nightmare, Peyton saw the armed guard standing on the right had raised his submachine gun and was firing in measured, deliberate bursts. Fountains of blood fanned the walls beyond the other two guards as the shooter methodically mowed them down. Now he was spraying gunfire at the people at the tables in front of him, sending up clouds of wood chips, blood, bits of equipment. Asperton began to rise, then fell back as a ghastly halo of crimson plumed around her head.

Dafna fired and the shooter jerked sideways with a grunt, but he swiveled his weapon back in her direction and she went down in a torrent of bullets. Now the man turned his weapon toward the center table and unleashed a long burst at Cardiff that sent the handcuffed programmer into a manic dance and tore his body to shreds.

Everything was slowing down, and Peyton raised his own weapon just as the shooter swung the smoking barrel in his direction and he got off a shot, but in the rising clouds of smoke he couldn't see whether the round hit home until an impact like the hoof of a horse hit him in the shoulder, and as Peyton went down the last thing he saw was the shadowy figure of the shooter dart out the exit and disappear, just as the security sirens began a rising mournful wail.

48

Logan had dragged the chair from the workstation in his suite and pulled it to the window. Now he sat with his feet on the sill, one ankle crossed over the other. The tablet he'd been scrolling rapidly through for the last fifteen minutes lay on the floor beside him; Grace, whom he'd kept busy conflating data and searching for needles in haystacks, had fallen silent.

He knew time was running short, but what Purchase had told him—and more critically, what Purchase surmised—convinced Logan he needed to step away from the madness and stitch these fragments of information together: lab notes, confidential files, journal entries intended for deletion, data disguised as innocuous that was, in fact, anything but. What he hadn't already learned, he absorbed as quickly as possible, Grace assisting by keeping to the most promising data nodes. Now he had to do what Grace could not help him with: put the disparate elements into a narrative . . . or, at least, the ghost of one.

He leaned back and closed his eyes, steadying his breathing. Grace had asked if he was planning to tell a bedtime story—and that seemed as good a description as any. Except this one was not likely to lull anybody to sleep. Clearing his mind, he sorted the myriad elements as best he could. And from those, he started to spin the tale.

. . .

Wing *Kaupei—no doubt that was not her birthname—had worked at Carewell for six years. Despite how thoroughly Chrysalis vetted those it hired, no details of her CV could be trusted. But from her work, it was clear the knowledge she claimed—molecular biology, with a subspecialty of paleopathology—was in fact one area of her expertise.*

It seemed likely she was also skilled at corporate espionage and social engineering, and from time to time took on assignments from an unknown but well-paying entity, perhaps even a nation-state.

Eight months earlier, Wing and Randall Pike had gone on an expedition to Alaska, in search of organic samples useful for pharmaceutical development. Pike had taken the trip before, but this time was different: ground-penetrating radar had previously picked up what appeared to be a Neanderthal gravesite embedded deep in the ice. Pike was a biologist specializing in epidemiology, and if in fact there was a mass grave, perhaps some useful information about ancient immune systems could be gleaned from it.

The expedition was successful beyond his wildest hopes, as Pike confided in a journal Wing had later deleted . . . only to be recently coughed back up, like a chicken bone, by the malfunctioning Helix. Not only did the cores find a mass grave, some thirty thousand years old—but they revealed tantalizing evidence of an unknown pathogen that had killed every last creature. As Pike studied the samples in his tent at night, he grew increasingly convinced this pathogen might not only have killed the Neanderthals in the mass grave . . . but it also could have been responsible for their die-off on a continental scale. A far cry from the conventional theory that interspecies hanky-panky—with Homo sapiens *Y chromosomes eventually replacing original Neanderthal DNA— helped speed them into oblivion.*

If Neanderthals had fallen victim to this pathogen, rather than going extinct through genetics and Darwinian evolution, it would not only be a breakthrough discovery—but it could benefit medicine as well, because all evidence pointed to the pathogen not affecting Homo sapiens. *Pike was so excited he broke radio silence once, to imply they'd found something important.*

Then, on the day of their planned return to civilization, a terrible tragedy: Pike accidentally fell into a crevasse, his body unrecoverable. Wing returned to her office in the Torus and analyzed the ice cores, only to find that—after further study with more sophisticated instruments—Pike's initial excitement was misplaced: the samples were valueless. A few weeks later, there was an electrical fire in the freezer compartment that held the cores, and Wing—her promising project literally up in smoke—was reassigned to a managerial job liaising with BioCertain.

This, at least, was what the record stated—along with Pike's diary, which was never supposed to be seen. But based on the data fragments Dr. Purchase had recovered, which revealed that a single core sample had survived the fire and been moved to another Carewell subdivision—DNA Synthetics—a very different story began to take shape.

Wing *confirmed that Pike's discovery—which he'd been correct about—would be a tremendous coup for Carewell. She also had corporate and government contacts outside Chrysalis that would be very interested in possessing it—and would pay handsomely.*

The most profitable endgame for a discovery like this would be a biological weapon.

Disguising her work and concealing her trail, Wing analyzed the remaining core sample, which she'd kept hidden away after the fire, and within a few weeks managed to isolate the pathogen so deadly to Neanderthals. It was a novel pathogen, with the zero transmissibility of a prion disease, yet following the familiar pattern of infection and DNA replication: a biologic whose effect was a cytokine "storm" interrupting normal action of the immune system. It acted quickly, almost as quickly as a poison—and it seemed invariably fatal.

The saving grace of this pathogen—which had perhaps led to the Neanderthals' extinction—was it had no effect on Homo sapiens. *But Wing had the expertise to change that.*

Scraps of metadata and header files, repurposed to look like innocuous lab work, showed that Wing succeeded in tweaking the pathogen to successfully infect humans. Apparently, it was startlingly easy. The two tests she ran—one "subject" a person in elder care, the other working in a sheet metal factory—showed the pathogen killed by causing the immune system to abruptly go into overdrive, dumping large amounts of enzymes into the nervous system that invariably caused fatal interactions with beneficial pharmaceuticals already present in the bloodstream. It was as if the immune system began to see these medications as a threat—but its response doomed the host body instead of saving it.

Logan opened his eyes. Here, the trail went cold. The PCR replication log that Purchase had stumbled across implied Wing had synthesized some of this weaponized compound. But given the danger of being caught, it seemed she'd performed the synthesis only once, after which she erased or corrupted all data related to the work: dutifully flagged as deleted by the Helix and now unintentionally, imperfectly, resurrected.

Wing's work had been remarkably dangerous and highly illegal. Logan wondered, could it be effectively marketed as a bioweapon? Its method of action, after all, was effectively like a poison: one victim at a time.

With one difference: this pathogen made it appear as though the infected person had died as a result *of his or her own defective immune system.* Spearman's sudden fatal attack; Janelle Deston's inexplicable car crash.

242 · LINCOLN CHILD

But what happened next? The tattered pieces of evidence did not explain.

Logan closed his eyes again.

Wing's handlers debated what to do with this sudden, sinister gift. Synthesizing additional doses would be difficult—and besides, governments to which one might sell such a poisonous compound probably had their own already. There was, however, one unique convergence Wing's handlers might exploit. Chrysalis was about to release a new product: the Omega II Voyager. How it worked was cloaked in corporate and technological secrecy. It was an audacious, game-changing, brilliant invention . . . but, like all paradigm shifts, would have to instill confidence, overcome consumer distrust.

If Wing's pathogen could somehow leverage Omega's mission-critical rollout, then it could best be weaponized as blackmail. If they planned carefully, salted the ground, then acted when Voyager was at its most vulnerable point of no return—and at the same time, manipulated all evidence to point to Omega itself as the culprit behind the mysterious deaths . . . then Wing's handlers would be in a position to extort an unprecedented amount of money from Chrysalis, in a great hurry, before vanishing from the scene and leaving wreckage and confusion behind them.

The scenario formed in Logan's head and he quickly ran through several others, rejecting them all. Every piece of data pointed toward this: the very things Wing had tried to delete or conceal, ironically, made her true intentions more obvious.

But there was still a significant problem: logistics. Wing could not have done this alone. Even if there were well-funded handlers on the outside, she'd need people inside the Torus to help with the implementation. Somebody in BioCertain would have needed access to the links maintained 24/7 with all smart implants to—somehow—kill board members Spearman and Bridger; poison Marceline; and then sacrifice Janelle Deston, all at precisely planned moments—and then—once again, somehow—be ready to kill a thousand more, all as a way of convincing and misleading Chrysalis.

"Jeremy," Grace said. "There's a priority—"

But even as the synthetic voice spoke, it was overridden by another: also female, this one human.

"Dr. Logan?" the accent was vaguely Middle Eastern. "Jeremy Logan?"

"Yes?"

"My name is Dafna. Security specialist, liaison to Orris Peyton."

Despite its brittle tension, the voice was rational and authoritative. In the background, however, Logan heard a confused turmoil of shouting and what sounded like a Klaxon.

"Where are you?" he asked.

"Security headquarters. We were interviewing Benjamin Cardiff. Then we came under assault by an infiltrator."

"Assault? How?"

"Disguised as a guard—machine-gun fire. He killed Cardiff, killed Kramer. Ms. Asperton is dead, four or five others. We wounded him and he had to retreat."

My God . . . all dead? Claire, too? "And Peyton?"

"Shot. Unconscious now. But last thing he told me, told me twice, was: *Call Logan.*"

49

"Call *me*? Do you know who this infiltrator's target was?"

"Yes. Benjamin Cardiff."

Cardiff. He'd sent the latest message, different from the others. Whose name they'd risked the integrity of the Helix to discover.

Claire. Dead?

Now Logan forced himself to think very quickly. No matter what obstacles he'd come up against in his career—phantasm, fraud, conspiracy—the endgame always came down to logic. He set up a mental chessboard, and—as he asked Dafna to give him every detail, no matter how trivial—he set up the players, one by one. Peyton. Cardiff. The mysterious shooter. Prawn. Janelle Deston. Purchase. Kramer. Wrigley. Claire Asperton . . .

Claire. Dead?

Suddenly, the missing pieces in the narrative he'd been assembling came into focus.

Oh my God . . .

Now, as he mentally moved the chess pieces, a plan began coming into view. Not so much as a plan, really; more like an organized retreat. "Dafna? Are you still there?"

"Yes. I am awaiting your instructions."

"How badly is Peyton hurt?"

"He's lost blood, but I've stabilized the bleeding."

"Can you move him to safety?"

A pause. "With an electric passenger cart, yes."

"Good. Now, listen very carefully. I want you to bring him to Infinium."

"Infinium? You mean, Arc E? Omega?"

"Yes. You must know the Torus well: take back passages an outsider wouldn't know. Use Peyton's security pass to get through any locked doors yours can't open, but leave your ID badges where they are so they aren't tracked. Try to get to Theater One, in the R&D division. You'll be met there—ask for Roz."

"But why—"

"I'll explain when we meet up. And one other thing. Bring Karel Mossby with you."

"The hacker? That I cannot do. He is locked in—"

"Dafna, I don't have time to explain. If I'm right, Mossby isn't safe from that intruder, either. You can't leave him in a cell. And we need him."

"But—"

"Peyton asked you to contact me. He was asking for help. *Right?*"

A longer pause. "Right."

"Then trust me. Bring Mossby. Cuff him to the cart if you want. But I need all three of you safe inside Arc E within the hour. Okay?"

"Yes."

Logan hung up. For a moment he sat in the chair, oblivious to the view outside, the faint alarm that was now beginning to sound even here, in the Tower—everything. He integrated what he'd just learned into the scenario he'd been piecing together. Scott Prawn, a supervisor on the fulfillment line: dead. Not fabrication . . . *fulfillment*. And there were the final words of the BioCertain programmer, Cardiff, as Dafna had just repeated: *I built the key; I can use it to unlock all this. You'd better keep me safe. Without me, those clients of yours are going to die!*

The trigger defaults to on, not off.

"Grace," he said, "get me Dr. Purchase."

His guardian angel seemed to understand the gravity of the situation, because she made the connection without persiflage. When Purchase answered, Logan spoke quickly, giving him instructions similar to those he'd given Dafna, and telling him to bring all the digital forensic tools he could carry.

Next, he reached out to Roz Madrigal in VR. As soon as she heard Logan's voice, she bombarded him with questions: What was happening? Why the lockdown, why the sudden station-keeping alarm? He did his best to calm her; told her who to expect; and begged her to keep them safe in the labyrinth of VR studios and labs until he got there himself. He also told her he'd take care of alerting Wrigley.

After disconnecting with Madrigal, Logan took a second to compose himself. Now came the most difficult—and most critical—conversation of all.

He asked Grace to connect him once more. A feminine voice, faintly accented, answered his emergency summons. "Wing Kaupei."

"Ms. Kaupei—Wing—this is Jeremy Logan. Please don't hang up. Listen to what I have to say."

Silence, rather than affirmation, came over the line.

"I don't know everything. Not yet. But I know a lot. Cardiff's dead—shot in the middle of being questioned. And the man in Fulfillment, Prawn . . . he's dead too, although you may know that already. Much of what you intended to delete has resurfaced— enough to explain how your extortion was intended to operate."

He thought he heard a catch of breath on the other end of the line.

"But I also know this. If somebody is killing the rest of your team, then you can't be safe, either. Whatever the case, the plan has gone south, and you're in danger. I can help you, Wing; *I can help.*"

When there was no answer, he continued, with all the reassurance he could muster. "I know from your perspective things are spinning out of control. That's my perspective, too. But the most important thing is *I can keep you alive.* This assassin, or operative, or whoever is stalking your team, it seems to be just one person. Chrysalis has far greater assets at their disposal. This is their home ground, Wing."

He paused. "We can still work this out. You won't have the death of a thousand innocents on your conscience. In the end, isn't that what matters? Wing?"

No response.

"Wing?"

And now he realized the line was dead, the connection terminated. Exactly when, he didn't know . . . but somehow he dreaded the thought of asking Grace.

50

On the twenty-seventh floor of the Chrysalis spire, Wing Kaupei had opened a bottle of Perrier Jouët Belle Époque brut and was now waiting for the storm of tiny bubbles in its neck to go quiet. Once they'd receded below the gold-foil capsule, she reached for the tall crystal flute that sat on a nearby table and poured herself a large glass.

The expensive champagne had been in her refrigerator for a month, purchased at the high-end wine store on the main concourse awaiting this special moment.

She glanced over at her Sentinel earpiece, flung across the room. This wasn't the moment she'd planned to celebrate, exactly—but it was indeed special.

Wing was no stranger to witnessing failure or tragedy. At Tsinghua University, she had been accepted not because she could afford tuition, but because she was the most promising student. On her way to winning full scholarships in molecular biology, she had seen many brilliant young people fall by the wayside. She was young herself, and seeing the dreams of others shattered with machinelike precision was unnerving. To compensate, she lost herself in physical activities, kung fu and especially—after that deadly art was banned by China in 2017—competitive diving. Her family was originally from the Shengsi Islands, where her father was head of a large fishing cooperative, and Wing had spent much of her childhood in the water. Fearless by nature, she excelled at the technical aspects of the highest DD dives from the ten-meter board, and her mastery of the difficult inward tuck made her a contender for the Olympic team—until her unique skill set attracted the attention of State Security instead.

For three years she was sent away, first to learn the forbidden arts of espionage, then to practice them in service of her country. Her skills in biology and pharmacology, as well as her innate courage and athleticism, made her valuable—until the day she learned her father's fishing cooperative, after protesting its takeover by a corrupt provincial leader, had been ruthlessly broken up and her father sent to Qincheng Prison, where he'd died under mysterious circumstances shortly thereafter.

This—and the unknown fate of her mother—had been deliberately kept from her to ensure she continued functioning at peak efficiency. But her headstrong, courageous, and at times impulsive nature caused her to go underground, and—hope replaced by cynicism—sell her services to the highest bidders.

In time, rebelliousness ebbed and she found a job that reawakened nascent intellectual interests: biochemical research at the Chrysalis labs. Here, she could bury herself in her work and even practice competitive diving: the Torus boasted a world-class pool, and she enjoyed perfecting the various elements of the sport: the approach, the flight, and the entry into the water. She was attracted to the grace, control, and elegance of the flying dive in particular, and disappointed that it was a lost art, infrequently performed in competition.

She finished her champagne, set the glass aside, and rose from the sofa. The French doors to the balcony of her private quarters—a perk of a scientist who'd attained her level—were partially open, the curtains fluttering in the crisp evening breeze. She walked past them and onto the balcony, grasping the railing and letting the smells of autumn, intensely fragrant at this altitude, fill her nostrils and rustle her hair. Several floors above, she could see the outlines of the large parapet where she'd spoken to Cardiff. Remarkable how little time had passed since then. She'd told him she clenched the railing due to fear of open spaces, but this was a lie: whenever she found herself far above the ground, she balled her fists instinctively, muscle memory of gripping the rails of a diving board rising up from her limbic brain.

Cardiff. He was a fool. But then, she was an even greater fool. She had found peace in the Chrysalis labs . . . but when a conglomerate that had employed her during the dark years reached out once again, she realized that, by chance, a perfect opportunity was literally at her fingertips. The Neanderthal vectors, the potential modifications—and the money they offered—proved simply too much to pass up. Agreeing to their proposal, and giving up the peace she'd found, had been the biggest mistake of her life.

Whether through lack of discipline, or years away from the espionage business, she had chosen two imperfect candidates for the necessary jobs—Cardiff and Prawn. Clearly, she had not sufficiently considered their characters. That mistake was hers, and she owned it. But the mistakes that killed those two had been their *own* shortcomings: conceit, impatience, and fear. And by way of collateral damage, their mistakes had doomed her as well.

She glanced at the darkening valley around and below, hands flexing automatically as they gripped the railing. She'd read about Jeremy Logan and some of his more headline-worthy accomplishments, and when she'd seen him with Dr. Purchase in BioCertain, she'd guessed why he was at the Torus. But he was wrong if he thought he could save her—or save anybody. For the thousand clients, it had been too late ever since their individual devices were most recently refreshed—and for herself, she knew the man calling himself Reginald Bryant was here for one reason only . . . and even were she to evade him, there would always be others. It had all scattered beyond her control.

And now, with the instinctual athleticism she'd always been

blessed with, she pulled herself up onto the railing and balanced easily upon it. The unimpeded view was breathtaking in the afterglow, and the night wind that had teased her hair a moment before now teased her ankles. As more and more lights came up in the Tower, she knew people might notice her. A shame that, if they did, they'd be too ignorant to appreciate her mastery of technique.

She took a deep breath, mentally preparing in the way she always did. And then, crouching slightly, she launched herself into space.

Immediately, she knew her initial mechanics—angular momentum and dive trajectory—had been well executed. There was nothing stopping her from achieving her favorite position, the nearly forgotten flying one-and-a-half. From the initial swan dive, she used the force of her approach to fold her limbs into a pike position, and her momentum to complete one and a half rotations. As she came out of this—eyes open, as she'd been taught—she saw the well-illuminated entry point was still quite some distance below her. This meant she could concentrate on maintaining the simple beauty of the flight—body vertical, arms tucked close—until at last the unappreciative earth claimed her.

51

Roz Madrigal looked over the motley—there was really no other word for it—group that had gathered in Theater One of the main soundstage, adjacent to the Chrysalis VR labs.

First to show up had been her boss, Wrigley. His slicked-back hair was askew, and the forty-eight-hour shadow he meticulously affected had been let slide an extra day or two. He told her to turn off all the lights on the soundstage, empty the R&D labs on the pretext of some last-minute electrical work in preparation for the morning rollout, and get ready to greet a few guests—quietly.

The tech staff had been working for days straight, and were only too happy to get an unexpected break—Wrigley, Roz said, would alert them when it was time to return. An Awareness alarm had been set off throughout the Complex, but this wasn't especially uncommon—a level-one alarm could be anything from a stuck elevator to a collision of passenger carts on the concourse—and nobody paid attention. Roz got the last holo-artist out and managed to collect half a dozen Li-ion flashlights just seconds before the next person appeared: Dr. Purchase of BioCertain. He looked nervous, and as she escorted him into the darkened theater, she felt it grow contagious.

Next was a thin, youngish Black man she had seen on rare occasions—at a rave or one of the restaurants—but whom she'd never actually met. He seemed reluctant to introduce himself, but

after an awkward moment said she could call him Virgil. He nodded at Dr. Purchase upon entering the theater, then walked into
the darkness and took a seat in the rear.

Five minutes later Jeremy Logan appeared, and then—
immediately afterward—the biggest surprise of all: Orris Peyton,
high priest of Chrysalis security, arrived in an electric cart driven
by a lithe, muscular woman with short black hair and cold, cobalt
eyes. Both were wounded. Peyton had a rudimentary tourniquet
around his right arm. The woman, who introduced herself as
Dafna, wore a pair of submachine guns slung crosswise over each
shoulder like fashion accessories. There was a shallow wound on
her neck that was bleeding freely, even as she dabbed at it with
some sort of compress. Even stranger was the sight of Karel Mossby,
who'd been barred from Infinium months before, sitting in the
rear of the cart with one wrist handcuffed to the seat frame. Dafna
unlocked Mossby and escorted him into the theater. Dafna, Peyton, and Virgil seemed to know one another, because Virgil immediately came down the aisle to check on Peyton, pulling a weapon
from his suit as he did so. Wrigley and Jeremy Logan joined them.

"What are you doing back here, you pariah?" Wrigley asked
Mossby.

"Everybody left their ID badges back in their own sectors,
right?" Logan asked.

Nods all around.

He turned to Dafna. "That query I sent you. Any luck finding
Wing Kaupei?"

The woman shook her head. "She is not in her quarters. A
search party was dispatched."

An urgent, whispered confab now went on for several minutes. Roz found herself holding her breath. If they'd only tell her
what was going on, she'd be a lot happier.

Finally, Wrigley detached himself. "Roz, would you mind

going to medical and getting a few things for the wounded? Hemo-static gauze, cotton wool, liquid bandages, betadine?" A pause. "Better bring some forceps and a couple fentanyl patches from the locker. We need to treat these wounds."

"One minute," Dafna said. "How far away is 'medical'?"

"The dispensary is just down the tech lab hallway."

Dafna nodded. "Be quick. Be quiet."

Roz dumped the flashlights she'd gathered on a chair and took one. As she turned away, a new conversation started up around Mossby.

"You know what you have to do?" Peyton gasped, clutching his arm.

"Your dominatrix here only told me about ten times. Locate the BioCertain line feeds supervised by this guy Prone."

"Prawn," said Dafna.

"Look for any meddling: video-frame jitter, or any other arti-facting that indicates looping. Isolate it. Restore the feed that was replaced by the loop."

"Right," said Logan.

"Piece of cake. Except for one thing: looping security vids is child's play, and undoing it is just as easy—but if whoever did it overwrote the original feed, then there's nothing left."

There was a pause.

"Normally, that might be true," Dr. Purchase said. "But the tangential backup system just suffered an, ah, abnormal shutdown. Certain material flagged for deletion can be recovered."

"'Tangential backup system'?" Mossby said, rearing back in mock surprise. "*Well!* You mean the secret project nobody knows about, but whose name begins with *H,* is screwed up?"

Nobody replied.

"This all sounds like loads of fun, but I don't see why I should help any of you," Mossby said. "I mean, not after what that bastard Kramer did to me."

Peyton started to speak, but the movement caused his words to morph into a groan of pain.

"Shut up, Karel," said Wrigley. "Okay, apprehending you was a mistake. You know it, and I know it. But just because security would never rest until they had you behind bars is no reason to whine about it now. We've got more important things to worry about."

"Wait a minute," Logan said. "You knew locking up Mossby was a mistake? That he wasn't a target?"

"He doesn't know that," Peyton said. "Obviously."

"See?" Wrigley said to Mossby. "They were running in circles, desperate for a suspect, almost *any* suspect. You were the raw meat. And, to be fair, you *did* keep trying to break back into the Palace even after I fired you."

"Hey, that's private!" Mossby cried.

"What palace?" Logan asked simultaneously.

"The 'Palace of Sublime Pleasures.' Shanghai, circa 1920. Karel's pet project."

"That's *private—!*" Mossby repeated.

"At first, I humored him. We learned a lot about coding virtual environments. But he just wouldn't leave it alone."

"And you never let me say goodbye to Rosebud," Mossby muttered petulantly.

Wrigley chuckled at the irony while Mossby went into a sulky silence. Meanwhile, Logan was busily putting this unexpected exchange together. *So, what? Mossby created some kind of personal bordello while Omega's persistent reality was under construction?* It made sense—perfect sense, in retrospect. No wonder Mossby got fired—and no wonder he kept trying to break back into Arc E. To see Rosebud, apparently. It seemed just the kind of thing Mossby would do. But he was too embarrassed, or proud, to admit it to security. Wrigley knew they were too riled up to listen anyway.

"So you were hacking away, breaking rules left and right," he said to Mossby. "But not to wreck Omega—to get back into your Palace of Sublime Pleasure."

"You'd do the same, if I had ever let you in," Mossby fired back, smart-aleck attitude returning to the fore. "These knuckle-draggers would never have understood. And speaking of that, Peyton, I think your boy Kramer enjoyed it—roughing me up himself. Doesn't he know how to delegate authority? Like, to somebody with smaller fists?"

Dafna jumped up and Logan stepped between them quickly, turning to Mossby. "You want a reason to help us? I'll give you a very good one. You might be able to save many innocent lives."

Mossby shrugged.

"There isn't much time. We're being hunted." Logan's voice rose in exasperation. "A *thousand* people could die."

"You know," Mossby said, "I read a statistic somewhere that said nearly two hundred thousand people die every day on our planet. That's, what, four hundred a minute? I mean, you nab me out of nowhere, lock me up for days, then administer a beatdown. For no reason. And now I'm supposed to help you save lives. I mean, really?"

"You can die, too," said Dafna, yanking the charging handle on her submachine gun and pointing the weapon at him. "How about saving your *own* life?"

Mossby licked his lips. "Hey, Chief," he told Logan, "this dominatrix is more persuasive than you are."

Roz was still standing near the door, listening in confused fascination. Now she heard Wrigley bark at her. "Roz!" He cringed at the noise he'd just made, lowered his voice. "Roz. *Hurry.*"

As she ran for the theater exit, she heard Mossby's nasal voice again. "Hey, another thing: a surgeon of my caliber needs the right tools for the right job. Like a fully configured supervisory workstation, with all clearances and a suite of forensic software."

"This way," Wrigley said.

. . .

Roz moved onto the stage, and the soundproofed door closed behind her with a deep *thunk*. Complete darkness surrounded her. She flicked on her flashlight and began making her way as quietly as she could toward the dispensary.

52

When Roz returned ten minutes later, heavily laden, she found the entire group had retreated to the control room: a long, narrow space, covered in uniform dark crimson felt and full of digital equipment—including a 128-track video mixing console—that wrapped around the back wall of the theater. As Dafna came over and began selecting various medical items, Roz noticed most of the others—except Snow, who seemed to be spending a lot of time on a portable radio—were grouped in a half circle around Mossby, seated at the supervisory workstation.

Everyone was fixated on the large central monitor above the workstation. It showed what looked like the feed from a security camera, monitoring the kind of clean room where the Voyagers were assembled—except that the objects moving along the two belts were not VR units but tiny containers. Robots, with cylindrical heads like the revolving nosepieces of compound microscopes, were bending over each container and—with long, thin hypodermic needles—filling them with precise motion. At one point, the belts stopped briefly while the robots backed away from the line and rotated their headpieces, bringing different hypodermics into place. Then the belts started back up again—carrying vessels of a different shape this time—and the robots went back to filling their chambers.

"Seen enough?" Mossby asked.

Nobody said anything, which Mossby took for assent. "This

is the doctored loop. Peyton, that's what your goons would have seen, if they'd been monitoring the security feeds."

He tapped a few keys. "Now: here's what was *really* going on."

The video started up again. Everything looked precisely as before—except this time a short, slightly overweight man in a lab coat was standing between the two belts. He had stationed himself in a staggered position relative to the robots. Like the robots, he too was holding hypodermics—one in each hand, in fact. They were of unusual design: while the needles were the same narrow gauge as the robots', the barrels were large and long, such as an equine veterinarian might use. He was injecting a small amount of the contents into each container, except that in order to keep up with both robots—one working the left line, the other working the right—he had to move very rapidly. There was no audio, but she could tell by his expression that he was nervous.

The line stopped, as it had in the first video; the robots backed away and swapped hypodermic chargers, changing meds again. Interestingly, the man did nothing but catch his breath. Then, when the lines started up once more—with different containers this time—he kept right on as before, injecting both lines with the oversize syringes.

After a few minutes, Mossby stopped the video. "Any questions?"

Logan's eyes were locked on the screen. "You're positive that's the same time, same location? No question?"

"No question. Security would have observed the first sequence, but the second sequence was what happened in real life."

"So Prawn *was* in there," Peyton said, gasping with pain as Dafna attended to his wound. "The bastard. I should have guessed, the way he was sweating during questioning."

"But what was he doing?" Snow asked. "Adding more medication? He didn't change meds when the second type of dosage chambers came down the line."

"It's far worse than that," Logan spoke up, silencing the room. He noticed Dr. Purchase at the end of the desk, lit by the glow of the wide monitor in the dim control room. Purchase's face had gone ghastly white, with the look of a man who'd just solved a puzzle—only to find it fatal.

"There's no time to explain the details," Logan continued. "We've got to find a technician named Wing Kaupei . . . *now*."

"So what's the problem?" Mossby said with a cocky grin. "Those were medical implants. And Prawn—that's his name, right?—was obviously dosing them with something he shouldn't have. Clearly, they've snuck some malware into a bunch of those implants, and unless you pay up by tomorrow, they'll release the payloads remotely. But look: they've messed up. Because now we know. This was all programmed to happen—so you just need to get the person who messed with the firmware of the devices to back out his changes."

"That person is dead." Logan looked at Dafna. "Just find Wing."

Dafna activated her Sentinel. "Get the search party on the line for me," she told her device. And then: "Forward Nine to Cortez. Do you have an update for me?"

The woman must have put the comm in broadcast mode, because suddenly the control room filled with a gruff voice.

"Cortez here," it said. "I was just going to check in." In the background, Roz could hear voices raised in alarm. "We located Wing Kaupei."

"You took long enough," Dafna snapped.

"Well, ma'am, she wasn't exactly in what you'd call a predictable place," said Cortez, sounding defensive.

"Where did you find her?"

"The lobby."

"What is so unpredictable about that, please?" Dafna asked.

"I didn't say in the lobby. On its roof."

A chill, like a breeze stirring dead October leaves, rippled through the group.

"Can you bring her here?"

"Forward Nine, that depends. Which piece would you like me to bring?"

Dead silence; then Dafna ended the transmission.

Sitting at the workstation, Mossby now had a more somber countenance. "That person you just mentioned—Wing? Was she the brains behind all this?"

Logan looked at him, nodded.

"And you said the person who could reverse the program is dead, too?"

Another nod.

"Oh," said Mossby. "Well, then I guess we could be fucked."

53

Reginald Bryant moved away from the windows of his suite. From this vantage point, he'd had the luck—if that, indeed, was the word—to see where Wing landed.

He sat on the end of his bed, looking at himself in a large mirror. He'd been lucky: the 9x19 round had passed cleanly through his side before the hollow point could mushroom. More than a flesh wound, but less than incapacitating: another inch or two closer to his spine, and it would have been a different story. As it was, he'd cleaned the entrance and exit, stopped the bleeding, and applied the kind of field dressing he had employed on others several times. The bandage would allow him to move with as much ease as possible.

He was shirtless, having discarded the bloody security outfit and donned the jumpsuit worn by Chrysalis electrical engineers. These workers had more leeway to move around the Complex than almost any others. Currently, its top was pooled around his midriff. Now he pulled it up gingerly over his shoulders, fastened it, added a fresh ID badge from the set in his suitcase, and examined himself again in the mirror. Good—very good. Nobody would pay him any mind, especially with a level-two alarm going off everywhere. And since he'd "broken his profile" with the addition of some facial hair and a little makeup, he shouldn't be flagged by any recognition systems, either.

Not that he would be in any case: he did not know much about the technological entity known as the Helix—only what scraps Wing had told him, but it seemed not only to be heavily integrated with all Chrysalis systems . . . but malfunctioning as well.

So much the better.

He stood up, moving this way and that, checking for pain. The jumpsuit fit well while concealing the weapons he carried. His side felt sore, of course, but he'd applied a strong topical anesthetic and there would be no more bleeding. He could move without a limp—and, if needed, move quickly.

He felt a sharp twinge, and he sat down again on the bed to apply a little more anesthetic. If he really wanted, he could just lie back on the bed, close his eyes, and call it quits. His mission had changed over the last few days due to unexpected events, but it was technically complete. Prawn was dead, and Wing—reading the tea leaves—had taken the honorable way out. Cardiff's apprehension had posed a problem, but he'd been stopped before he said anything too incriminating.

But in his mind that didn't mean his job was done: it simply meant a new objective. The cartel that employed him—a hybrid of corporate extortionists and ruthless venture capitalists—valued thoroughness almost as much as loyalty and success. He'd made sure that Prawn, Wing Kaupei, and Cardiff had paid the price of failure. But he also wanted to punish the target itself for noncompliance. This was important to his employers: it would be helpful in future negotiations. Asperton, the woman they'd chosen as the Chrysalis contact, had already been punished for lack of cooperation—as had Kramer, chief of security. A thousand more would die tomorrow, but nobody need know that was the plan all along.

Even so, entries remained on his punishment checklist. The man he'd watched interrogate Cardiff: he was overall head of Logistical Integrity. And the brains behind the Omega project, that useful smoke screen, Wrigley: losing that visionary would be a massive blow. Then there was the high-profile troubleshooter, the so-called enigmalogist. Jeremy Logan. From what Bryant could piece together, it was Logan, more than anyone, who'd stirred up this wasp's nest. Logan interested him—he sported a background and skill set that was unique. Bryant would find it just as sporting to kill him.

Eliminating those three would constitute a fitting punishment—and free him of any residual taint from an operation gone wrong due to the shortcomings of others.

He stood up again, moving just a little slowly. The pain was now less noticeable, and his movement unimpeded. He turned his attention to his suitcase. It was time to deal with the checklist.

54

"It just turned eight thirty."

These were the first words Logan had heard uttered in at least twenty minutes. Coming out of a semi-stupor, he looked up and saw it was Dafna who spoke.

Everyone he had gathered together the evening before—Peyton, Dafna, Mossby, Dr. Purchase, Roz, Snow, Wrigley—were sitting around tables or on the control room floor, in the ghostly quasi-illumination. Beyond, Theater One was dark. Shortly after midnight, in direct consultation with Christie and the rest of the board, Peyton had escalated the entire Complex to Awareness level three: all personnel were to be either on shift, or in their quarters, until further notice. This meant the VR workers Roz sent away had returned to their desks, but she'd made sure to pass the word around that Theater One and the production lab were temporarily off-limits. Not that anyone would have time for wandering around: with Voyager going live in half an hour, every Arc E employee would have their hands full. Logan now looked at Roz, sitting on the carpeting, knees tucked up beneath her chin and arms hugging her shins. Although this was her territory, she ironically had little to do with the current crisis. Logan had chosen this space as a rally point because he knew it had extensive network access and a robust infrastructure . . . and, since the extortionists had chosen Voyager as a red herring, Omega seemed, perversely, the safest place to assemble.

This little group was the last line of defense. If they didn't act, Voyager clients would start dying at noon.

The time for the eight o'clock message promised by the extortionists had come and gone. The usual recipient, Asperton, was dead—and Logan sorely missed her calm, guiding presence. Peyton had taken the lawyer's Sentinel, and adjusted it so he could receive any incoming messages. But there had been none.

Logan cleared his throat. "I think it's a safe assumption they're not going to reach out to us anymore. But we have to assume the clock's still ticking. The default programming for these murders is on, not off. So let's quickly run through what we know—and then figure out what the hell to do with these last few hours."

There were sighs; a groan from Mossby. But nevertheless all eyes turned toward him.

"Dafna," Logan said, "what have you turned up about the conspirators?"

"There were three spies that we know of. Cardiff, the Bio-Certain programmer; Prawn, the lead on the BioCertain fulfillment line; and Kaupei, the scientist. All are now dead. The killer was not a Chrysalis employee. I would guess he was a sleeper agent—inserted to make sure things went according to plan."

"Did you kill him?"

"He was wounded, but got away in the confusion. Maybe he hid in a closet somewhere and bled out. But we have to assume he's alive."

Logan turned to Purchase. "What, exactly, concerned you so much about that doctored video?"

"In the *real* video, the line supervisor—Prawn—breached clean room protocol and was injecting a solution into the MMD loads. If you look closely, you'll see that Prawn wasn't filling the load chambers. He was filling the *reservoirs*."

"What?" several voices echoed at once.

"Cue up that video again and zoom in," said Purchase. "Slow."

Mossby took a seat at the console and restarted the undoctored video, this time at half speed, zooming in with remarkable clarity on Prawn. Now, Logan could see that the objects running down the belts contained two chambers: a large, forward chamber and a smaller one at the rear. The robots were systematically filling the forward chambers with medication; Prawn, meanwhile, was filling the rear chambers—with whatever was in his fat hypodermics.

"Okay," said Peyton after a moment. "So what?"

"We make devices for all kinds of medical administration: insulin, allergies, pain relief, psychotropics, and so on."

It was the last two Purchase mentioned, Logan thought grimly, that had done in Bridger and Spearman. He'd finally managed to get through to Spearman's doctor, who confirmed receipt of a new medication load for Spearman directly from Carewell just three weeks before. Bridger, Spearman, Williams . . . all artfully sacrificed to make it appear their tour of the Voyager rollout was the reason for their deaths.

"Over the last year," Purchase was explaining, "our designers conceived the idea of an extra medication chamber."

"Why?" asked Snow, who had finally put away his radio.

"Safety, backup, redundancy. For the same reason you have a reserve switch on a boat or motorcycle. Even though our devices are carefully monitored and the med loads replaced, it seemed wise to design the units with a spare reservoir . . . just in case." Everyone was looking at Purchase now, and he began to sound defensive. "With our implants getting smaller by the year, that left room for such a reservoir. In some units, it would be helpful to have a backup dose of the primary med. In others, it could contain epinephrine, or lidocaine, or other drugs vital in critical situations. If and when we brought those online, they could save lives."

"You said 'if and when,'" Wrigley said. The VR head had been looking increasingly restless—probably because nine o'clock was approaching and he wasn't supervising the initial rollout, which—without word from the extortionists—they had not dared delay.

"Reservoirs are included in many newer implant models now, but we haven't yet made them operational. We're still—"

"In short, the implants out in the world, as well as those being filled in this video, are all supposed to ship with their secondary reservoirs empty," Logan said. "But while the robots were filling the primary chambers with medications, Prawn was . . ."

Logan stopped. "Dr. Purchase," he said, "I think you'd better tell the others what you told me. About the Alaska expedition, and Wing Kaupei's work with Neanderthal DNA."

Purchase did just that.

"Jesus," Peyton said after Purchase fell silent. "So Wing synthesized the poison, got Prawn to fill the emergency reservoirs with it, and Cardiff to loop the security videos and establish the ransom communications. And made it all look like the Voyager rollout was to blame. But Prawn panicked and was killed by that fucking ninja embedded in security."

"Meanwhile, Cardiff secretly programmed a thousand implants to dump their emergency reservoirs, but he didn't tell anyone how to undo the programming—for self-preservation, maybe. His big mistake was the bad guys didn't care." Wrigley sighed in exasperation and apprehension. "And the whole scheme basically went south on them. They're all dead—"

"Except for their cleanup man," Dafna interrupted. "We don't know if he's dead or alive."

"The point is, they wanted a shitload of money by noon," said Peyton. "But since their agents all failed, it looks like they've walked away, the clock still ticking."

"And by midnight, a thousand Voyager clients will be dead," said Wrigley. "Even though it's the implants doing the killing, it's *my* product that will forever be tainted."

A short silence hung in the room.

"Mossby," Peyton said. "Can you verify what Cardiff told us? About his altering the implant firmware so it releases the poisoned reservoirs, and having the only key? I mean, we *saw* what Prawn did on video. But we only have Cardiff's word."

Logan watched as Mossby worked in silence for a few minutes.

"The system's acting wonky," he said. "For some reason, I can only access the console logs. Cardiff's fingerprints are all over Bio-Certain, but he only performed firmware downloads three times. Actually, the first two look like trial runs. Judging by its size, the third drop was live. The real deal."

"And when was that?"

"About a month ago. September fifth, three fourteen p.m."

"Who did it go out to?"

"Based on what Dr. Purchase said, I'd guess every client whose implants are new enough to have reservoirs." Mossby pushed himself away from the workstation.

"But Prawn only dosed a thousand devices, max," said Snow.

Mossby shrugged.

"Why don't we call?" Dr. Purchase said into the silence.

When everyone looked at him, he continued. "Everyone with an implant. We could get the list of drug-implant clients who are also early adopters of Voyager, and tell them—"

"Tell them what?" Peyton said. "Yank out their implants? Turn them off? Instead of one thousand, you'll kill—"

"The Helix," Mossby said.

All eyes swiveled toward him.

"We all know it's down there. I'll bet it stores everything." Mossby's eyes flashed with sudden excitement. "It's how you found out it was this Cardiff dude who sent that last message—right? And we know now that Cardiff also pushed out the malware. So, what's the first thing his malware's going to look for when it's activated? Tampering. But we still have two-way communication with all those implants out there. We *know* when Cardiff sent out his update. So we just use the Helix to locate the code from his firmware lock, null it out, then send out a new update that turns it off. Bingo! A simple story for simple people."

"Can't be done," said Snow.

Mossby frowned. "Why the hell not? You saw how I used those deleted packets to restore the video—"

"That's the problem: the deleted packets. When we froze the Helix to track the source of Cardiff's message, the input buffers overloaded and corrupted a chunk of header files. Data was becoming garbled, erased files were appearing in searches. Temporary fixes just started a cascade effect. It's built on a photonic framework: if we'd let it run wild, the optical cabling would literally melt. So, with no other short-term options, we shut it down."

"*What?*" said Mossby and Purchase simultaneously.

"Three hours ago." Snow unshipped his radio, waved it in emphasis. "We shut down the Helix."

55

In the tense silence that followed, the sharp warnings Asperton and Peyton had exchanged over temporarily freezing the Helix echoed in Logan's head.

It could crash the entire architecture. It's never been tried. You'll be yanking a hatch off a jet in midflight.

There are protocols for shutting it down—but with all the data streaming into the Helix, all needing to be processed and stored in real time . . . there's no mechanism for pausing.

His sixth sense—which had saved him so often in the past—whispered there was something else buried in that rush of conversations.

What am I missing, Kit? he asked his wife across the barrier that separated the living from the dead. *I know there's something.*

"Omega," he abruptly said out loud.

Everyone was deep in their own thoughts, and there was no response. Wrigley was standing in a far corner and speaking animatedly into his Sentinel, consumed with how the rollout—now a full hour in—was progressing.

"Omega," Logan repeated, loud enough for everyone to hear.

Peyton looked up. "What about it?"

Logan turned to Wrigley. "What's the status of the rollout?"

Wrigley took a moment to respond. "Thank God for all the unit testing. So far, so good: just normal hiccups. This 'go slow' business is making it difficult for my PR and customer support teams."

" 'Difficult,' " Purchase muttered. "Wait until noon."

Logan turned back to Peyton, more animated now. "Hear that? We're overlooking something—the Voyager rollout is under way."

"Yes, we know—and we have roughly two hours to celebrate before the shitstorm starts."

"No, no . . . you're missing the point!" Logan turned to Snow. "What about you?"

"What about me?"

"Do you remember what you said in security control, when you suggested freezing the Helix? Asperton asked: What about Omega? And you said—"

"I said it was indirectly integrated, so I could put a moat around it, but nothing more."

"Yes, put a moat around it—and *sequester* the data. Call me an idiot, but to me that implies the Omega portion of the Helix is still undamaged and operational. If it wasn't, the rollout would be stalled. Nonfunctional."

"So? That rogue code has nothing to do with Omega or the Helix. It's already in place, set to go off at noon. *Stopping* it is the problem."

"Jesus, will you listen? This Helix can do almost anything except cure cancer. You *would* have been able to locate and emasculate the malware, like Mossby suggested, if it was running. So if Omega's portion is still intact, why not leverage that to backtrack through the system and disable the coding?"

Peyton shook his head. "The whole blockchain structure is shut down. Even if it wasn't, the consensus algorithms would prevent us moving from Omega to the rest of the Helix system. They were built to be compartmentalized—that's why Snow was able to put a moat around it in the first place."

"What I'm saying is, your new Omega technology might be able to defeat that."

"The problem is *access*, Logan. The system is effectively brain-dead." Peyton paused. "Can I call you an idiot now?"

"No," someone said from across the room. It was Roz Madrigal—who'd hardly said two words since they'd hidden themselves away in this control room hours before. "I see where Logan is going with this. And he may be right."

"All right, Roz," said Wrigley, suddenly paying attention. "Tell us how Logan is going to part the Red Sea."

"Well . . ." She looked around nervously. "I know a little about the structure of the Helix. I mean, we rubbed shoulders with those Arc X techs practically the whole time we were retrofitting Bio-Certain's synaptichrons."

She stopped abruptly, aware the subject was verboten.

"Oh, go on," Peyton said. "You've dipped a toe in the dog shit—you might as well jam your foot all the way in."

This caustic remark seemed to stiffen her spine. "Omega technology uses fiber optics for pushing video fast enough to mimic HD-quality immersion. The Helix uses photonic—optical—computing for data transmission." When nobody spoke, she continued. "It's like Logan said. You might be able to find a way in with Omega's network, which is still functional, to access what you need from the Helix . . . *without* bringing it online."

"Can't be done," Peyton snapped. "Different systems, different architectures—and different interfaces."

Roz glanced at Logan with a knowing smile. "I don't think Jeremy is talking about accessing the Helix through a standard interface."

"No, I'm not," Logan said.

Now everyone in the room was listening intently. Roz raised her finger. "You're forgetting *this*," she told Peyton, and, very deliberately, she gently tapped the Sentinel unit cradled around her ear: once, twice.

"What is that supposed to mean?" Peyton asked.

"It means," said Logan, "if we can't access the software bomb that's ticking somewhere in the Helix by any normal way, we'll try it the *virtual* way—with Wrigley's VR technology."

Twenty minutes later, after giving Mossby time to run a few diagnostics, everyone was standing by the exit of the dimly lit soundstage.

"All right," Wrigley said to the assembled group. He seemed to be thriving on the adrenaline of the morning. "We've been live for ninety minutes, and our tech support teams are in panic mode dealing with typical rollout shit: they won't pay any attention to us."

"Where are we going?" Peyton asked.

"The cage."

"Why the hell are we leaving—"

"It's the only place we'll have the necessary equipment and computing extensibility. Come on, let's hurry the hell up."

"Hold on," Purchase said, nodding at Dafna. "What about her 'cleanup man'? If she's right, and he's roaming the Complex with unfinished business, that means we're the business."

"What, then?" Logan asked. "Let those thousand people die? We've already kept our heads down for hours trying to figure out an answer, and now we just might have one. We can't worry about unknown variables."

"*Time to move,*" said Wrigley, checking his watch. "I'll lead, and you follow like you're bigwigs, here to check on how the rollout's going." He turned to Mossby. "Tuck in your goddamned shirt. And hide the damn machine guns!" he told Dafna.

He glanced around a few more seconds, then pushed open the door.

They were confronted by a babel of voices, almost deafening after hours in the soundproofed control room. Logan walked quickly down the tech corridor behind Peyton, trying to look both curious and important at the same time. Dozens of workers were talking into their Sentinels, typing on keyboards, huddling in groups around screens.

"Roz," Wrigley said over his shoulder, "Mossby's going to need a shitload of equipment to complete this VR linkage—we've never done anything like this before. Can you gather it for him?" She nodded. "You, Snow—we'll need your Helix expertise if this is to have any chance of working. You, and *you*"—he looked back at Peyton and Dafna—"are going to cover our asses. If somebody is really still out there, you'd better drop him fast, before he shoots us, too."

"I'll loop in somebody stationed down at the Helix," Snow said to Peyton. "Someone who can access the right linear block."

Peyton nodded. "Loop away. We already have a date and time stamp—September 5. And we know who pushed out the malware."

"*And* from where," added Purchase. "Those implant updates can only be sent from one console in BioCertain."

They rounded a corner, walking faster now, and Wrigley spoke again. "Karel, my old ex-friend, you're now officially the pilot. If you need any help and Roz or myself aren't around, ask Purchase. Or Logan. They're just spectators, anyway."

He pushed open the door to a large room all too familiar to Logan: plain beige walls, a scattering of wheeled devices . . . and the grid-like cage, sitting alone in the middle with only cameras and action dollies for company.

Wrigley waited for the door to shut behind them. Logan, however, kept walking—across the concrete floor toward the cage.

"What do you think you're doing?" Wrigley demanded.

"Just what you requested. I'm going to part the Red Sea."

"*You?*" Wrigley said. "Roz should go."

"Roz is needed here. As are you."

"You don't know the first thing about this," Wrigley snapped.

"*I've* been inside. I know as much as anybody. Fact is, nobody can say whether this will work or not, because it's never been done. Using VR to leverage the common architecture of Omega and the Helix? It's unknown territory. It's also our only option."

Wrigley started to object, but Logan cut him off. "And I've got Christie's carte blanche—remember? With authorization to give any order, or take any action, to fix this mess. We'll need everyone here, sharing their expertise. And that means all of you outside the cage, monitoring the simulacrum. My job is to be guinea pig."

All eyes turned to Wrigley. After an excruciatingly long moment, he gave a slight nod.

With that, Logan took a seat and glanced at Roz. "Ms. Madrigal, would you do the honors, please?"

Roz quickly ducked into the cage, removed Logan's Voyager unit, and began arranging the equipment as she'd done once before.

"Wait," Wrigley said abruptly. "Give him the phase three prototype."

She paused. "We're still alpha-testing some of its—"

"We're likely to encounter problems at the air gap, and it's got a better chance of navigating those than the enhanced Voyagers."

After a hesitation, Roz left the cage, then returned with an unfamiliar device in her hand. It had two seams closed imperfectly by torx screws—all too obviously a prototype, advanced or not. He felt a momentary, almost undetectable pinch of discomfort as she set it in place. Then, after a quick check of the hardware, she backed out and closed the cage, hurrying toward Mossby, who was sitting at a control console near the far wall.

Logan looked around for a second. Peyton and Dafna were guarding the room's main door, submachine guns in hand. Wrigley had settled behind a large center console. Snow was at Mossby's side, talking into his two-way radio.

"Ready, Jeremy?" Roz's voice sounded in his ear.

Logan glanced at the clock: twelve noon exactly. Then he took a deep breath. "Go ahead, Alice," he told her. "Send me down the rabbit hole."

56

Logan's vision blurred, then dimmed, as it had done during the original demo. But when it came back into focus again, he felt something must be wrong. Because he wasn't in Neiman Marcus, being fitted for a shoe—but rather still in the cage, surrounded by all the same people. Outlines blurred slightly as the figures moved, like the combing artifacts of interlaced video.

"It's not working," he said.

"Why?" Wrigley sounded in his ear. "Because you haven't gone down a rabbit hole? This isn't a demo. Actually, I don't know what the hell you'd call this. We're going to be giving you instructions—as we figure them out—and you're going to follow them."

Logan glanced in Wrigley's direction. *Reassuring.*

"See that door at the far end of the lab?" Wrigley's voice sounded loudly in his ear.

"Yes."

"Okay. Exit the cage and head through it."

It was only now—as Logan stood up a little gingerly, opened the door of the cage, and began to move around the room—that the truly virtual nature of this new reality was driven home. Because he knew that in the "real" world, he was still seated. It was a strange, unpleasant sensation, as if someone was projecting a movie against the inside of his eyelids. Looking back, he had the truly peculiar experience of seeing his own self, sitting in the cage . . . but abruptly, the combing and jittering increased.

"Don't look at yourself!" Wrigley warned. "Unless you want to end up a *real* guinea pig. That might cause a feedback loop we've never even simulated. Head for the door. And quickly. Remember, this isn't a demo: it's not going to be anything like the first time around."

Logan tried to ignore the visual artifacts and concentrate on walking toward the door. Wrigley was right—even the sense of movement felt different.

He felt the floor beneath his feet, and the doorknob in his hand. He opened the door, stepped out, closed it behind him. He was in a narrow corridor, with storerooms to one side and labs to the other. This was obviously a back-office area, because it seemed completely deserted—with the rollout currently under way, it was all hands on deck in the primary workspaces. He felt a certain relief, now that he couldn't look back at himself sitting in that cage.

"Walk down the passage and open the second door on the right," Wrigley told him, his voice so loud Logan almost winced.

Following the directions, he stepped into an empty equipment space. "Why are you shouting?"

"Because of the passthrough."

"What?"

"The passthrough, for God's . . ." Silence as Wrigley got his impatience under control. "It's VR terminology. Video passthrough controls how much of the real world you can still see, so you won't bump into things. Audio passthrough does the same. I have the gain turned up because the farther we get into unknown territory, the greater the interference is going to be."

"What kind of interference? Can I compensate?"

"A, I don't know, and B, you can't. Now: turn to your left. Do you see a door labeled KEEP CLOSED AT ALL TIMES?"

"Yes."

"Open it."

Logan did so, to find himself staring at a veritable forest of cabling. There was an occasional thick trunk line, but the majority were slender: coaxial or the even narrower fiber optic. At about chest height was a service box, riddled on both sides by wires and cables entering and exiting.

He could hear voices from the prototype unit: conversations that, though sounding inside his head, were actually taking place in the lab. Then Wrigley's voice returned. "See that metal box within all that cabling?"

"Yes."

"I want you to reach out, open it, and put your hands inside."

Logan opened it. "It's full of wires."

"Of course it is. You should see a thick blue one, striped white, with a plastic access port bisecting it."

"Got it."

"Okay." A brief moment of conversation between Wrigley and Mossby. "Hold on to it tightly. This . . . this is going to feel a little weird."

"What is?"

"You'll find out. Look—just *hold on*."

Logan grasped both sides of the little plastic port, feeling foolish. Nothing happened for about ten seconds except an increase of babbling from the production lab. Then Logan felt a strange sensation in both hands. His fingers were flexing of their own accord. A moment later, he realized that wasn't quite right: the plastic port was swelling alarmingly.

And then he understood. In this virtual reality, he was shrinking—faster and faster.

57

Logan grabbed onto the box for dear life as he felt himself lifted off the ground, making a bizarre ascendance while first the cable closet, then the metal box, and finally the access port itself grew larger and larger. Instinctively he compensated, ducking this way and that, to find that within thirty seconds he was standing on the floor of what, moments before, had been a plastic housing no larger than his thumbnail.

He realized Wrigley was shouting in his ear again. "Logan?"

"Yes?"

"Where are you?"

"I'm in a place where the words 'Made in Japan' are taller than I am."

There was a faint echo of laughter, a rush of excited conversation. A moment passed before Wrigley spoke again.

"Jesus Christ, it worked! Talk about thinking outside the box—I should get a Nobel for this."

"It was Roz who thought outside the box. And I'm the one who survived this Kafkaesque shriveling. I might have been lying on the floor now, squashed like a roach."

But Wrigley was still so excited that he didn't rise to the bait. "If I'd tried to explain, it would have taken ten minutes—and you'd probably have fallen. Now: turn to your right. See the exit cable?"

"Yes."

"What can you make out? Is it dark?"

"No—it's illuminated by a light. Faint, pulsing occasionally."

"What you're seeing are optical signals—well, virtual recreations of signals. Okay, listen closely." A pause for more rapid-fire discussion. "I'm told there are three steps to this—four, if you count what you've just done. We have to get you—or your simulacrum—to the physical juncture where the fiber optics supporting Infinium terminate at the OEO."

"What?"

"The optical-electrical-optical . . . just think of it as the no-man's-land between the optics running through our systems and the optics running through the rest of the Helix."

"Understood."

"The pathway that leads there is far too complex for you to navigate. So we're going to send an optical pulse through the prototype Omega III you're wearing: one that will require interfacing with the unsequestered part of the Helix. At least, that's the theory. Now, hold on and prepare yourself."

"For what?"

"To be honest, I don't know. We're off the map right now. Just hang on while Mossby figures this out."

Just hang on. Logan hadn't known, of course, what was involved in leveraging Omega's VR technology to access the Helix, but . . .

Suddenly—without warning—he was propelled forward at terrifying speed, like a bullet from a gun. He shot down a dozen, then two dozen, then countless cylindrical passageways, threading abrupt curves, the walls around him narrowing, lights changing intensity with unbelievable rapidity. He dropped; blew down a particularly long, narrow tube; dropped again, farther this time. Worse than this unexpected breakneck journey was the utter strangeness: there was no sound, no feeling of motion, no rush of wind in his ears or G forces pressing against his chest.

. . . And then as suddenly as it began, it stopped, and Logan found himself facing a wall. But it was like no wall he'd ever seen: it throbbed as if alive with energy, and its color changed subtly from black to purple before returning to black. He put out his hand to touch it, but some instinct prompted him to pull it back again.

"Logan?" Wrigley was calling.

"Yes?"

"What just happened?"

"I don't know. I don't ever want it to happen again. I must be ten miles from where I was."

"I think it worked!" This was said, not to Logan, but to the others in the lab, because once again he could hear an excited confusion of voices. "So what's in front of you? A portal of some kind?"

"Looks more like a door, but . . . well, given the 'photonic' computing, that's probably right. Because this thing seems to be almost shimmering—like an oasis."

"That's the portal. Now, you'll need to cross the terminator and enter the primary ring of the Helix. Then it's just a question of locating the right data block, and . . ."

Wrigley went silent. There was some kind of commotion, it seemed, going on in the background of the lab. Logan could hear raised voices.

"Wrigley?"

"I'm here."

"You were saying: locate the right data block, and—?"

"And that's where Snow and Mossby come in. In fact, Snow's going to pick it up from here. I've taken you as far as I can."

"So what do I do? Open the door?"

"I'd, um, suggest jumping." Wrigley seemed distracted. More noise in the background, apparently shouting, but Logan could still make out Wrigley: "I heard you, *I heard you!* Are we ready on this end?" A distant affirmation.

In a moment, he was back on. "Okay, Logan? Jump!"

Logan jumped.

There was a brief moment of pain in his head—a pain like he'd never experienced, as if his cerebral cortex was a balloon and some force was inflating it, pressure building by the microsecond—and then he felt his virtual self, which seemed to have been falling, land on a dark, smooth surface. He stood up. The intense pain had vanished as quickly as it had appeared.

"Logan?" A different voice was speaking to him now—Snow. "Can you hear me?"

"Yes."

Snow whistled with awe. "You passed through the barrier?"

"I think so. And it hurt like hell."

A pause. "That might have been some manifestation of the signal conversion. Or perhaps the 'sinkholing' necessary to direct you into the right traffic flow. But congratulations—you just crossed the moat."

"Congratulations is one word for it. Tell me I don't have to come out the same way I went in."

"You don't. Where are you, exactly?"

Logan looked around. "At the end of a single large cylinder. It's dark, but ahead I can make out some illumination."

"All right, that's . . . yes, I suppose that's how it would appear. You're in Helix Prime now, and I'm going to guide you to the exact node storing the data of Cardiff uploading his rogue code. Dr. Purchase gave us all the specifics before he left. Hopefully Mossby can take you the rest of the way."

"Okay, I—" Logan paused. "Purchase left? Why?"

"He'll be back. He just . . . well, we've just learned two clients have died."

"Clients?"

"Of the Voyager rollout."

Virtual or not, Logan felt his shoulders slump. He'd entered the rabbit hole at noon precisely . . . and been so distracted by the task at hand that he'd almost forgotten the full impact of the hour—or why this desperate attempt was so urgent.

A thousand could die. It seemed that threat was becoming reality.

58

Purchase knelt over the porcelain bowl again, feeling another dry heave coming on. He'd long since brought up everything in his stomach, but the heaves seemed disinclined to stop—he'd kept on flushing, and retching, and flushing again. Ten minutes had passed, and here he was, still kneeling on the tiled floor, one hand on the toilet seat and the other around the tank, hugging it as tightly as a child would a teddy bear.

They'd told him to calm down and stop shouting. They'd said this was no time for hysterics. Peyton and that frosty one, Dafna, hadn't even wanted to let him out of the lab. But when they'd seen the greenish pallor rise in his face, they'd moved aside instead of getting doused in puke. The rear hallways of Omega R&D had been mercifully empty, and he'd just managed to make it into a men's room stall before the geyser came.

Calm down. Stop shouting. Easy for them to say. It wasn't their brainchild that had been weaponized. Implant research was his baby. It was his life. And he'd helped shepherd it from the crude offerings of other medical design companies to what it was today, without taking the easy route of other firms he could name, who relied on the 510(k) pathway or pre-market approval of "predicate devices" to avoid clinical trials. He'd insisted on the most stringent tests, made sure BioCertain's offerings passed the strictest clearances: his own. And with only one aim: to improve lives, to *save* lives. But thanks to cruel fate, those same implants were being used to kill.

All this time—as his own investigations had revealed more and more, as the ramifications of what the others told him sunk in— he'd been able to compartmentalize the possibility that his devices would kill people today. But his Sentinel didn't compartmentalize. It had merely signaled, with an unusual alert tone, twice—then gone on to provide him with details. A man, seventy-three, whose heart stopped following sudden, unexpected diabetic ketoacidosis. A woman on their newest beta-blocker, who'd abruptly gone into V-tach and then just as abruptly to sudden cardiac arrest.

They wouldn't—shouldn't—have died so quickly. The man exhibited the first symptoms at four minutes past noon; the woman, at 12:07. They were both dead by ten minutes past.

Now he pushed himself up to a kneeling position, supported by his legs instead of the porcelain. Wrigley had been hit hard, too—he'd seen it in his face. But VR had only been the red herring. He, Francis Purchase, was in charge of the devices ultimately responsible. It meant his career, of course, but that was nothing compared to . . .

His Sentinel sounded again: that same unusual tone. *Christ, not a third one already—*

It was at that moment he felt a gloved hand curl around his mouth, and cold sharp steel press against his neck. "Dr. Purchase," came a muffled voice.

It was a statement, not a question.

"No yelling," the voice continued. "Just bring me up to speed—as fast as possible."

The voice had an accent Purchase couldn't place. As the pressure on his lips eased slightly, he struggled to process what was happening. "Up to speed," he repeated.

Suddenly, the man—it was obviously a man—shoved a device

into Purchase's field of view. It was a security-issue Chrysalis transponder, with half a dozen signals locked in on its screen. "Mossby. Peyton. Logan. They're nearby. What are they doing? Tell me, now, and maybe I'll let you live."

Purchase felt himself drifting into shock. Was he perhaps going mad? It didn't matter. His professional life was over—which meant he had nothing to live for.

A fierce pain lanced into his neck. It dug deep, scraping one of the cervical vertebrae—or at least, that's how it felt. The blade retreated; the pain remained. Purchase felt blood begin to run down to his shoulder, then his chest, in a thin, warm stream.

Fear brought him back to the present moment.

"The one thing you don't have is time," the voice said. "Give me the objective, layout, complement—you have five seconds to start talking."

Purchase, now focused on the pain in his neck, parsed the military terminology. "You'll let me live?"

"I said I *may* let you live. But if you don't tell me everything, immediately, I'll hose this stall with your blood."

For a moment, Purchase's jaw worked silently. Then—feeling the pressure of the blade on his throat again—he managed to find his voice.

59

Roz Madrigal sat on a tall stool beside Wrigley. The most critical part of their work was done—guiding Logan to the Helix interface—yet they remained, glued to the monitoring stations.

She stared at Logan, seated in the cage, various leads snaking away from his arms, chest, and the prototype Omega III module framing his right ear. His eyes were sometimes open, more often closed—but even then, she could see rapid movement behind the eyelids. Everybody who experienced Omega VR moved in one way or another: usually, it was just involuntary jerks of a finger, a shift of the head to avoid some imaginary object—and, of course, the inevitable smiles brought on by the novel experience. But Logan was far more active. At times his legs churned, as if running or climbing; he gasped occasionally, from effort or pain—and whether his eyes were open or closed, his head was constantly in motion, searching for a path through the digital maze his avatar was navigating.

She had retrieved some equipment Mossby requested, along with a few items she handed off to Dr. Purchase and Snow, the security spook from Department X. She'd set up Logan in the cage and guided his progress with Wrigley. But now there was nothing more she could do. The necessary framework had been jury-rigged: either it worked, or it wouldn't.

Dafna remained at the main entrance to the lab, gun at the

ready, while Peyton limped painfully from station to station, gazing around, now and then murmuring to Mossby.

A beep—low and insistent—began once again to issue from the monitoring device Dr. Purchase had asked for, tied into a Bio-Certain feed that would alert him to any malfunctioning Voyagers. This was the fourth time it had gone off. When it first sounded, the implants designer nearly had a fit; the second time, he'd rushed from the lab. A part of her resented him for setting up the device, which was obviously linked to implants that began to malfunction. It was already well past the noon deadline—why this perverse need for confirmation? She realized that he, like the rest of them, had been hoping this was a bluff . . . or that, perhaps, the deadly mechanism would fail.

"Will somebody shut that damned thing off?" Snow said. "I'm trying to guide Logan to the right node."

Almost gratefully, Roz slid off the stool, walked over to the device, and shut it off.

"He'll probably just turn it back on when he finishes puking," Wrigley said. "Assuming he ever does."

Peyton stopped his pacing near Mossby's workstation. "You've got everything you need?"

"Everything but Cardiff's malware."

"Mind hazarding a timeline?" The security honcho had, Roz noticed, become much more deferential to Mossby in the last hour or so.

"I need the code fully intact—and for that channel Purchase established to BioCertain's command terminal to stay live. Assuming Cardiff's code isn't encrypted, I just need to analyze it, repurpose, compile it into an upgrade wrapper—and send it out."

"To every client?"

"It's the only way. Any devices with backup reservoirs will immediately render them unusable. Any implant that doesn't will just ignore the code."

Peyton nodded.

Roz, listening to this exchange, now realized Wrigley was trying to get her attention. She glanced toward him.

Wrigley nodded toward the alarm she'd just muted. "That's the fourth. If these assholes keep their promise, they're going to be upping their kill rate significantly to reach a thousand by midnight."

A cold calculation—but Roz had been thinking the same thing. "Perhaps it needs time to scale up. Maybe I should head out and check on our people. They have enough on their plates keeping the rollout on track. If certain clients start going off-line for no reason . . . it could turn into a madhouse."

"That's good thinking. And Roz? Be careful."

As she made for the exit, she heard Snow speak in his radio. "Grady? Get ready down there—it won't be long." Then he lowered the radio and addressed the room. "All right! People, give me some quiet, please. I'm guiding this bad boy home."

60

As a child, Logan had been plagued by several recurring dreams. One—steeped in the supernatural—had ultimately led him to his vocation as enigmalogist. In another, he'd been trying to escape some off-world penal colony. He'd fled down a series of dimly lit, horribly long corridors, with the kind of low gravity that allowed astronauts like Gene Cernan to bunny-hop across the surface of the moon. Except the low-gravity hops in Logan's getaway nightmare had been agonizingly long: minutes spent gliding through air before he could land and take another jump. For most people who flew in their dreams, the sensation was exhilarating. For him, it had been just the opposite.

Especially cruel, then, that the transit of the Nexus reminded him so strongly of that dream. Unlike his high-speed, uncontrolled passage through the optical pathways of Omega, he was in control of his movements here—almost too much so.

For the last twelve minutes, Snow's voice had been guiding him down the photonic backbone of the Nexus. That's what Snow called it, and Logan hadn't asked for a clearer description. What he knew for sure was this time, they couldn't slingshot him to a destination. Now that he was outside the digital moat around Omega, the best Snow could do was optimize his route along the server farm, from one rack to the next to the next, while monitoring his approach to the one that contained what, more and more, began to feel like buried treasure.

The corridors—in reality, thin hollow cables barely wider than a thread—were all the same, save for their stenciled letters, and were all ridiculously long and straight. A combination of leaping and hopping—far enough to gain the most distance, without prematurely impacting the ceiling—was the fastest method of propulsion. At first, it had been almost unbearably slow. But he'd soon gotten the hang of the strange virtual gravity and was able to move along the backbone efficiently. One bound per rack; a brief transit of darkness, lit somehow by Snow; and then another bound through another rack. He felt like Major Heyward in *The Last of the Mohicans*, with Snow as his Natty Bumppo, guiding the way through a dim and trackless wilderness. He preferred not to consider what was actually taking place: via what was essentially a high-tech optical hack, he was using Wrigley's VR to move—with all the size of the tiniest mite—through the endless row of blade servers he'd seen, lined up in a lazy curve deep beneath the Torus. Somewhere nearby, walking alongside the racks of CPUs and following Logan's virtual progress via radio with Snow, was Grady, one of the worker bees who tended the Helix, making sure everything was on track and eventually—when the correct linear block was reached—who would do the physical work of downloading a specific node and transmitting its contents to the waiting Mossby.

"How much farther?" he asked Snow.

The answer that came back was garbled. This had become increasingly frequent the farther he proceeded. "Repeat, please?"

"Just keep on trucking. I'll let you know."

Shit. If Snow was being coy, that meant he still had a ways to go.

Although the brain that controlled the Helix had been shut down to avoid some catastrophic chain reaction, the physical ring itself remained nominally powered; in essence, idling. It seemed endless. Logan tried occupying himself by counting the server racks he'd transited. Eight hundred ninety, eight hundred ninety-one—

"Logan," came Snow's voice. "Stop at the next set of interstices."

He'd been at this repetitive motion so long, it felt like an effort to pause. Logan passed through the brief darkness between racks. "Okay."

"That stenciling on the locking mechanism. What does it say?"

Logan had to pivot his head ninety degrees upward to take in the entire thing. "Four Nine Able Foxtrot . . . Three Two Charlie."

"Okay. Go another two racks and read back its ID, please."

Twenty seconds later, Logan repeated the process. "Four Nine Romeo Victor Zero One Zulu."

"That's it." The garbled background noise of the lab grew briefly more distinct, and Logan heard Snow, conferring with Grady down there—*here*—by the Nexus. "I'm going to open a portal. Get ready."

Logan waited. A moment later, a black circle suddenly opened right before his feet. "Christ!" he shouted. "You didn't say it would be in the *floor*. I might have fallen."

"You're not going to fall. You're going to jump in—*now*."

Logan followed these instructions before he could think better of it. After about ten seconds of dropping past long, ghostly structures, he hit another floor—and bounced slightly.

"Ouch," he said. In his childhood dreams, he'd never felt his feet actually hit the ground as he ran. How strange that a fiber-optic tube—real, yet artificially reconstructed in this VR simulacrum— seemed so much more tangible.

"You're almost there. Now you're going to need to help us out. I'll explain as best I can. Around you, if my calculations are right, are the SSD drives storing Cardiff's activities of September fifth, around 3:10 p.m. We know which ones contain the program he uploaded to the medical implants, because under a microscope the code-storage drives differ slightly from the drives holding visual feeds. But we can't just go digging around randomly. So we're essentially going to do a little brain surgery—and you'll guide the scalpel. Follow?"

"No. Yes. I guess so."

"There should be a single optical passage ahead of you now—narrower than the backbone you've been traveling through. Do you see it?"

"I'm at one end of it." Rising to his feet, he realized just how narrow the transparent tube was—he'd have to crawl.

"Good. That's a fiber-optic line that channels data to integrated circuits. The true 'information superhighway'—currently dormant, of course."

"Of course." Logan wondered what would happen if the Helix wasn't dormant, and he was caught in a cramped tunnel suddenly busy with data. He shook these thoughts away.

"You're looking for ICs in rows of four," Snow said. "Ending in . . ." A pause. "Ending in nine-nine-four-nine." He repeated the number.

Logan started crawling, looking through the tall forest of silicon that rose dimly on both sides like silent sentinels. Among the mass of wires, transistors, diodes, and other confusing guts of the circuit boards, he could see numbers etched into the facing edges. They were small, even to his eyes. "They *all* end in nine-nine-four-nine."

"Good. Now: look for a specific set in which the conductive pathways on the underside of the boards are purple instead of green. Those are the ones we want. You'll find five, maybe six total."

Conductive pathways. Jesus. Logan moved forward more slowly, peering at the slabs of silicon. He could see what Snow was referring to: green lines like mazy rivers between projecting nodules of solder. As he crawled on, the green lines turned to purple.

He checked the number on the edge of the closest board. Nine-nine-four-nine.

"Found them," he said.

Snow's voice was suddenly tight with excitement. "How many?"

"Five, I think. Yes: five."

"All right." There was some background chatter. "Now listen. I want you to back up and brace yourself. You might feel an unusual sensation, a buzzing, or maybe heat. That will be your Omega device sending my man Grady an exact position. Next, Grady will extract the ICs you've located. You'll need to confirm he got the right ones—and that he got them all. Ready?"

"What happens once I've—" Logan fell silent. A tickling started up, inside his skull just behind his ear. It became warm, like a thermal pad. And then the warmth grew intense, and still more intense, until it felt like the inside of his skull was being microwaved. Just as he realized it was the prototype Omega III unit that was causing this, and he raised his hands instinctively to pluck it off, there was a massive tremor, like an earthquake. Part of the silicon forest ahead of him vanished, to be replaced by a flood of overpowering light. Through this light came an object so frightful in bulk that for a moment, Logan didn't notice that the pain in his head had vanished.

It was a huge pair of calipers, surrounded by spidery arms forming a diamond-shaped frame. On the ends of the calipers were feet of soft rubber, large as bookshelves. As Logan scrambled backward, and the calipers plucked out one of the monolithic slabs of silicon, he realized what they were: a pair of IC extractors, used to safely pull integrated circuits from their sockets. His heart was racing like mad. This was a situation beyond anything he'd ever imagined, and he willed his pulse to slow as he watched the extractor remove the five chips, one after the other.

There was a pause. Then the piercing light melted away; another brief earthquake followed; and the narrow corridor was once again cloaked in darkness.

"Did he get the right ones?" Snow asked, voice still tight.

Logan crawled forward, blinking in the dimness. "All five."

"*Fuck,* yes!" There was a babel of chatter as Snow apparently began talking to several people at once—Mossby, Grady the worker bee, others Logan couldn't distinguish. He let himself go limp in the narrow tube, back resting against the smooth virtual wall. They weren't done yet, he knew: Mossby still had to successfully extract the rogue computer program from the chips just removed, recode it, and upload the fix to the client implants—but for the moment, all Logan could think of was the miraculous journey he'd just undertaken to retrieve those precious bytes. Buried treasure wasn't a bad metaphor, after all. And it had taken the accumulated expertise of so many people, a synchronicity of technologies never intended to mesh, to—

Then he paused. The sounds of excited chatter in the background had changed. Over the garbled audio channel, he now heard what sounded like screams.

"Snow?" he called. "Hey, Snow! Can you hear me?"

He listened intently. They were undoubtedly screams—along with cries of pain. And there was something else, intermingled with the confusion and static: the steady, rhythmic chatter of machine guns.

61

Roz had followed Wrigley's orders and made a quick circuit of the customer service area. It was as busy as when she'd walked through nearly an hour earlier, if not more so. She glanced over a few shoulders of the people operating the workstations, looked at a dozen screens, and listened in on some conversations taking place between Chrysalis employees taking a coffee break in the adjoining canteen. She picked up no anxiety, no whispers of dangerous gossip. Either they were lucky, and the clients with sabotaged implants didn't line up yet with those participating in the Voyager rollout . . . or there were too few for anyone to start noticing.

Finishing the circuit, some instinct told her she could be of more use back in the lab. They'd done so much jury-rigging, and almost anything could go wrong—in an operation where *everything* had to take place in the right order, with no errors, to have any hope of success.

She moved quickly back down the corridor, stopped at the heavy door of the production lab, and gave two raps. It was cracked open by Dafna, who eased it back enough to allow Roz to enter.

She gazed around as Dafna closed the door. Everything was more or less as it had been when she'd left. Logan was still in the cage, all too obviously—from the jerky, awkward movements a mime might envy—within the simulacrum. Wrigley was monitoring him in a distracted fashion, and when he heard her return he glanced over, clearly relieved when she signaled *so far, so good.* Mossby was at the command workstation, and Snow was just joining him: they exchanged a few quick sentences; high-fived each other; then sat down together at the terminal, Snow handing Mossby his Sentinel and the hacker quickly syncing it to a data port on the far side of the desktop.

Peyton, she noticed, was still pacing the room. The blood from the wound in his shoulder had soaked through his jacket—he really should not have been moving. He was just approaching the rear door leading to the maintenance hallway.

At that moment, as if animated by her thoughts, the maintenance door opened. Peyton stopped pacing just before colliding with it.

Purchase stood in the doorway. He'd looked strange enough when he dashed out of the lab in a fit of nausea, but now he looked even stranger. His eyes were bulging, almost rolling in his head. A towel was wrapped around his neck and chest, like he was heading for a sauna. If she hadn't known better, she'd have thought he was sleepwalking.

As she stared in confusion, the implants director suddenly lurched forward and sprawled onto the concrete, the towel unfurling into a field of red. He had been shoved from behind by someone using him as camouflage, or shield, or perhaps both. The stranger behind Purchase was wearing the outfit of an electrical engineer, with a circle beard and dark hair. But he moved with such horrifying quickness she could make out no other features. Turning toward Peyton, rooted in place with surprise, the intruder administered a quick, knife-hand chop to his injured shoulder. As the infrastructure chief gasped in pain, knees buckling, the stranger grabbed the submachine gun from Peyton's shoulder, raised it while performing a one-eighty visual recon of the room, and then aimed a long burst at Dafna. Roz, just a few feet away, felt herself abruptly drenched in a spray of warm blood. Dafna had swiveled her machine gun into position, but with her boss in the line of fire she'd hesitated just long enough for the assassin to shoot her first.

For Roz, time began to slow down. As Dafna crumpled beside her, Roz saw Mossby dive from his chair and crouch beneath the console, arms rising protectively over his head. Wrigley dove behind a heavy equipment cart. Snow was leaping behind the console adjacent to Mossby, one hand balanced on its upper housing while the other pulled a handgun free. But even as she watched him, explosions of red began to blossom: first on Snow's left arm and then his left side, and what had begun as an agile leap turned into a tumble, ending brutally as Snow fell amid the equipment behind the console.

The intruder looked directly at her, barrel smoking, as if deciding whether to expend a few more rounds. He smiled faintly, or so she thought, and let his gaze continue past her, eyes registering Dafna bleeding out on the floor, passing the supine form of Purchase, then stopping at Peyton—who was rising to his feet, reaching into his jacket. The intruder let go with another sustained burst that dropped the security executive in a ghastly cloud of blood.

At last, the man turned toward the cage that held Jeremy Logan. For a moment, the device itself seemed to confuse him. But then, Roz saw something kindle in his eyes. And as he raised his weapon toward the oblivious Logan, Roz found her voice and began to scream. The man turned back toward her, and in that brief moment of hesitation the mortally wounded Dafna rose on one elbow, automatic weapon rising with her; Snow appeared over the upper edge of the command console, left hand bloody but right hand full of a big nine millimeter—and twin eruptions of noise and smoke shrouded the scene of carnage as Roz dropped to the floor like a wounded bird, a dead faint claiming her.

62

"Snow!" Logan called, pounding on the floor of the narrow tube. "*Snow!* Can you hear me?"

There was no reply—just the sound of automatic fire; a piercing scream; and then an even more furious eruption of gunshots. Logan, in a sudden ecstasy of frustration and claustrophobia, writhed in the tube like a maggot trying to shed its larval skin.

And then, as quickly as it deserted him, reason returned. He did what he should have done as soon as the chaos started— reached up to the prototype unit snugged around his ear and, with a sharp yank, pulled it free.

A brief darkness blurred his vision, and when it cleared he found himself once again inside the cage—in a scene of shocking chaos. Thick smoke—gunsmoke, from the stench of it—rose in waves from various locations in the room. As it cleared, he made out bodies on the floor, blood pooling into large puddles: Peyton. Purchase. Dafna. And a man in a Chrysalis service uniform that he didn't recognize.

My God.

Springing into motion, he pulled the hardware from his chest, head, and arms, jumped out of the chair, and exited the cube. The main door of the lab suddenly opened and a sea of faces looked timidly in from the corridor. This was followed immediately by screams.

"Close that door!" Logan turned to see Snow emerging from behind the command console. A moment later Mossby, too, rose from under the desk. Snow was clearly injured, but Mossby, though in shock, seemed unscathed.

Now Logan noticed Roz. She'd been lying beside Dafna, whose wounds were clearly fatal. But other than being covered in Dafna's blood, Roz seemed unhurt. She rose from the floor and began moving in a zombie-like shuffle. Next, Wrigley loomed into Logan's vision. He stepped to the door, forcing the onlookers back into the hallway, and closed it again.

Despite the carnage surrounding him, Snow seemed fixated on one thing: Mossby, and a Sentinel attached to some kind of input device and keyboard next to him.

"Well?" Snow gasped.

Mossby looked around; grimaced; then turned his back on the bloody scene. "Give me a minute, will you?" he said. "Christ, it's like the O.K. Corral in here."

Logan, joints as stiff as if he'd been in the cage a week instead of an hour, walked over to the shooter, picking up a large drum wrench on the way in case there was something that needed finishing. But the man was clearly dead, blood and brains blown out in a corona of gore. Peyton lay nearby, white shirt sodden with blood. His eyes fluttered open. For a moment, they focused, recognizing who was looking down at him, and Logan was sharply reminded of just how young the logistics chief was. Then the eyes closed and the limbs went slack.

"It's undamaged," Mossby told Snow. And then, a moment later: "I've got the code. It's not encrypted."

Logan began moving toward them, slipping twice in the blood that covered the floor. Roz had recovered her wits and was trying to stop Snow's bleeding. He remained bent over the coder, ignoring the ministrations.

"A lot of people just sacrificed themselves for this," Snow said. "And a hell of a lot more will die if you don't get this right."

"Will you shut up and let him parse the code?" Wrigley shouted. "Jesus."

Snow sat back, balancing a little erratically on the edge of the worktable.

"Call medical," Wrigley told Roz. "And call in our backup team. Third shift. We have to do damage control, get those people out there refocused on the rollout."

Mossby sat up straight, fingertips trembling slightly. "Okay. I can fix this cleanly. Just bypass the kill function with two instructions: a jump and a NOP."

Snow took a breath, nodded.

Logan came forward, still holding the drum wrench. He, Wrigley, and Snow encircled the coder like a protective shell. Mossby worked fast now, fingers flying over the keyboard. "Debugger's not complaining," he muttered. "I'm running it against three . . . four . . . five implants in a test environment." More typing. "Compiled and wrapped."

He cleared his throat.

"What now?" Logan asked.

"Commit." And Mossby pointed to a blue key at one corner of the keyboard. "This will activate the transmission interface Purchase wired into BioCertain's 'push' mechanism. In two minutes, three thousand implants, give or take, will get upgraded firmware. Rendering their backup medication chambers—if they have them—permanently inactive."

There was a brief silence.

"Well?" Wrigley asked.

"Well, what?"

"Go ahead. Commit."

Mossby looked stricken. "I'm not going to do it."

"But . . ." Wrigley hesitated in confusion. "You altered the code. You just gave the green light!"

"That's not the point," Mossby said, almost pleading. "It's not my *job*!"

Logan understood. Gently, he pushed through to the keyboard. "I guess it's my job, if it's anyone's." He glanced at Wrigley. "After all, it was you who said to part the Red Sea."

Logan extended a finger and touched the blue key. "So here goes."

63

Jeremy Logan entered the hotel lobby and paused, letting his eyes grow accustomed to the subdued light. It reminded him of the "snug" of an old English pub, only more elegant and on a larger scale. To the right, past a carven archway, was the front desk, discreet and pleasantly spare. He took three steps down into the lobby proper. It was a long and relatively narrow space, with a coffered macassar ceiling and plush, hand-knotted Persian carpets over the onyx floor. Small tables—the perfect size to hold drinks or cards for a game of bridge—were artfully placed along both sides of the room, each surrounded by deep wing chairs. Here and there along the walls, tall ferns rose from oriental vases, and oil paintings hung on the walls, illuminated by sconces and small brass chandeliers set close to the ceiling. To one side, halfway down the lobby, a fireplace with an oversize marble mantel was set into the ornate woodwork. The low, narrow design of the place practically oozed a cozy, sub-rosa sensibility, assuring the sounds of conversation would remain low and the passersby—other than waiters—infrequent. It seemed as if the space itself had been artfully planned to yield up, from time to time, new discoveries: a small, recessed bookcase here; a shadowbox of Tiffany glass yielding onto some objet d'art there.

Only a few of the dozen or so tables were occupied, and Logan quickly saw the party he was here to meet: sitting in one of the few banquettes, in the rear by the copper-fronted elevators. As he approached, they rose to greet him: Orris Peyton; Roz Madrigal; Virgil Snow—and Matthew Wrigley. They all looked more or less as he remembered them, save for Roz. It took him a moment to realize this was because he'd only seen her in her work garb of faded jeans, never a dress. And yet, come to think of it, though their faces were familiar, there was nevertheless something slightly exotic about the company as a whole: perhaps it was the unfamiliar setting, formally dressed around a table in an elegant lobby. Logan decided not to analyze. This had been their invitation; he'd accepted it; and as he looked from face to face, he absorbed the slight blows to the memory each brought back.

In the end, seven clients died from anaphylactic shock or other fatal conditions brought on by toxic drug interactions. BioCertain had dealt with these quietly, with generous compensations on an individual basis, and nobody—no ambulance-chasing lawyer or story-hungry journalist—had put it together . . . or, if they had, Logan had not been told. The fact was, until this invitation he'd heard very little from Chrysalis. He'd learned of the deaths only through inference and his own investigation: the dosing process had been accelerating as he left the cage, and perhaps there were a few others he knew nothing about. The Voyager rollout itself, however, had been a success—a rather spectacular one, in fact—and now Wrigley's pet project was the darling of the tech world and social media, its initial bugs quickly squashed and new iterations pushed out to clients on an almost weekly basis. Rival tech companies had been left trying to explain why they'd been caught so flatfooted, while the big, high-end retail chains had lined up, fighting for an opportunity to establish a "shopfront" in Wrigley's virtual, persistent environment. But Logan had learned all this from what he'd read in the papers, or online via his Voyager: already growing quickly obsolete, though his guardian angel Grace, through the magic of software updates, remained forever young.

"Sorry," Peyton said, indicating the glasses in front of everyone, "but we already ordered." There was an open bottle of Pol Roger, and another on ice in the wine chiller standing tableside. A waiter dressed in black and white came up, slipped a fresh champagne glass in front of Logan, bowed at an ever-so-proper angle, then vanished again.

Sitting closest to him, Snow picked up the bottle and drained it into Logan's glass. The atmosphere felt closer to that of a reunion than a postgame analysis, and Logan decided to let his hosts take the lead. He picked up the glass, noticing how the stem was already growing cold from the beverage; how the tiny bubbles rose to the surface in remarkably straight lines, only rarely colliding in a temporary, helix-shaped swirl.

He carefully tucked the word "helix" into the back of his mind and took a sip. Very dry. Very good indeed.

At this, everybody else raised their glasses in unison. "To the man of the hour," said Wrigley.

"And the day," Roz added. "And the week. *And* the month." A light laugh circled around the table, and the waiter glided up to remove the empty bottle, twist the wire cage and remove the cork from the fresh one, and refill people's glasses.

"Congratulations on your runaway success," Logan said, turning to Wrigley. "It's the same old story: I should have invested in Infinium back when I could."

"Don't worry," Wrigley said. "Your compensation should make up for that oversight."

Logan smiled politely. His fee had been handsome, though not quite at that level.

Something caught the group's eyes and he saw them looking away from him. Logan followed their glances and saw Claire

Asperton walking slowly toward them, a glossy black cane gripped tightly in one hand.

Logan had seen his share of ghosts and he instinctively caught his breath, allowing the shock to wash over him. She was significantly thinner, and there was a long scar running up one side of her neck that spoke of skillful but extensive surgery. But she was smiling, and other than the cane and the slow gait, the loss of weight conferred a more youthful appearance.

"Jeremy!" she said, hugging him. "What a pleasant surprise."

"Surprise is an understatement," Logan said. "I thought . . ."

"What? That I was dead?" Asperton slid into the far side of the booth. "Many others thought the same—even the EMTs, for a while. Luckily, there's a first-class emergency center in the Torus. I . . . I only wish we could have saved more."

A brief silence fell over the table. Logan, taking another sip, thought of Dafna, and Purchase, and the others, including the Chrysalis clients whose lives had been so needlessly lost. Then he thought of the others who'd died—the ones who carried out or enabled the dreadful plan. Clearly, the organization who'd backed them had retreated into the darkness from which they'd emerged: Wrigley, Roz, Peyton, and the rest would not be gathered here otherwise.

It seemed his job to break the silence. "It's so nice to see all of you. I don't often get a chance to see clients once an assignment is finished."

"It's not quite finished," said Asperton. "There are two items still outstanding. Here's one." She reached into her bag, withdrew an envelope, and pushed it across the table.

Logan held it for a second, admiring despite himself the thickness of its paper, its pleasant toothiness—as a printer might say—against his fingertips. Then he opened it. Inside was a nonitemized remittance sheet and a check. He glanced at the check twice—to make sure he'd counted the number of zeroes correctly—and then, before the moment became gauche, slipped it into his jacket.

"I've already been paid," he said.

"We thought you deserved something extra," Snow said. "We were all going to chip in our bonuses . . . until John Christie got wind of it and wrote the check himself."

"Thank you," Logan said, surprised and moved.

"I think I speak for the table," Claire said, "when I say we wouldn't be here if not for you. And I mean that literally, figuratively—and virtually."

Once again, glasses were raised; toasts were made; vintage brut consumed. "This is a beautiful hotel," Logan remarked. "I had no idea it existed. May I ask why you chose such a place for this reunion?"

"We heard you liked hotel lobbies," Roz said.

Logan raised an enquiring eyebrow.

"It was in *Vanity Fair* last year," Snow added. "That interview you gave. They wondered where, since you'd traveled so widely, you'd choose to spend the rest of your life. You said something about an elegant, discreet, dimly lit hotel bar, where the staff were all familiar and the patrons few."

"I think," Peyton added, "you also said something about 'an air of habitual restraint.'"

"Right. I'd forgotten about that interview." Logan looked around. "Well, whoever chose this did a good job. It's exactly what I had in mind."

"I read that you'd taken a vacation," Asperton said. "From breaking ghosts and solving enigmas, I mean. You'd gone back to teaching at Yale."

"For the semester that just finished up, true," Logan said. "But I've deferred the rest of my teaching schedule until next year."

"Is that a fact?" Roz asked. "So you've taken on some new assignment?"

"No," Logan said.

"*Yes*," the rest of the table countered in almost perfect chorus.

"You mentioned two items of outstanding business," Logan said, changing the subject without bothering about subtlety. "This was one—thank you again." He patted his jacket pocket. "May I ask what the other is?"

"That's more Matthew's department than mine," Claire said. She drained her glass. "Matthew, care to do the honors?"

"Sure." Wrigley stood up, his owl-like glasses shining in the light of the chandeliers. "Jeremy, mind coming with me?"

As Logan stood as well, he caught the others at the table exchanging glances. Roz Madrigal's eyes met his. She blushed, then looked down.

As Wrigley led the way back through the lobby, Logan caught the strains of "That Same Old Song and Dance" coming from a grand piano in a distant corner of the bar. Odd he hadn't noticed it before. "What's up with Mossby?" he asked. "Any fresh warrants issued for him lately?"

Wrigley laughed. "He's in the Torus, back working for me. If there was ever a coding geek with no life beyond the digital domain, that's him. He asked me to give you the finger for him. And that he'll see you around."

"Hardly likely."

"You'd be surprised."

They ascended the steps and reached the maître d's stand near the front of the lobby. Beyond this spot, Logan had not ventured. But now Wrigley took his elbow and led him onward, through the revolving doors of the hotel and into the cool whiteness beyond.

Outside was the echoing gallery of an elegant shopping mall, replete with canned classical music and shoppers laden with bags. Everything was immaculate. Logan looked around, taking in the upscale names of the surrounding shopfronts: Williams-Sonoma, Saks, Crate & Barrel, Gucci. Then he noticed the large brass name-plate on the front of the hotel itself. It was unmarked.

"Why isn't there a name?" he asked.

Wrigley turned. "Sorry?"

"The hotel. Why isn't there a name?"

"I don't know. What should it be?"

"What—" Logan began. "I don't know what to say."

Wrigley shrugged. "Why not say hello to Brenda?"

Logan frowned. Then he looked over Wrigley's shoulder, toward the posh entrance to Neiman Marcus across the plaza. The woman who had helped him try on shoes—Brenda, the woman who existed only in the VR demo Roz and Wrigley had given him—was standing beside it. She had a shoebox under one elbow, and she was waving.

"Hello, Dr. Logan!" she called over the bustle. "I've got new oxblood Ballys in your size—12EEE—if you ever need more!"

Instinctively, Logan raised his hand—stopped himself—then, a little self-consciously, waved back.

"You're one of her favorite customers," Wrigley said, with another laugh.

"My God." Logan turned back to him. "This is it. Phase three."

Wrigley nodded. "Getting Voyager pushed out and into production was the logjam. Since then, we've moved like lightning. Thirty retailers have partnered with us, and . . . well, that NDA you signed only extends so far. But I can tell you that all of this, including the first fifteen stores, goes live in a month. But *this* place"—he waved a hand toward the hotel entrance—"this is yours alone. It's Omega's gift to you, along with our sincere gratitude. Ten million virtual shoppers a day might pass it by. They can peer in the windows all they want. But unless you invite them in, it's your private world. But you need to name it."

Logan, almost overwhelmed, didn't answer at first.

"Just please not the Bates Motel."

Logan barely heard. "The Tabard."

Wrigley frowned. "If you wish. But why that?"

"Because that's where Chaucer's characters began their pilgrimage."

"Good enough for me. I'll talk to Mossby about making the global change. And now, I've got to go. Sorry: late for a meeting." And he held out his hand. "Goodbye, Jeremy. As Claire said: if not for you, we'd have lost all this—and so much more yet to come."

Logan, still struggling to take everything in, shook the proffered hand mechanically. But then, when he glanced up, Wrigley had vanished. Brenda was still waving at him from the entrance to Neiman Marcus. And then she turned and walked back into the store.

A little woodenly, Logan made his way into the hotel, where he was greeted with familiar graciousness. He stepped down into the lobby proper. A few guests relaxed here and there at the tables they'd occupied before, but the banquette that had housed the Chrysalis staff was empty, its table clean and gleaming.

"Another glass of champagne, Dr. Logan?" The waiter was at his side, linen-wrapped bottle in his hands.

"Why not?" And Logan slid into the banquette, marveling anew at the crackling of the smoothly worn leather seat; the rustle of the cocktail napkin as it was placed on the table before him; the glass of champagne that was carefully set upon it in turn, its surface reflecting the glow of the chandeliers. He shook his head wonderingly, then took a sip, recalling fragments of the recent conversation. *We wouldn't be here if not for you. And I mean that literally, figuratively—and virtually.* And his own words: *Whoever chose this did a good job. It's exactly what I had in mind.*

He thought of how his eyes had met those of Roz Madrigal; how she'd blushed and looked down, as if guilty of something. *Exactly what I had in mind . . .*

On the table, the cocktail napkin shivered slightly, as if losing focus for a moment. When it came into focus again, it bore a logo in elegant script: THE TABARD.

Logan looked up, and—sitting at the bar near the entrance to the lobby—he saw Kit, his wife. Or Kit as she'd looked ten years earlier, when she was still in the full bloom of health. She caught his eye; smiled.

At least, he thought she did. His own eyes seemed to be growing unaccountably misty.

This was too much—too much. Raising his hand to his right ear, he unseated the Omega device.

Immediately, he was back in the living room of his sprawling house off Compo Beach Road in Westport: evening coming on, surf crashing faintly in the distance. The transition from virtual to real had grown nearly seamless—but, as Logan had just learned, that was the least of Chrysalis's recent miracles.

He glanced at the open gift box on the table before him. It had arrived by messenger, hand delivery only. The gift card had read simply: *Hotel lobby, 5 p.m.*

Now he looked at what had been inside the box: the bluish-green device cradled in his right hand, stamped OMEGA VELOCITY, PROPRIETARY AND TRADE SECRET. It was larger than his Voyager device, but only a little.

Too much? That's what he had thought a moment before. Now he wondered if he'd been right.

This place is yours alone. Your private world.

He turned the Velocity device thoughtfully over in his hands: once, twice. And then, he effortlessly refitted it around his ear.

"Hello, Jeremy," he heard Grace say. "Welcome back."

"Thanks," he replied, his eyes shifting out the bay window toward Long Island Sound. "I'd like to visit the Tabard, please."

"My pleasure." And even as the words were uttered, his view of the Sound vanished.

ACKNOWLEDGMENTS

If any single person—myself included—is responsible for seeing this book into print, it's my long-time editor and friend, Jason Kaufman. Jason read, advised, suggested, waited patiently, helped steer the story through an abrupt early course change, read again, waited almost as patiently, and then—after a brief but exhausting late-game period of absorbing several new inspirations of mine—deftly edited the final manuscript with microsurgical skill.

Many others contributed to the development of the novel—more than I can remember or name. My particular thanks to my writing partner, Douglas Preston; my agent, Eric Simonoff; Patrick Allocco; numerous research clinicians, surgeons, and pharmacologists who declined to be named—and of course my family, Luchie and Veronica. If Jason coaxed the book into being, it was my wife and daughter who kept the *corpus* that conceived and wrote it alive and, arguably, sane.

The simulated world made possible by the Omega Velocity, as well as the entities that have chosen to populate it, are of course imaginary. One hopes this does not remain the case forever.